Sue Rich

POCKET BOOKS

New York   London   Toronto   Sydney   Tokyo   Singapore

An *Original* Publication of POCKET BOOKS

POCKET BOOKS, a division of Simon & Schuster Inc.
1230 Avenue of the Americas, New York, NY 10020

Copyright © 1994 by Sue Rich

ISBN: 0-671-79408-6

First Pocket Books printing April 1994

10 9 8 7 6 5 4 3 2 1

POCKET and colophon are registered trademarks of Simon & Schuster Inc.

Cover art by Ken Otsuka

Printed in the U.S.A.

To my beautiful children . . .

Royd Ray, Greg, Sherie, Audie, Roger, Connie, Sandy, Jim, Sheila, Jay, and Loni.

And to my husband, Jim . . . for giving them to me.

I love you all.

CHAPTER

1

Arcane Island in the Bahamas, 1851

"She's dead? *Murdered?*" Valsin Masters stared down at the month-old newspaper he held in his hand, at the blurry front-page sketch of the woman who had shared his home for several weeks.

Pain moved through him in slow waves. *Oh, Sara.* He lifted his gaze to watch rivulets of rain trickle down the glass veranda doors. The wide, thick lawn and junglelike foliage beyond were barely visible through the spattered panes. Though it was a summer shower, he felt chilled. She had loved this island. Beautiful, gentle Sara.

Dead Sara.

His hand trembled as he recalled how her smile and musical laughter had brought a whisper of joy into his lonely world. A sweet warmth that, for a little while, made him forget his self-imposed isolation. Made him forget the reason he'd imprisoned himself on Arcane.

He crushed the edge of the newspaper in his fist. Who had done this to her? Why? A tidal wave of anger rose inside him, and he quickly took a controlling breath.

"Sin?" his manservant, Donnelly, said from the open doorway. He gave a light cough, a sign Sin recognized from childhood. Donnelly was troubled.

Dropping the *Nassau Guardian* on a chair, he faced the older man, who now stood across the study, on the other side of a gleaming cherrywood desk. "Yes, Donnelly? What is it?"

Age-spotted hands worried the crisp white folds of his jacket. "Do you think Sara Winslow's death has anything to do with the other one?"

Sin had already asked himself the same question, yet had feared the answer. "I pray not. Because if the two deaths *are* related, then this deed is somehow connected to me."

Thin wisps of gray hair bounced on the old man's puckered brow as he shook his head in confusion. "Why would anyone want to murder your lady friends? It doesn't make sense."

"Murder is too polite a word for what happened to Beth," Sin rasped. He could still remember the devastating details of Elizabeth Kirkland's killing last year. She had been stabbed through the throat . . . and so much more.

"What did the paper say?"

Sin shoved his hand into his pockets and fingered a blue quartz crystal, the object his mother always called his worry-stone because he fondled it when unsettled. "The *Guardian* didn't give any details. Only that Sara's body was found near the wharf."

"Do you want me to make another trip to New Providence and find out what happened?"

"No, I don't," Sin answered truthfully. "But I *have* to know." Reluctantly he released the crystal. "Rest for a few days, then have the *Midnight Wind* readied. I want you to sail Monday, on the morning tide."

"Come with me, lad. Get off this island for a spell."

"No."

"Curse it, boy. You've hardly left this hellish place in five years—except for making trips to them jungles to bring back things like that." He jerked his thumb toward a black leopard sprawled lazily before an unlit fireplace.

The panther, a former resident of an African rain forest, raised its head and curled its upper lip at Donnelly. A row of menacing teeth flashed, then the animal stretched out on its side again.

The servant sniffed in a show of annoyance, then returned his attention to Sin. "All this isolation isn't good for a body. Why, even before we came here, you locked yourself away inside the walls of the plantation in Savannah like some hermit, refusing callers, canceling engagements."

"And *you* know the reason."

"No I don't—"

"This discussion is at an end," Sin commanded sharply, not mentally or physically up to any more conversation. Memories of what happened in Savannah were too painful. "Just go." Turning his back on the man who'd been like a father to him, he concentrated again on the water-streaked panes.

A heavy silence passed, then he finally heard the study door close. Releasing a pent-up breath, he thanked the fates Donnelly hadn't pressed him this time. The way he felt right now, it would have surely pushed him beyond control—and that's something neither he nor Donnelly wanted. Ever.

He glanced down at the crumpled *Guardian,* at Sara Winslow's exquisite face, and another surge of pain and anger threatened his control. What if the murders *were* connected to him? What if someone had discovered his secret? Was trying to get to him by killing those women? His hands began to shake, and he drew them into fists, fighting desperately to regain his composure. Beads of perspiration slipped down his temples, and he knew the battle was lost before it began.

He stared at the *Nassau Guardian* lying on the chair. A fierce heat grew behind his eyes, and the headlines blurred into a charcoal line. The newspaper fluttered . . . then burst into flames.

* * *

Charleston

Moriah Morgan paced the small confines of her fiancé's book-lined office, the high collar of her taffeta mourning gown clinging in the damp climate. She hated the way propriety demanded she wear such disagreeable garments, and she knew Sara would have shared the sentiment. She had despised anything depressing.

At the memory of her sister, a swell of pain rolled through her. The ache in her chest made it hard to breathe, and she quickly drew in a lung full of air. Still, the question that had plagued her for over a month demanded an answer. Why would anyone want to kill someone as beautiful and full of life as Sara? She'd never hurt a soul. Quite the opposite. Moriah couldn't even begin to count the times her sister had aided a hungry family, or a homeless runaway, or toted home a drunk lying in the street, just to give him a decent bed for the night.

She clenched her hands and fought a surge of tears. Oh, God. Why would anyone want to destroy such a gentle, caring person?

The sound of shuffling paper reminded her of her whereabouts and why she'd come here. Blinking the moisture from her eyes, she looked at her betrothed, Carver Miles, who sat behind his desk, staring at some notes he'd penned while in Nassau. At her insistence, he'd gone to the main port of New Providence Island to investigate Sara's murder.

He withdrew a page, then glanced up. "This is not pleasant, my dear. So do try not to faint."

As if she would, she thought mutinously. Only her oh-so-proper mother did that, and he just couldn't accept the fact that Moriah wasn't like her.

He planted his forearms on the edge of his desk. "Somehow, your sister's death is related to a very similar killing last year. A woman named Elizabeth Kirkland. Let's see . . ." He rustled the parchments again, causing the thin black tie at his neck to sway against his white shirt. "It says here that the injuries to your sis and the Kirkland chit were quite the same. Both had been beaten severely and had rope burns on their wrists. There were also signs of torture, and, of course, each had a stab wound at the base of the throat, obviously made with a knife or dagger of some sort. Rather gruesome killings, all in all."

The room dipped, and she clamped a hand over her mouth in an effort to dispel the nausea climbing her throat. Until this moment, she hadn't realized how brutal the crime had been. *Oh, Sara. How you must have suffered at the hands of that vicious maniac.* She swallowed, trying to hold back her tears.

Her fiancé adjusted his spectacles. "While I was prying into the situation, I learned one or two things the women had in common—if you think you're up to hearing the details."

Knowing that nothing could be worse than what she'd just learned, she nodded. "I'm listening."

"Well, one peculiar similarity is that both women had just returned from a lengthy stay on Arcane Island with a man named Valsin Masters, or *Sin* Masters, as I've heard he's called."

"A lengthy stay? What are you talking about?"

He lowered the paper to the desk. "Moriah, my dear. Surely you aren't that naive. You must have known that your sister was nothing more than a whore . . . er . . . woman who sold her services—as did the Kirkland baggage. After all, that *was* another factor they had in common."

"What? Sara wouldn't!"

He tapped the papers. "But she did. It's all right here. The names of her companions, the fee she charged, and the length of time she spent with each. I was quite thorough, my dear." His gaze traveled her length as if he suddenly wondered at *her* virtue.

Furious, she snatched up the document. "Let me see that." Torn between horror and disbelief, she stared at the vividly detailed information. A sword slicing into her heart couldn't have hurt any worse. "Oh, Sara." Her tears refused to be contained and slid down her cheeks until they became trapped by the corners of her mouth. She hastily brushed them away, not wanting Carver to see her vulnerability. Forcing her chin upward, she gave him her haughtiest glare. "Where did you get this absurd information?"

His thin brows lifted, indicating how much he disapproved of her forwardness. Not that she gave a fig. She'd never be the proper wife he sought. Why she'd even attempted to change was beyond her.

He tugged at his cuff in a show of vexation. "Some of the particulars were given to me by Madam Blanche Rossi, proprietress of the rendezvous house where Sara worked—where she offered her services to monied gentlemen," he expounded. "The rest came from those named on the page, and from your sister's former companion, a Miss Callie Malcom."

"You've made a mistake," she told him emphatically. "My sister was not a harlot. Damn it, Carver, *she wasn't.*" Angry and hurting, she stormed out of his office. She knew her outburst had probably ended their relationship, but she didn't care. She was tired of pretending to be something she wasn't in order to snare Charleston's most sought-after bachelor—just to please Mama. And she wasn't concerned about what her mother would say about her failure. She wouldn't be around long enough to find out. No. She was going to Nassau. Sara's murderer was on that island, somewhere, and she intended to find him.

She kicked a stone out of her path on the boardwalk. While she was at it, she'd clear her sister's name, and shove the proof up Carver's aristocratic nose.

Unfortunately, trying to track down a murderer on her own was not one of her better ideas, she decided a week later as she stepped into a hired carriage and gave the driver the address where she wished to be delivered. To get a straight answer out of condescending, cajoling males was nearly impossible. And, of course, none of the gentlemen named on Carver's list would even admit to having met Sara.

Exhausted and hot, she leaned into the coarse cushions and fanned herself with a lace handkerchief, wondering if Mama might have been right about the foolishness of this journey.

But what else was she to do? Damn it all, the bumbling authorities had come to a dead end. They had no clue as to who killed her sister. For pity's sake, they couldn't even locate Valsin Masters, the mysterious man Sara supposedly visited shortly before she died.

The thought of anyone believing her sister was a . . . a . . . *loose woman* made her furious all over again. And hurt. Aching from grief so deep it sliced into her soul, she steadied herself in the rocking coach and shoved aside the curtain to stare out at the passing scenery, her fingers in a stranglehold around the worn linen.

The emerald grandeur of Nassau, sitting atop a steep hill, didn't impress her one whit. Nor did the fact that the Bahamas' main port was bustling with activity. All that mattered was proving Carver and the others wrong and finding her sister's murderer—though not necessarily in that order.

The carriage wrenched to a jarring halt, and she glanced out the opposite window to see a shabby-looking house set back in the trees. Realizing she'd reached her destination, and that this was where her sister had supposedly stayed, she wanted to shout her denial. She couldn't imagine Sara sharing a hovel like this with anyone.

Warily she stepped out and asked the driver to wait, then knocked on the sagging door. A rustling sound and hushed voices drifted from inside. A moment later, the warped panel squeaked open and a lovely mulatto peeked out.

"Callie Malcom?"

Drowsy emerald eyes squinted. "Yes?"

"My name is Moriah Morgan, and I—"

The girl gasped. "Lord have mercy. Just a minute." She shut the door.

Shocked by the woman's strange behavior, she didn't know what else to do but wait.

Hurried movements came from inside, then another door opened and closed. Curious, she stepped to the end of the porch and glanced around the corner of the shanty.

A man raced into the trees, his shirt in one hand and the other at his waist, holding up his unbuttoned pants.

Blood gushed to her face, and she quickly returned to the entrance, wishing she'd never seen the man—or this horrible place.

The door tugged open. "Miss Morgan, please come in," the girl said, gesturing to a chair in the surprisingly neat room as she belted her robe. "Won't you sit down? Would you care for tea? Coffee? Chocolate?"

Hesitantly she eased into the chair. "No. Nothing, thank you. I won't take but a moment of your time."

The woman took a seat across from her. "I know you're Sara's sister. She told me about you. But I can't imagine why you'd want to see me."

Moriah was surprised that Sara had mentioned her. She usually didn't speak of her family to strangers. "How did you know her?"

"I was her companion."

"I was told she shared your home with you. I must have been misinformed."

Callie's direct gaze met hers. "She did stay with me for a short time."

"Why? I mean, I don't understand why she moved in here." She winced, hoping she hadn't sounded offensive.

"It was my idea," Callie offered, apparently unaffected. "When Sara's husband died, the creditors took her home, the hotel business they'd loaned Mr. Winslow money on, everything. She didn't have any place else to stay."

"She could have come to me," Moriah defended, fully aware of what those vicious creditors had done when Buford passed on of consumption.

"I didn't mean to upset you. And I didn't mean *no* place exactly. Just nowhere here in Nassau. She didn't want to leave until she found out what happened to her husband's little sister."

Moriah was at a loss. She hadn't even known that Buford had a sister. "Did Sin Masters have something to do with Sara's sister-in-law? Is that the reason she went to his island to investigate?"

"I think so. That's why she joined the lineup at the rendezvous house."

Lineup? A sick feeling cramped Moriah's stomach. "What exactly is a rendezvous house?" *Oh, please, let Carver have been wrong.*

Callie twisted her long, slender fingers. "It's a big house on Bliss Island where gentlemen select a . . . temporary partner."

"I see," Moriah said, seeing much too well. Damn it, Carver could have been mistaken—just this once. "How did Sara find out about this place?"

"I told her. I worked there before Sara took me in." She glanced at the bed. "When she did, I hoped I wouldn't ever have to go back to . . ." She shrugged. "Guess someone like me never escapes the life she was born to. Not even the fancy tutor Sara paid for helped me get out." She forced a chuckle. "Even proper speech doesn't change what you are."

Sympathy filled Moriah, and in that instant she saw in Callie what her sister had seen. The beautiful mulatto was kind and intelligent, yet so beaten. In a gesture of friendship, she placed her hand over the slim brown one. "There's always a chance, Callie. All you have to do is take it."

Moist, pain-filled eyes met hers. "That sounds just like something Sara would say." Her voice cracked. "I miss her so much."

Fighting her own grief, she silently agreed, then sat quietly for a few minutes before regaining her composure. "How did you meet my sister?"

"I quit Madame Rossi's to go out on my own, hoping

to make more cash so I could buy me a place." She waved her hand, indicating her house. "It isn't much, but it's mine. Anyway, I had just paid off the loan when one of my customers got out of hand—beat me up bad. Sara found me wandering the streets in a daze, and just like that, she took me in. She told Buford I was her new companion. It didn't matter to her what I'd done for a living. She cared about me. Saw to it that I was patched up and made to rest until I'd healed. We became friends." She stared at her clenched hands. "Good friends."

Moriah swallowed her sorrow, not wanting to break down in front of a stranger.

"After that," Callie continued, "she gave me a real job as her companion." A small smile touched her bow-shaped lips. "Not that there was any work involved. Laughing and talking and shopping and doing her hair was hardly labor. The hardest chore I did was lace her into a corset."

For the first time in weeks, Moriah felt something besides a hollow ache. She recalled her and Sara's comical attempts to squeeze Sara's womanly figure into a whalebone small enough for a child, not to mention their riotous battles over Moriah's refusal to wear the killing garment. Sara had often called her a rebellious little brat, then playfully bombarded her with flying pillows.

"You're trying to find out who killed her, aren't you?" Callie asked suddenly.

Pulled from the pleasant memory, she glanced up. The girl's astute comment didn't come as a surprise. "Yes, I am."

"I want to help."

"How?"

"By finding some answers." The mulatto leaned forward, her gaze intent. "And we both know where to begin looking." She stared for a long time, as if gauging Moriah's depth, then said very quietly, "I know how to get to Sin Master's island."

CHAPTER
2

Sin watched Donnelly cling to the rail on the gangplank as he disembarked the *Midnight Wind.* After a near mishap two years ago, he had made certain a rail and wood runners were installed on all the ramps on his vessels. Though he'd never admit to the aging servant the improvements were because of his increasingly unsteady gait. The knowledge would crush the old man.

Sin glanced at the narrow entrance to the hidden cove that protected his island, wishing he could do something about the jagged coral beneath the surface of that opening as easily as he'd taken care of his manservant's problem. Of course, he knew he was being ridiculous.

His gaze wandered across an expanse of sparkling white sand, over the skeletal outline of a half-built freighter, then up to scan a line of thick trees that bordered the outer finger of the secluded inlet, making the inner bay nearly impossible to see from the open waters. A sigh of thanks slid past his lips that the sloop had once again made it safely through the tight passage. The ship's captain, like Donnelly, was getting on in years and had lost many of his former skills. An old battle waged within him over the fate of his maturing friends, but fortunately, he knew the decision didn't have to be

made today. There was a much more pressing matter—
what Donnelly had learned in Nassau.

Not wanting the servant and crew to know how
anxious he'd been over their safety, he headed for his
study to await Donnelly's arrival.

Long, feather-shaped ferns brushed the legs of his loose
white breeches as he negotiated a wall of thick foliage
that concealed the manor from view. Warm salt air,
sweetened by jasmine, honeysuckle, and lilac, made his
shirt cling damply to his skin as he edged aside the spiky
leaf of a banana tree.

When he emerged from the thicket of shimmering
green, he experienced the burst of pride he always felt
when he saw his home sitting in a shallow valley amid
lush, manicured lawns. The white, two-story mansion
had massive, seven-foot-thick stone walls and great
arches supporting a veranda that encompassed the entire
house.

Alabaster wood railings encircled the upstairs balcony.
Although the upper level housed the servants, it was
every bit as grand as the rest. Each room, up and down,
had glassed-in doors that led out to the portico or
balcony, doors that were shuttered up during a hurricane
or unusually vicious storm.

It was picturesque by anyone's standards, he mused.
So serene. For a heartbeat he paused, wishing he didn't
have to disturb the quietude of his island sanctuary. That
he didn't have to know what Donnelly had learned. The
information could very well change his life.

As he stepped into the immense foyer, he was greeted
by the delicious smells of steaming banana pudding and
baked bread, and by Beula, the cook. Her round, flour-
streaked black face brightened when she saw him.

"I was beginning to wonder if you'd ever come out of
dat study. Dorothy said you hadn't left dat room since
Donnelly went away on dat boat."

Recalling the housekeeper's rather vocal censure of his
life-style, he smiled. Beula wasn't any different.

"I swear, young'un, you is goin' to wilt away if you don't get yourself straight. It ain't right for a body to cut hisself off from others the way you done." She wagged her head of springy gray curls nearly hidden beneath a white bandanna tied at the back of her neck. "No, suh. It ain't right for a body to be so lonesome and unhappy-like."

He wasn't disturbed by the woman's scolding. He'd received much worse in the past when she was his nanny. He tugged on the end of her bandanna. "I'm not unhappy, Beula. How could I be with you around?"

She huffed loudly, but he could tell she was pleased. "When Donnelly arrives, have him come to the study, would you?" He kissed a fleshy umber cheek. "After that, I'd love to sample some of that pudding and bread I smell."

She slapped his shoulder playfully. "You rascal. I don't know what a body's to do with you. When you turn on dat charm, you could ask for the moon and get it. And you know as well as me, I cain't rise above your wicked sweet talk." She shook her head, mumbling as she walked away. "Lord-a-mercy, I never could. No wonder you got away with so much as a chile." She made a snorting sound. "I shoulda been more strict. Yes, indeedy, I sure shoulda been. Den maybe you'd listen to reason now."

Still smiling, he made for his study, knowing full well he'd never gotten away with a damned thing in his youth. Beula had been worse than any taskmaster.

He was standing at the veranda doors with his back to the room when he heard Donnelly enter. Immediately the pleasantness he'd experienced with the cook was forgotten, and he grew tense as he faced the older man. "I don't want preliminaries. Just tell me how Sara died."

The servant shifted uncomfortably and eyed the distance to the door just behind him, as if determining an escape route. "The magistrate figures the same person murdered both women. The wounds were the same, the method of torture . . . everything."

No! Damn it, no! Sin's mind bellowed. A low quaking moved through his limbs, and a vase of flowers on the desk started to rock precariously.

"Get out," he ordered hoarsely. The urgency of the command spurred the old man into motion, and he quickly bolted from the room.

An instant later, the vase erupted in an explosion of crystal splinters. Books flew from the shelves. Window-panes shattered.

With every ounce of self-control he possessed, he fought to restrain his rage. *Stop. Sweet Christ, make it stop.*

Finally, slowly, the floor beneath his feet grew still. For a heartbeat, he was afraid to breathe, afraid to move, fearing he'd loose the beast again. Then, at last, the grinding tension left him and he relaxed, dropping into a chair.

He planted his elbows on the desk and gripped the sides of his head with his hands, then took several calming breaths. His fingers dug through the strands of his hair as he tried for the thousandth time to understand what had brought this curse upon him. What had he ever done to deserve such punishment?

He stared at the shambles. The sight of such savage destruction twisted his insides. It was the first time this had happened since he came to Arcane. The first time since— He pounded his fist on the desk. Damn it to hell, wasn't there any way to escape this evil?

He rose and kicked aside a book, then paced to the center of the brick floor. And what about Sara? Who had killed her? *What did it have to do with him?*

Feeling a swell of frustration tighten the muscles down his spine, he quickly busied himself by picking up several volumes from the floor and shoving them back into the bookcase. If he wanted to find the answers, he had to remain calm and think rationally. He had to make plans—not spin off into another rampage.

After righting the rest of the room and feeling more

settled, he stared out at the soothing view just beyond the porch. A soft breeze rustled the leaves of a palm near the flagstone edge and wafted the sweet scents of orchids and passion flowers. Mosquitoes hummed in the sticky afternoon heat.

He considered his options. He could always go to Nassau himself and carry on his own investigation, but that meant contact with outsiders, something he dare not risk. Too, he could send Donnelly, but at his age, he wasn't really up to the task. He was okay for a jaunt of a day or two, but not for the length of time—or the effort—a full-blown investigation would take.

Of course, there was Lucas, the overseer for the cane fields, but, though the man's intelligence was keen, folks in Nassau weren't likely to answer sensitive questions from a man of mixed color, especially the old-timers who'd opposed the abolition of slavery barely seventeen years ago.

He closed his eyes, trying desperately to think of who might have committed such a horrendous deed—and what it had to do with him. Only one answer came to mind. Someone must have learned his secret. But why would the person kill the women he hired? To draw him out? To destroy him as he had once destroyed? The horror of that fateful day tried to creep into his mind, but he determinedly forced it away. The memory was too painful to resurrect . . . and no one but himself knew what happened that afternoon.

No, the murders weren't committed because of what transpired five years ago. He was sure of that. Still, he couldn't imagine who might have learned of his curse. Other than the islanders, crewmen, and servants, all of whom he trusted with his life, and the priest he'd confessed to a few years ago, there wasn't a single person who knew. Except Mudanno.

He immediately dismissed the fledgling notion. She might be a voodoo witch, but she wouldn't resort to out-and-out murder. In an odd sort of way, she would consider such an inauspicious deed beneath her—especially because of its brutal nature. No. This was a man's doing. Besides, the killings took place in Nassau, and as far as he knew, the lustful, power-hungry priestess had never left the island.

Dispirited, he paced the veranda. There had to be a way to make the killer show his hand. A way to lure him into the open. Sin stopped midstride. An idea took hold . . . and rooted. His eyes narrowed as the scheme expanded into a full-blown plan.

"Donnelly!" he bellowed. "Get in here."

Hobbling footsteps clopped down the hall, then the door swung open. Chest heaving, the servant glanced around hurriedly. "What's wrong?"

"Sit down and catch your breath, then I want you to go on another errand."

The thin, graying man sank into a chair facing the desk. "What kind of errand?"

"Bring me another woman."

"What?"

Sin lifted a brow. "I didn't realize you had a hearing problem."

"I don't. I just can't believe that you want—"

"Another woman? Why not?" Sin asked casually as he stroked the head of the panther, who'd wandered over from the fireplace. "The request never shocked you in the past."

"Women never started dying before, either."

The impact of Donnelly's hurtful remark staggered him. Silence deadened the thick, humid air that hung between them. Finally Sin found his voice. "This woman won't meet any unscrupulous ends. I promise you."

Donnelly looked stricken. "Sin, I didn't mean . . ." He slid crooked fingers through the wisps of hair barely covering the top of his head. "When do you want me to go to Bliss Island?"

It was on the tip of his tongue to shout *never,* but what else could he do? The murderer had to be caught before someone else got hurt. "I want you to leave for the rendezvous house today."

"I will *not* wear this," Moriah said flatly.

The mulatto glanced down at the shimmering lavender dress that clung to Moriah's curves like wet tissue.

She squirmed beneath the girl's scrutiny. The gown draped off the shoulders, dipped so low in front, one could see the darker line of her nipples.

"It's perfect," Callie argued. "That is, *if* you wish to be chosen as Sin Master's next woman and taken to his island."

Moriah paced the carpeted hotel room, irrationally wishing she'd never let Callie send that message to Madame Rossi on her behalf. Churlishly she stared at the response she'd received less than an hour ago. Already she knew the contents by heart. This evening there would be another lineup, and if she wanted to participate, she must be at the rendezvous house by six o'clock. Good heavens, who would have ever thought the woman would reply so quickly? That Moriah would have no time to come to terms with the situation before she blundered into it. "What if he doesn't choose me—even if I do wear your dress?" She voiced one of her many fears—or hopes.

Callie gave a low, soft laugh. "Then the man is either nearsighted or senile. There isn't a single woman at Madam Rossi's that could compare to you in that gown. Probably not even anyone on New Providence Island. Mercy, girl, haven't you ever looked in a mirror?"

"Well, of course. But I assure you, I haven't seen anything staring back at me that warrants such praise."

Green eyes rolled heavenward. "Never mind. Just take my word for it, you'll be irresistible."

"I feel naked."

"You look sensational. Now, come on. I've made arrangements to have your trunks stored here at the hotel, your bags are packed, and the carriage is waiting downstairs to take us to the docks. Captain Quizzie's ferry leaves for Bliss Island within the hour."

"You've thought of everything," Moriah said testily, wishing her insides didn't feel like carnage left behind by a hurricane.

"Not quite everything," her pretty friend mumbled as she strode out the door.

Afraid to ask what she meant by that, Moriah followed at a slower pace.

Three hours later, she fought a rush of terror as she stared at the porch steps leading up to Madame Rossi's elegant two-story house. The call of a beautiful parrot who sat on the railing did nothing to calm her nerves. The island's thick, steamy air clogged her throat. Perspiration slid down the back of her neck. She'd never be able to callously sell her body for a man's pleasure. She couldn't. "Callie?" Her voice quavered.

"It's all right," the younger woman soothed. "Sara made it up those steps, and so will you."

For the first time, she wondered if her older sister might have been the stronger of them. Then, recalling Sara's brutal death, she squared her shoulders and mounted the steps. *This is for you, sis.*

When she followed a maid into a red, velvet-draped room, she tried not to show her shock at the scantily dressed women lounging casually about the room.

Trembling with nerves, and unsure how to proceed, she swung around to Callie.

The mulatto had disappeared.

Fear streaked along her spine. Callie couldn't have deserted her. She just couldn't!

"Well, well. What have we here? Aren't you a looker."

Stunned to find a large, buxom woman standing beside her, Moriah couldn't speak. She didn't know what to say.

Dressed in a low-cut satin gown of ruby that clashed horribly with her orange hair, the woman grinned broadly. "Gotta say, ducky, if you're half as good as you look, you're a real money-maker. I sure could use a beauty like you around here full time."

"I'm M-Moriah Morgan. I came for the lineup."

The madam cackled. "Do you want me to send the others home now or go through the motions?"

Assuming that was a compliment, she felt her face grow warm. "I'll wait with the others." What choice did she have, anyway? And where the blazes was Callie?

Moriah had barely gotten seated and cursed Callie again when she heard a man's voice coming from the hall. Her heart rate picked up speed. This was it. Holding her hands tightly clenched in her lap, she watched the doorway.

A thin, balding old man stepped into view.

She barely contained a gasp. *This* was Sin Masters? Sweet heaven, he was ancient!

"Mr. Roarke. Good to see you again," Madam Rossi gushed as she hurried forward. "Got your message last night saying you'd be here today." She waved a heavily ringed hand. "Already got the flock together for you to size up." She winked. "And a grand flock it is, too, even if I do say so myself. I know your man'll be pleased."

"I'm sure he will, madam. Now, if you don't mind, I'll have a look."

Realizing this wasn't Sin Masters but his agent, Moriah didn't know whether to be relieved or frightened. She lifted her lowered lashes to watch Mr. Roarke as he paused before each woman.

He didn't touch them, thank goodness, or speak to them. He merely looked, then went to the next one.

When he stopped in front of her, she shyly met his gaze.

A flicker of disapproval lit his eyes, before he quickly averted them and moved on.

Did her appearance disappoint him? Or her supposed occupation? She sensed it was the latter, but, of course, that was absurd.

Not knowing what to do next, she glanced around the

room, and finally spied Callie, standing just outside the door.

The mulatto shrugged as if to say she didn't know why the man had passed her over, either.

Her spirits sank. He wasn't going to pick her. He didn't even like her. Damn it. What could she do? *Think, Moriah. Think!*

But her brain wouldn't work. Nothing came to mind. Having suffered enough humiliation for one day, and not about to endure another second, she rose and made her way to the door, her head held high, her back straight. She'd find another way to get to Sin Masters.

"I'll take her," Mr. Roarke's voice rang out.

Unable to stop herself, she turned to see which one he'd chosen.

He was staring at her.

Madam Rossi beamed. "A whopping choice, Donnelly. I know your man'll approve."

Mr. Roarke didn't respond. He merely moved closer. "What's your name, miss?"

Overcome with a surge of embarrassment, she couldn't meet his eyes. "Moriah Morgan." Now that he'd actually chosen her, she was beginning to feel ill. What had she done? What had *Callie* done? she amended. Shooting the mulatto a fearful glance, Moriah knew she couldn't bear to journey to Arcane without her reassuring presence. She thought quickly. "A-And I h-have a personal maid that I'd like to bring with me." She peeked at Madam Rossi. "At no extra charge."

A gray eyebrow climbed the man's creased brow, then he shrugged. "That's highly unusual, but I don't foresee a problem. Be ready at first light. I'll pick you both up here."

Feeling as if she'd just been handed a death sentence, she gave an unwilling nod.

When Mr. Roarke left the room, Madame Rossi whirled around, her face puffed with anger. "What's this about a personal maid, missy? I don't cotton to no shenanigans. Sin Masters is too good a customer to mess with."

"Ain't no shenanigans, ma'am," Callie said as she stepped into the room. "I's Miz Moriah's maid. She don't go nowhere without me. Plain and simple. Why, land sakes, who'd dress the chile?"

Moriah blinked in surprise at Callie's illiterate dialect, but didn't dare question her.

The orange-haired woman's eyes narrowed. "What are you playing at, Callie Malcom? You ain't no more a lady's maid than I am."

Not at all concerned about the woman's accusation, the girl smiled sweetly. "I am so a lady's maid . . . or I was 'afore I come ta work for you a couple years back, Miz Rossi. And da missy here—" she pointed at Moriah "—she needs me. 'Sides, a whore with a maid makes folks take notice, and she's right good at what she does." She winked conspiratorially. "Ain't heard nothin' but praise from the gents."

Why didn't the floor open up and swallow her? Moriah thought, her cheeks flaming. When she got Callie alone, she was going to *choke* her.

Madame Rossi squinted. "You that good, girl?"

It was extremely difficult to speak with her tongue plugging her windpipe. "S-So I've been told." How utterly embarrassing.

The large woman crossed her arms. "Well, we'll just see about that." She flicked a smirk at Callie. "I have in mind a *gent* who'd be right pleased to give little Miss Morgan a trial run tonight."

CHAPTER
3

"What do you mean it's all right?" Moriah glared at Callie. "She expects me to . . . to . . . *fornicate,* for heaven's sake!" Wondering how she'd ever let the girl talk her into wearing this horribly revealing peignoir, she stared down in disgust at the sheer peach folds. And the perfume! The garishly furnished bedroom virtually reeked with the smell.

"Moriah, stop fretting. I told you I'd take care of it. You just meet the man at the door and invite him in."

"In *this?*" she sputtered, her hand tightening on the flimsy material.

Ignoring her outraged gasp, Callie continued. "When things get serious, excuse yourself to blow out the lantern." She nodded toward a lamp sitting on a table near a freestanding wardrobe. "Then slip over to the closet. I'll be inside and we'll switch places."

"But he'll know."

"No he won't. Men who come to this place have only one thing on their mind. In the dark, they wouldn't play close enough attention to tell one body from the next."

"But you—you—"

"It's not like I've never done it," Callie said with a

tinge of bitterness. "I've been satisfying men's baser urges since I was thirteen."

Moriah felt the depth of her pain. "Why?"

She shrugged. "I didn't have a pa, and when Mama died, I needed money to see her buried proper."

The unsteady rhythm of her voice revealed there was much more to the brief story, but Moriah wouldn't press. If Callie wanted her to know, she'd tell her when she was ready.

A loud pounding rattled the door.

Fear rippled through her. It was the customer.

"Take a deep breath," Callie coaxed. "Just act natural. He's not going to jump you the minute you open the door." She crossed to the wardrobe and opened one of the front panels. "Just remember what I told you to do." She smiled encouragingly and stepped inside before shutting herself in.

Moriah's palms went damp.

The pounding came again.

Swallowing, and reminding herself she was doing this for Sara, she shakily opened the door.

A man, possibly in his late twenties, stood in the entrance, his hat perched at an angle over sandy-blond hair. With feet spread, his thumbs tucked into the waistband of baggy britches, he flashed her a lewd smile. "Evenin', lass. Name's Clancy O'Toole." He ran his gaze over her body. "Ooo-wee. Are ye nae somethin'? Why, me friends'll be jumpin' ship ta get here when I tell them about the likes 'o your beauty."

Embarrassment hit her so hard, she had to grip the doorknob to keep from reeling from the force. She had never met such a crude man. "W-Won't you come in?"

He peeled off his hat and stepped inside, kicking the door shut behind him.

Unsure how to proceed, and wanting to forestall the inevitable as long as possible, she turned her back to him. "Would you care for a drink?"

A hand came up under her arm from behind and

cupped her breast. "I'm nae spendin' me hard-earned cash for a drink, lass."

Her knees nearly folded. No one had ever touched her so intimately. The floor began to rock, and a loud thundering hammered in her ears. The humid air became as thick as quicksand.

He spun her around and caught her by the nape of the neck, then planted his mouth on hers.

She stiffened beneath the wet pressure, then nearly cried out when she felt his fingers squeeze her rear. Frantically she thought of Callie's directions and broke away from him. "Wait," she said, gulping in air. "I need to blow out the lantern."

"Nae, darlin'. I'll be seein' what I'm payin' for." He reached for her.

She quickly sidestepped. She *had* to put out the light. Glancing wildly around, and seeing no means of assistance, she lifted her chin and drew on pure nerve. "If you won't allow me to extinguish the light, then, sir, I'm afraid you'll have to find another companion." She knew if he left now, Madam Rossi would never allow her to go with Donnelly Roarke, but she had no other choice.

For a heartbeat, he didn't move. Then, mumbling, the sailor shoved her aside and crossed to the lantern and blew out the flame.

The room plunged into darkness.

She panicked. How could she get to the closet? He was blocking the way!

She heard him come closer, heard the heavy thud of his shoes, the rasping of his breath.

Fearfully she edged toward the door.

A hand grabbed her shoulder.

She choked on a scream, then nearly buckled with relief when she realized it was Callie.

"Get into the closet," her friend whispered urgently, and gave a gentle shove.

"What's that ye say?" Clancy blurted.

Barely able to breathe from the bile rising in her throat, Moriah inched along the wall until she reached the open cubicle. Scampering quickly inside, she closed the door, then curled into a ball and hugged her knees to her chest. Still, Callie's voice rang as clear as if she stood next to her.

"I said, I'm over here, Clancy. And I don't plan to wait much longer."

Oddly, Moriah noticed the girl's tone had changed abruptly. She sounded distant, almost as if she'd mentally removed herself from the situation.

"Ye willna have ta wait for me, darlin'," he chuckled amid thumps and bumps as he obviously tried to hurry across the room and undress at the same time.

"Ah, Blessed Virgin," he crooned. "Ye feel too good to be true, darlin'. Give me your hand, lass. Feel what ye be doin' to the likes o' me shaft. Ah, sweet saints. Yes. That be it."

Guilt and embarrassment attacked Moriah at once. It was all her fault that Callie had to subject herself to this man's despicable whims. He'd make her *touch* him. Do heaven only knows what to the poor girl. The heat inside the cabinet grew stifling, the sounds more pronounced. Her stomach churned, then lurched. She clamped a hand over her mouth. She couldn't get sick *now*.

Horrible slurping and smacking echoed through the room. "Ah, your boonies be tastin' like pure honey, lass."

Her stomach gave another giant heave. Frantically she rammed her hands over her ears, praying to blot out the sounds. But it didn't help. She could hear the man's moans and pants. Hear him tell Callie where to touch him . . . what to do. Things that, until tonight, she would never have imagined. She could almost feel the girl's suffering, her degradation.

An eternity later, the last of the man's cries of fulfillment died down and the room grew quiet. Devastated, she leaned her head against the closet wall, fighting tears.

A moment later, the closet door opened. "Are you okay?" Callie asked so softly, she barely heard the words.

"I'll never be okay after what you had to endure for me," Moriah said bitterly, though equally hushed.

The girl patted her hand. "Come on, light the lantern and get him out of here."

As Callie closed herself in, Moriah numbly made her way over discarded clothing and did as instructed. A yellow glow filled the room, and she noticed the musky smell of sex that hung in the air, giving her stomach another uncomfortable wrench. Unthinking, she turned toward the bed.

Clancy lay sprawled across the covers. Stark naked.

Horrified, she jerked her gaze away. Never in her life had she seen a nude man.

The sound of the frame creaking forced her attention again to the sated man, but she refused to lower her gaze beyond his shoulders.

Clancy blinked sleepily in the light and scratched the sparse hairs on his chest. "Ye got a fine touch, darlin'," he said sagely. "I ken I never be havin' me a better piece o' tail." He dragged on his britches, then stood up and seized his shirt. "I ken you're bound ta have a boatload o' lackeys waitin' their turn, and me dawdlin' be costin' ye money, but I want ye ta ken, I'll be back on me next stop. And I'll be sure'n tell your boss lady." He stomped into his shoes, then straightened and walked toward her. One eye crinkled into a suggestive wink. "Next time I'll be bringin' enough coin for a whole night . . . or two." He squeezed one of her breasts roughly. "Be seein' ye, lass."

How she kept from collapsing right then and there, she'd never know. But as he left the room, there was one thing she *did* know . . . she'd never be able to suffer at the hands of a man the way Callie had tonight. All the horrible things he had said and done echoed through her head. Ugly, vile things that she knew she could never endure. Never survive. Things that a man like Sin Masters would expect of her.

The seriousness of her situation struck her full force. If she went to that island, there would be no escape from the atrocities. No escape at all.

Her chest began to hammer painfully. She couldn't go

through with this sham. Frantically she swung her gaze to the door. She had to get out of here. *Now.*

"Sara wouldn't have given up at the first setback," Callie said quietly.

She stiffened, her hand trembling on the cool metal door latch. Part of her, the side that wanted to run away from this horrible place, ached to silence the girl. The other, the one that knew Callie was right, sank with shame. How could she have even considered abandoning the quest to find her sister's murderer?

Drawing on all the composure she could muster, which wasn't much, she squared her shoulders and released the latch. "I hope both you and Sara will forgive my momentary lapse."

Emerald eyes softened. "There's nothing to forgive. You're only human. And if I were . . . like you, I'd have already been gone." She gestured toward the bed. "That wasn't something an innocent should witness."

She averted her gaze from the tumbled sheets. She still didn't want to think about the things she'd heard. "It'll be expected of me when I arrive at Sin Masters's island." She tried to keep the quiver from her voice.

"No, it won't."

"What do you mean?" She turned to see Callie straightening the bed.

Finished, the girl sat down. "The switch worked once; it will a second time."

"You mean you'd— Why?"

She stared off into space. "It isn't right for an innocent woman to be forced into a man's bed. With me, it doesn't matter anymore."

The defeat behind those words tore at Moriah's heart. "No. I couldn't let you go through that again." She shook her head. "I'll simply have to find a way to divert the gentleman's attention, or . . ." She couldn't bring herself to complete the sentence. The mere thought of allowing a man to touch her—*to violate her*—made her ill.

She met the other woman's gaze. Though Callie's

expression didn't reveal her inner thoughts, the way her eyes melted with pain strengthened Moriah's resolve to exclude the girl from this outrageous scheme. The mulatto would never again suffer at the hands of a man because of her.

Whirling from the door, she stalked to the lifeless fireplace, suddenly noticing the stifling heat filtering into the room from an open window. Thick black night shadowed the opening. "What time is it?"

"Just past midnight. You should get some sleep. Dawn comes pretty early."

She eyed the bed. She would *not* sleep there. "I'm not tired."

As if sensing her reluctance, Callie retrieved something from her knitted reticule and crossed to a table near the window. "Do you know how to play cards?"

"No."

"Then maybe you should learn."

And learn, she did, Moriah mused the next morning as she stared in the mirror at the bluish gray smudges beneath her eyes. But what had she expected? She'd spent the entire night sitting in a hard chair, learning the finer points of poker.

"You look beautiful," Callie commented as she latched the last hook of her high-buttoned shoes.

She didn't feel beautiful. She felt degraded—and scared. "Thank you." She tugged once more on the indecently low bodice of the scant, rose-colored gown Callie had unpacked from a trunk. She'd insisted Moriah wear the daring garment if she planned to convince anyone of her supposed profession. Sighing, she faced her friend. "Are you ready?"

"Why, Lordy, yes, Miz Moriah. I's ready as a plucked chicken bound fo' da soup pot."

"Callie, do stop."

The girl grinned, an endearing crease framing one corner of her full mouth. "I need the practice."

Wishing she could be as lighthearted about this situation, Moriah headed for the door.

Not a soul occupied the parlor, only the scandalous portraits of women lining the satin walls.

"Where is everyone?" she asked, baffled by the lack of inhabitants.

"Sleeping, I imagine. Most of them probably had a long night."

"Of course." Heat burned her cheeks, and she quickly took a seat. But she couldn't stop the images of those poor women suffering beneath cruel male hands.

Callie touched her arm. "Would you like me to have Sassy prepare you some tea and biscuits?"

"I don't think I could swallow them."

"Want to play another game of poker?"

"Oh, heavens, no. Not that. Please."

"Why not? Seems to me that you won the last six hands."

Moriah smiled. "I've always had the luck of angels."

"Then let's hope it continues." The voice was Mr. Roarke's, and it came from the doorway.

Moriah jerked around to find him standing beside Madam Rossi. Warily she wondered at his odd statement.

"You ready, girl?" the heavy woman asked, her manner now full of approval.

Knowing exactly why she was so amicable made Moriah ill. Shakily she nodded and rose. But inwardly she knew she'd never—*ever*—be ready for what was to come.

By the time they reached the docks, her nervousness had intensified twofold, especially when she saw the sleek black, two-jibbed sloop rocking at anchor. It looked sinister and evil . . . just as she imagined its owner would.

Once aboard the *Midnight Wind,* Moriah and Callie were shown to a cabin below. Immediately she felt a jolt of anxiety. There were no windows.

"Mr. Roarke? Could we perhaps have other accommodations? I fear I tend to get claustrophobic in windowless rooms." *Not that I've ever been in one,* she added silently.

"Lass, I'd let you stay above if I could. But the truth is, Sin doesn't want anyone knowing where his island is. I'm afraid you'll have to remain down here."

"Why? I mean, why is the location of his island so secret? Is he a criminal?" Her throat tightened as the words came out. Good heavens. She'd never thought of that possibility.

The older man chuckled. "No, miss. The lad's not a criminal, or a smuggler, or a refugee. He just demands privacy."

She slid a peek at Callie, who seemed completely unaffected. "I see."

Mr. Roarke nodded. "Just knock if you require anything. And there's a basket of fruit on the bureau to tide you over till we reach the island." He pointed to one of two cots braced against either wall. "Might as well get comfortable. Even if the winds are with us, we won't get to Arcane till near dark." Touching his hatless brow in a gesture of respect, he left, closing the door behind him. An instant later, she heard the lock turn.

Panic gripped her, and she whirled around. "Callie?"

"It's all right, Moriah. I heard about this from one of the other girls." She offered a small smile. "One who went to Sin's island—and lived. I saw her last year before the killings started." She tossed her knitted reticule on the opposite cot and sat down. "Anyway, Brandy, that was the girl's name, said that she was locked below until the sloop docked in some hidden cove on Arcane Island. Arcane means secret, by the way. Or knowable only to one with the key. Kind of appropriate, don't you think?"

"But why?"

She shrugged. "Guess it's like Donnelly says. Sin Masters *demands* his privacy. Aside from that, Brandy said that he was one of the most attractive men she'd ever seen . . . and one of the best lovers."

Warmth gushed to Moriah's face. She would never become accustomed to the way these people spoke so casually of intimacy. "When did you say Brandy went to this island?"

"A few months before Beth Kirkland died, may the poor soul rest in peace."

"Did this Brandy mention anything unusual? In the man's behavior, I mean?"

"No. But then, you'd have to know Brandy. As long as she's not mistreated, she doesn't see a whole lot beyond the color of a gold piece."

"Then he didn't mistreat her?"

"I don't think so. Mostly she talked about his dynamic appearance and insatiable prowess . . . and something about *animals* that I didn't quite understand."

"Animals?"

Callie shrugged as if she didn't understand either.

The boat gave a sudden lurch, and Moriah grabbed a post at the end of her cot to steady herself. As she realized the sloop was under way, the fear she'd kept so carefully contained surfaced ferociously.

There was no turning back.

Knowing she couldn't possibly go on like this, she gathered a firm hold on her composure. "Since this looks to be a long journey, I think I'll catch up on some of the sleep I missed last night."

Her friend didn't have to be prodded into agreement, and within moments, they were both disrobed and stretched out on their respective bunks. But for Moriah, sleep wouldn't come. She lay there for several hours before her eyelids at last grew heavy.

The boat careened sharply, jarring her to instant alertness. She blinked rapidly, trying to understand what had awakened her. Then she heard the loud thunder of crashing waves and felt the sloop pitch wildly.

Wearing only a thin chemise, she clung helplessly to the post at the foot of her cot. "What's happening?" she shouted over the roar of the ocean.

Callie, usually so calm, looked terrified in the wavering lantern light. Huddled on her bed, she clung to its frame. "It's a gale!" she yelled in answer.

She'd thought as much, but prayed she was wrong. She

glanced apprehensively toward the locked door. Surely the storm would be over soon. Or Mr. Roarke would let them out. And certainly they must be nearing their destination by now. Shouldn't they?

Footsteps thundered overhead. Men shouted frantically.

Her pulse began to hammer. Something was terribly wrong.

A loud, horrible scraping sound wrenched through the pounding waves. Wood cracked and splintered. Water gushed into the cabin. A beam jabbed into her side. The cot bucked wildly, propelling her into the opposite wall. The frame pinned her beneath the water.

She clawed frantically at the twisted metal holding her against the bulkhead, but it wouldn't budge. Her chest labored. Pain throbbed in her side. Her mouth opened in desperate need of oxygen. Nearly delirious with panic, she strained upward. Grasping fingers searched for something, *anything,* to save her. Fire burned her lungs. She had to breathe!

Her hand touched a curved object. A ceiling hook that had once held the lantern. She latched on to it and pulled with fierce determination. Pain speared through her ribs, but her head broke through the surface, and, thank God, sweet air rushed into her starved lungs. Choking and gasping, she sucked in great gulps until her senses began to clear.

When she could at last think clearly, she became hauntingly aware of the utter, dead silence . . . of total darkness. "Callie?" she croaked out. Gingerly she eased one hand away from the hook and moved it back and forth in front of her, trying to locate her friend.

"Over here," Callie groaned from across the cabin. "I think I'm up near the ceiling."

"Me, too." She moved her hand again, gauging the distance between the water lapping at her chin and the overhead panel. Since the cabin was filled, they must be in an air pocket of some sort. But she couldn't hear the storm anymore. "Why is it so quiet?" she asked uneasily.

"The whole ship must be under," the girl whimpered.

Horrified, Moriah visualized the sloop sinking to the ocean floor, the crewmen savagely battling the angry sea as they fought to save themselves without thought to the women trapped below.

"We're going to die," Callie cried, her voice pitched with raw panic.

Wishing beyond anything else that she could comfort the girl, she searched for the words. But they wouldn't come. Callie was right. They *were* going to die.

Water sloshed against Moriah's cheek. "Callie, are you trapped in any way?"

"N-No. I'm h-holding on to my upended cot."

"I'm pinned by a bed frame. You're going to have to swim over here and try to free me."

A sob broke from the girl's throat. "I can't! I can't swim!"

Oh, dear God. Those three words had just sealed their fate. She tightened her hold on the hook as she listened to Callie's pitiful sobs, knowing that tormented sound would be the last she'd ever hear. If only she could move, reach the girl, hold her . . . until the end. Maybe dying wouldn't be quite so terrifying in the arms of a friend.

CHAPTER

Sin had been standing on a rocky, wooded hill, overlooking both the ocean and cove, and watching the heavens with growing concern. The setting sun illuminated thick clouds rolling in from the south. After five years in this area, he knew what they meant. A violent squall.

He had searched the shrouded waters for the *Midnight Wind,* willing it into view. But there hadn't been any sign of the sloop. No sign of Donnelly or Captain Jonas.

Shoving his hands into the pockets of his breeches, he fingered the quartz crystal. He shouldn't have sent them. He glanced at the half-finished freighter he'd been forced to start building after the old sea captain lost the other one in a similar gale a few months ago.

He clenched his hands, vowing that this would be the man's last voyage.

A sudden gust molded his shirt to his chest. Salty spray from a wave crashing into the rocks below spewed up to sting his eyes. He narrowed them and focused on the darkening sky. *Come on, damn it. Hurry.*

The heavens opened up in a torrential downpour, but he refused to move until he saw his friends safely to shore.

A leaning mast pierced the gray torrent just beyond the bay's opening, giving him a moment of relief. Then he saw the ship, riding high on a foaming wave, teetering on its side—*and heading straight for the jagged coral.*

"No!" he bellowed, scrambling over boulders and fallen branches as he rushed frantically to reach the cove. Sheets of rain plastered his shirt to his torso, poured hair into his eyes. He slipped twice on the slick granite, but still he didn't slow.

Scratched and bleeding, he at last reached the calmer waters of the inlet, then skidded to a halt, watching helplessly as the sloop's starboard side slammed into the coral.

The sound of splintering wood exploded across the inlet. Water spewed upward like a geyser. The sloop bounced against the rocks, then dipped as it began to slip beneath the surface. Crewmen shouted and dove overboard, swimming frantically for the beach.

Sin hit the water at a dead run, his only thought to help his men. As he pumped his arms savagely he saw Lucas and the field workers running toward them.

With the help of the islanders, the sloop's crew was swiftly plucked from the bay. Sin himself had dragged Donnelly ashore, and he shook as he fiercely embraced his old friend. How close he'd come to losing him. But he hadn't, nor had he lost any of the crew. They were battered, some nearly drowned, but alive. The typhoon had come and gone, and the only price had been the damage to his ship. A small cost indeed.

Donnelly coughed and sputtered something, but Sin didn't listen. "Come on. Let's get you up to the house." He motioned for Jonas to follow, then turned to his overseer. "Take the others to Woosak," he ordered, referring to the old native woman who served as their only doctor. She didn't possess any modern medical skills, but at the moment, she was all they had. At least she'd give the men blankets and hot drinks. "After that, Lucas, come up to the manor."

"Washed overboard," Donnelly rasped out. "Couldn't get to them—" He doubled over in a fit of coughing, his body shivering from shock.

Concerned for the older man, he ignored Donnelly's rambling.

At that moment Beula and Dorothy arrived with armloads of quilts. After one glance at the manservant, Dorothy shoved all but one of the covers into Beula's arms and flung the remaining one around Donnelly's shoulders. "You blithering fool," she scolded affectionately. "You're too cursed old to be out in weather like this. You wanna catch your death?"

He fought her hold. "The women!" he cried, then slumped forward.

Sin went to reach for him, but froze. *The women?* His brain connected in sudden understanding. Donnelly meant *woman*. He'd been so concerned over his men, he'd forgotten all about her. Damn!

Lunging to his feet, he tore off the soggy clothes that would slow him down and dove naked into the sea, thankful that the submerged ship wouldn't be too difficult to find since he'd seen where it went down.

The current ripped at his arms and legs. Coral clawed his body. But he couldn't stop. If there was a chance to save her, he had to try. With sheer force of will, he pushed downward until he reached the sloop resting on the bottom.

Feeling his way around the deck, he fought the need for air as he located the hatch that led below. He wrenched it open and shoved himself down into the narrow corridor. Using his hands, he pushed along the walls until he came to the cabin where he knew the girl would be.

The door was locked.

He tried jiggling the latch.

It held.

Helplessness surged through him. His chest burned for oxygen, but he couldn't quit now. It was his fault she was down there. He braced his back against the corridor wall and rammed his foot into the stubborn door.

It didn't give.

Again he kicked. Again. Again.

At last the door gave a watery, eerie groan, then burst open.

Without hesitation, he plunged inside, searching wildly for the woman. His hand met a smooth leg. The need for air driving him on, he grabbed the limb and pulled downward, then latched on to a struggling body. Frantically he swam back down the corridor and out the hatch. His chest jerked in spasms. Desperately he pushed upward, willing the surface closer, stretching, straining, clutching the woman.

An instant later, he shot up out of the water, coughing, sputtering, gasping for air.

The woman beside him choked and spewed mouthfuls of salty sea, then turned into a clawing tigress. "No! No!" Her strength depleted, she slackened in his arms.

What was the matter with her?

Several field hands stood on the beach holding blankets, and helped them out.

"Will ya look at what Donnelly done brought back for da massa," one of the men muttered in astonishment.

Sin turned to look at the girl, bundled in a blanket and shivering, and met the green eyes of an enchanting mulatto. Surprised at Donnelly's choice, yet not displeased, Sin offered her a smile.

She seemed incoherent for a moment, then started stuttering unintelligibly between chattering teeth.

"What is it?" he asked with concern. She was horrified about something.

"Moriah! She's still down there!"

Another woman? "Son of a bitch! Dorothy, get her to the house." He whirled around and dove back into the bay.

His descent to the submerged sloop was easier this time, but exhaustion had taken its toll on his lungs' capacity to retain air. Already his chest tightened with a burning cramp.

Knowing he'd better find the woman quickly or both of

them would drown, he shoved into the cabin and ran his hands rapidly over the walls. Finally he touched a woman's flesh. He closed his fingers around her ankle.

She kicked out.

Surprised and extremely thankful she was still alive, he worked his way up her leg. His palm outlined a shapely thigh, a firm little rear, then cold metal. Shocked, he continued upward. His hand curved around a small rib cage, then trailed up over a full breast and a slender upraised arm.

His head broke the surface, and he gulped at thin, stale air. Oxygen that had obviously kept the woman alive.

"Where's Callie?" she cried frantically. "She was here, but she disappeared! She can't swim. Find her. Oh, please. Find her!"

"Calm down," he ordered, his hold tightening on her trembling arm. "If Callie is the mulatto, then she's safely onshore."

"Oh, thank God."

"Are you all right?" he asked, concerned by a sudden frailty in her tone.

She took a deep breath, as if to control herself. "After being battered in a shipwreck, nearly drowned, barely able to breathe for an hour, and pawed by a gentleman I don't even know, I imagine I'm as well as can be expected."

He tried not to smile at the sharpness in her husky voice, wishing that he could see her face and wondering if it was as pleasing as the rest of her. "Then it's high time we headed for shore," he said gently.

"I can't move. Otherwise, I imagine I would have gotten out by myself."

He admired her spunk, but he didn't miss the underlying fear that shook her voice. "Of course."

"You said Callie is all right?"

"Yes. I told you, she's already onshore. Now, where exactly are you stuck?"

"Right here."

Well, that told him a lot. Reaching out his hand, he accidentally brushed her breast.

"Not there, you fool. Here."

Not knowing where *here* was, but willing to find out, he slid his hand around her back and down. Her waist was lodged between the bulkhead and what felt like a piece of broken bed framing. Instantly he ascertained that there wasn't room for her to slip through in either direction. He retraced her side until he came to her upraised arm.

"What are you holding on to?"

"Remove your hand from my person," she hissed. "And for your information, I'm clinging to a ceiling hook."

He felt water lap against his grin. "Well, don't let go. I'll try to free you."

He gripped the metal at her waist and yanked hard. But it didn't move. The thin air made him light-headed, his own limbs nearly useless. He placed a hand on either side of her, then slid them forward and gripped the frame again. Bracing his foot against the bulkhead, he jerked hard.

Nothing. The metal remained embedded in the wall.

The air began to thicken. With two of them breathing, it wouldn't last much longer.

His chest pounded at the hopelessness of the situation. He couldn't leave her and come back with tools. There wasn't time. Yet if he stayed, neither one of them would come out of this alive.

"Damn you," he swore viciously, pulling on the frame with everything he had. "Damn you. *Damn you.*"

"Sir. Do try to control yourself."

He ignored her. "Come on, goddamn it!" The metal began to vibrate against his palm. It rocked, then suddenly burst free.

"You did it! Oh, thank God."

"Or his rival," he muttered. "Come on, let's get out of here." He wrapped his arm around her waist. "Okay, take a deep breath. Here we go." He submerged with her, then, moving as rapidly as possible, led the way back through the silent vessel and out into open water. Knowing the thin air wouldn't hold either of them long, he kicked savagely, propelling them toward the surface.

Within a few feet, he felt her claw frantically at his shoulders and knew she was out of air.

She convulsed violently. Jerked. Then her struggles weakened, and she went limp.

Fear nearly stole his remaining breath. She couldn't die now. Not after all this.

His own lungs near bursting, he shoved up, up, until finally, after an eternity, he shot out of the water. Barely giving himself time to take a breath, he swam for shore, the woman's lifeless body held close to his side. He dragged her out onto the sand and shook her viciously. "Damn you, breathe!"

Her head rolled to the side. In the moonlight, he could see a dark rim surrounding her full lips. He could feel the stillness in her chest.

Impotent fury engulfed him. Angrily he dragged her up against him. "Breathe," he groaned helplessly against her mouth. "Breathe." His eyes burned hot, willing her, *demanding* her to breathe.

Suddenly she gasped and coughed, then jerked away. Grabbing the sand with both hands, she bent over, relieving herself of great amounts of salt water.

To him, the retching sound was the most beautiful he'd ever heard. She was alive. The burning in his eyes eased, and he touched her back, rubbing gently until the spasms passed.

When she finished, she hung her head forward, breathing hard. "Th-Thank y-y-you."

"My pleasure," he said warmly, wiping her face with one of the discarded blankets.

She pushed his hand away and curled over onto her side, then drew her knees up to her chest. "I'm so tired. So sleepy . . ."

After what she'd been through, he could imagine she

was. Rising, he slipped on his pants, then returned to her. "Come on, princess. Let's get you to the house."

She didn't respond.

Covering her with the blanket, he scooped her up in his arms, suddenly aware of how tiny she was, how delicate. How nicely put together. A heavy warmth moved through his lower body, and he quickened his pace across the sand.

"Is she all right?" Dorothy questioned as he stepped into the tiled foyer.

Not in any mood for queries at the moment, he brushed past the older woman. "Bring some hot tea." With each step, his concern mounted. Was she really just overly tired? Or had her near drowning caused another problem? Knowing he wouldn't leave her side until he knew the answer, he carried her to his chamber and gently laid her down on the bed, then lit a lantern.

A soft, amber glow wavered over her gleaming raven hair. Though it was pinned into a tight bun atop her head, the escaped strands looked like silk against the orchid quilt.

"I thought there was only gonna be one girl," Dorothy said as she entered carrying a tray.

"So did I." He glanced toward the housekeeper. "Set that on the table and fetch Donnelly. He's got some explaining to do."

She did as instructed, then moved to the dresser and withdrew one of his shirts. "I should get her out of those wet clothes first." She tossed the garment on the foot of the bed. "I had the other woman taken upstairs to the servants' quarters, but she looks like she's in better condition than this one."

He waved her out. "I'll do it. You just send Donnelly."

Looking as if she wanted to argue, she clamped her mouth together, then left the room.

He shook his head. She never had approved of him bringing his mistresses into the manor. Having been his mother's personal maid before she died, Dorothy worked diligently to maintain some semblance of decorum here on Arcane. Often she was quite vocal in her disapproval.

Not that he minded. The task seemed to give her pleasure. And in this instance she was right about one thing. Moriah needed to get out of that soggy chemise.

His gaze lowered to her full, thrusting breasts molded by the wet silk. The darker centers peaked impudently. It was all he could do not to trace the hard little tips with his fingers.

One of the damp ties clung to a smooth white swell, taunting him to loosen the lacy streamer and touch the enticing woman who lay beneath.

Temptation warred with integrity. He did not molest unconscious women—even if he'd paid for the right to do so.

A sultry breeze swirled through the room, caressing his senses, igniting his passion, and taking his reason. The burning need to run his palm over her breast consumed him. He fought the impulse, fearing he might not be able to stop, but the potent, long-denied urges of his male body wouldn't be stilled.

Slowly, hesitantly, he lifted his hand.

A gentle, sweet warmth stroked her, pulling her from the depths of a peaceful black void. Her nipple tightened as an arousing palm lazily explored the shape of her breast. Of course, she knew the sensation had to be a dream, but it felt wonderful. She arched into the pleasing heat, trying to get closer.

A sound, like a quick intake of breath, penetrated her foggy brain. With sluggish effort, she lifted her heavy eyelids and tried to focus, but as the haze cleared, the roaming hand stilled, then disappeared. She regretted the loss, but immediately came to full awareness when an unfamiliar room filtered into view.

Lacy white curtains billowed out from the sides of an open veranda door as a moist breeze, thick with the scent of jasmine, drifted across the bedchamber. A symphony of chattering monkeys floated on the sultry air, telling her more effectively than any words that she was not at her home in Charleston.

A trickle of fear pulsed through her. Where was she?

She shifted on the bed and examined a tall, richly polished wardrobe, a gold-trimmed washstand and gilded mirror. She'd never seen anything so fine . . . or so foreign. Uneasily she glanced at the door, centering a satin-covered wall. The beautifully carved oak panel merged at the floor with lush wine red carpet.

Her fingers sank into the folds of a quilt as she turned her head to inspect the other side of the room.

Her gaze collided with a pair of breathtaking, liquid brown eyes.

"Hello, princess."

The low, provocative timbre of the man's voice moved over her flesh like that slow hand. Tiny wings fluttered inside her chest, but she quickly snipped them. She was still dreaming. In a moment she'd wake up, and this god of sensual masculinity would be gone. No mortal being had hair that silky black, or features that strong and flawlessly perfect.

She stared at his tantalizing mouth. The seductive shape, with its slightly fuller lower lip, revealed both strength and fierce passion . . . the kind that uncurled a woman's insides. No. This man was not mortal.

"Who are you?" she said, trying not to let her voice quiver with reverence.

"Sin."

Her heart tumbled over itself. If this man was *sin,* she couldn't wait to go to hell. "Where am I?" Maybe she was already there.

"In my bed."

Oh, sweet heavens. The erotic undertones in that statement set fire to her blood. Thank goodness this was only a fantasy. "I'm going to hate waking up from this dream," she mumbled, wishing she could actually touch the magnificent illusion.

His mouth curved into a bewitching smile. "This isn't a dream, princess." He brought her hand to his lips. Hot, moist heat brushed over her fingertips. "We're both very, very real."

Tingles skittered up her arm. *Real tingles.* She snatched her hand back, suddenly frightened. "Who *are* you? Where am I?"

The warmth faded from his eyes. "I'm Valsin Masters, and you're on Arcane Island . . . my island."

Alarm stole her voice. Her memory came back in a violent rush. Sara's death. The storm. The shipwreck, and why she was in this man's home. "Where's Callie? Is she all right?"

"She's fine. I believe she's been put to bed upstairs and is eating supper at the moment."

"Thank heavens." She edged sideways, trying to gain a little distance from him. "How are the crewmen?"

"A little battered and bruised, but they all survived." The underlying relief in his tone was unmistakable. Then his mouth tilted in a wry smile. "And before you ask . . . my ship did not. It's lying at the bottom of the cove."

"Is it salvageable?" Good heavens, she couldn't be stranded on this island—*with him.*

"We won't know until we bring it up." He crossed to the door and opened it, then turned back. "I'll have my cook, Beula, bring your supper." His carnal gaze traveled over her curves outlined by the quilt. "And, as much as I might wish it otherwise, I imagine she'll find something for you to wear." With his broodingly handsome features set, he nodded and left the chamber.

She let out a breath. How did she always manage to get herself into these messes? Unfortunately, she knew the answer. Her dogged, bullheaded determination.

Another breeze swept through the room and feathered over her breasts. She looked down sharply. The quilt was gathered at her waist, leaving her upper chest uncovered. Embarrassment slashed through her. He had seen her like this. Nearly naked.

Vaguely she recalled thinking a man was touching her

when she awakened. No, she quickly refuted. *That* was a dream. Dear God, it must have been.

Still, she could recall the way he'd touched her in the submerged cabin. The way he'd run his hands up her leg and thigh. Slid his palm over her breast.

A tingle shot through that particular area, startling her. She yanked the quilt to her chest, refusing to believe that she could have enjoyed a man's touch. Why, she'd rather suffer the tortures of hell than have that man paw her again. Mother always said that men were intent on but one thing, and after the vulgar cavorting she'd overheard last night at the rendezvous house, she knew the truth of those words.

Yet somewhere in the deepest part of her, she couldn't imagine Sin Masters behaving the way Clancy O'Toole had. But he *had* purchased her the same as Clancy, she thought with loathing. They were both rutting boars, only *he* was more refined, that's all.

Attempting to climb from the bed, she winced when her side cramped. She twisted slightly, trying to see the damaged area. Through the thin chemise, she could see a dark blotch. Knowing how easily she bruised, it didn't surprise her.

She massaged the area gently, allowing her thoughts to explore ways she might use the injury to her advantage. Surely her host wouldn't physically abuse an incapacitated woman, would he? She smiled. Of course he wouldn't. Not if he was any kind of gentleman.

The hand at her side trembled slightly. But what if he wasn't? What if her injury didn't mean one whit to him? She drew in a steadying breath. Well, it was certainly worth a try. Besides, what other choices did she have?

But she mustn't let herself dwell on that. She'd made it to the island, and she had a job to do. She would learn if this man who had just saved her life had, in truth, also been responsible for taking Sara's.

CHAPTER
5

~

Blanche Rossi took a ferry to Nassau, then hired a carriage to take her to her brother's house. She didn't wave at the occasional customer she passed on the street as she normally did. At the moment she had more important concerns. Though the girls at the rendezvous house hadn't realized the coincidence yet, she was sure the last two whores she sent to Arcane had been killed because of something associated with Sin Masters. And it had to stop.

She relaxed against the carriage seat, thankful that today was Wednesday, the usual day she visited her brother. But this time, unlike the others, she sought his advice. Walter would be pleased, she knew, and he just might be able to help. If the murders didn't cease, she would lose Sin's business, and that could ruin her financially.

For five years she hadn't had to struggle, fight off creditors, or listen to the girls complain about being overworked. With the amount Sin paid her for a companion, she'd nearly made enough to open a second house, and was on her way to becoming a very wealthy woman.

Narrowing her eyes on the opposite seat, she recalled

how surprised she'd been when he'd sent for another woman so soon after Sara's visit—and elated at the additional cash. Normally she only heard from him a couple times a year. Could it be that he, too, was becoming suspicious about the deaths of his former mistresses and was waiting to see what would happen to the next one?

She drew her hands into fists. Damnation, she couldn't allow anything to upend Miss Morgan. Blanche's livelihood depended on the chit living to a ripe old age—and the only way to assure that was by finding the killer.

When the carriage halted in front of her brother's cottage, she strode up the steps and knocked briskly.

Instantly Walter's tall, skeletal frame appeared in the darkened entry. "You're late," he pointed out in his usual wounded tone.

"Is supper on the table?"

"No."

"Then I'm not late." Brushing past him, she marched into the dining room.

A single taper flickered from a holder in the center of a naked table. He never bothered with a linen cover or decent dishes, she noticed with disdain. Tin plates and bent forks . . . and heaven only knew what kind of meal *this* time. Mercy, what she had to endure for the sake of her only living kin. And why didn't he light more candles?

She took a seat, wanting to get this over with as quickly as possible, and spread a napkin over one knee, then tucked a corner of the linen under her belly to hold it in place. "What's for supper?"

Walter, who had followed her, smiled, showing his uneven teeth. "Impatient today, aren't we, love?"

"I'm a busy woman."

He gave a mock bow, causing his black pin-striped suit to mold to his narrow shoulders. "Then I shall take your leave for the sake of expediency."

Blanche rolled her eyes. If she weren't sure he was her own flesh and blood, she wouldn't claim relationship. He was downright strange. But, to give him credit, he did have a sharp mind, one that might aid her now.

When minutes passed and he hadn't returned, she adjusted the bodice of her crimson-colored gown, then drummed her fingers on the table and studied the dimly lit room. Other than the table, only a plain sideboard and an aging organ graced the room. Through an archway directly across from her, she could see the adjoining chamber where Walter kept his memorabilia. Crucifixes and statues of Jesus and the Virgin Mary took up every available space from the floor to tabletops to bookshelves. Beside each sat a short, unlit candle. In the middle of the room stood a lovingly polished pulpit.

How different they were, she mused. Since they'd been raised by a mother who had plied the same trade Blanche now did, one would have thought she and her brother would be more alike. But they never had been. Not even as children.

He had always been the righteous, good little boy, bent on saving the world. She, on the other hand, had followed their mother's path . . . out of need to provide for her brother.

When she finally married one of her "men friends," Blanche thought she'd at last be somebody—and she was as long as Chadwick Rossi had his ship. But when he lost it in a storm, and times got tough, he started bringing his former crewmen to her . . . for a price.

After her husband died in an accident on the wharf, and realizing the life she was destined to couldn't be changed, she fastened her sights on a new goal. She scrimped and saved until she had enough money to buy the rendezvous house.

Walter followed his own calling and became a man of the cloth.

"Here we are, love. A meal to savor." With a flourish, he set a plate in front of her, then moved to his own seat.

She stared at the contents, desperately trying to swallow a groan. Half-cooked salmon lay atop a bed of wilted lettuce. Beside that sat a chunk of bread covered with a runny fried egg. A mound of pasty grits completed the unappetizing supper.

He smiled boyishly. "I bought wine to go with our meal." He lifted a basket off the floor and took out a bottle, then poured dark ruby liquid into their water-spotted glasses.

"You've outdone yourself," she managed, then took a hefty drink.

Walter nodded approvingly, then bent his head in prayer.

She listened to the heartfelt, *elongated* blessing with as much patience as she could muster.

At long last, he raised his head, then picked up his fork and began eating the now cold meal.

Blanch stabbed her own fork into the grits.

"So, sister mine, how is your business progressing?" he asked around a mouthful of slimy egg, but his eyes relayed the same reproachful message they always did when discussing her occupation.

That he disapproved of her profession had never been in question, but for some time now, she hadn't had to listen to one of his sermons on sins of the flesh. Maybe he'd given up . . . or had at last come to accept her way of life. Smiling, she gestured with her fork. "Couldn't be better. Hired three new girls, real lookers, too, and made another bundle off Sin Masters."

"Oh? You sent another woman out to that mysterious island?"

"Yep. A downright pretty one, too. Odd, though. This one took a maid."

"You sent two women?"

She took a bite of salmon and rolled it around in her mouth. "Yep. Didn't get no extra pay, though."

"Too bad, love." He picked up his glass. "Are they from around here?"

"The maid, Callie Malcom, is, but I'm not sure about Moriah. I think she was staying at the Nassau Hotel, so she might not be."

"Moriah?"

Blanche took a swig of wine to wash down a bit of egg. "Moriah Morgan, Sin's newest mistress."

"Oh. Morgan, huh? No, I don't believe I know of any family by that name in these parts."

Setting her glass down, she decided now was as good a time as any to approach her problem. "Walt, someone's been killing Sin's women."

His thin brow shot up. "What?"

"The last two, Beth Kirkland and Sara Winslow, were murdered after they returned from Arcane."

"Do you think your client is responsible?"

She shook her head. "I've been sending women out there for over five years. Only the last two came to harm. No. I don't think he killed them, but I do believe it has something to do with him—in a roundabout sort of way."

He studied the bare table. "Were the women murdered on Bliss Island?"

"No. The bodies were found here in Nassau. That's why I was wondering if you might be able to help."

"How?"

She waved a hand. "I don't know. Snoop around. Ask questions. See what you can discover that the sheriff might have missed." She grinned. "After all, people are usually more open to a priest."

He smiled, and raised his glass in a toast. "I'll see what I can do, love. But don't expect a miracle."

Sin met Donnelly coming down the hall and, without a word, motioned him into the study. He had several questions to ask the old reprobate, mainly, why were there two women? Didn't Donnelly realize that it would be hard enough to protect one from a murderer when she returned—much less *two?*

"How're the lassies?" his friend queried as he sat.

"Well enough, considering." Easing into his own seat, he picked up a letter opener and slid his fingers along its smooth metal surface. "I'm waiting for an explanation," he said without looking up.

The leather upholstery creaked beneath the aging man's shifting weight. "About what?"

"Why there are two women." He stared into the lined face. "How do you expect me to take care of them both?"

Donnelly waved a long, thin-fingered hand. "Oh, that. One's the maid."

"Callie, I presume?"

"Yes. Miss Morgan wanted her to come along, and I didn't see any reason to deny the request."

He curled his fingers around the metal. "Didn't you?" he asked softly, trying very hard to control the urge to strangle the man. "Not even knowing what awaits them when they return to New Providence?"

He paled. "I never thought of *that.*"

The letter opener bent under the pressure of Sin's grip. "Damn it, Donnelly. If the man killed Beth and Sara to try to lure me out, he'll go after Moriah *and* Callie when they return."

His watery hazel eyes grew wide at first, then his whole expression relaxed. "Send one of them back at a time."

Sin stared at him, wishing he could shake the man without doing damage. "And which one do I sacrifice first? The mulatto because of her race? Or the raven-haired beauty because of her profession?" Not that he'd consider either one. He damned sure wouldn't.

A knock sounded at the door.

Not waiting for Donnelly's answer, he gestured for him to leave, knowing he'd communicated his displeasure. "Get out of here. We'll discuss this later. And see that Dorothy sends baths for the women."

Donnelly hurried to the door and opened it, then quickly brushed past Lucas, who stood on the other side.

Lucas Burke had been a part of Sin's life since childhood. He could still recall the first time he'd seen the proud, thin child standing on the auction block. His mahogany skin and somber gray eyes declared his mixed heritage and simmering hostility. His shoulders had been stiff with arrogant defiance, his chin raised in challenge. When Sin's father bought the boy, Lucas had no idea he'd be set free the moment the papers were signed. Or that Sin's father would take to him, see him educated, and eventually train him to manage the numerous estate fields.

He stared fondly at his overseer. "What is it?"

"Damned if I know. You sent for me, remember?"

Warmth moved along his neck. He'd been so muddle-brained in the last hour, he'd completely forgotten the command. "Shut the door." He tossed aside the bent letter opener and shoved a hand in his pocket. His fingers clutched smooth stone.

When Lucas had seated himself, he leaned forward, his muscular brown arms resting on bare knees. "Well? What's put you in such a foul mood?"

"Incompetent help."

White teeth flashed against walnut skin. "What'd Donnelly do this time?"

He met his friend's amused eyes and felt the anger drain away. "Nothing more than usual. I guess I'm just testy after the shipwreck. How are the men?"

"In heaven. Woosak gave them an ample supply of rum, warm beds, and several willing women."

Sin nodded his approval. "They deserve it. They came through a hell of a storm."

"Unfortunately, your sloop didn't."

"I know. But thankfully no one was hurt—not even the women—and tomorrow I want you to gather some men, see what we can salvage from the wreckage."

Lucas's curly head dipped to one side. "Women? There's more than one?"

"The prostitute I sent Donnelly after . . . and her maid. And before you say it—*no*, I didn't plan this. The second woman is a complication I hadn't figured on." Having let Lucas in on his scheme to catch Sara's murderer, he knew his friend understood the problem a second woman presented.

"What are you going to do?"

"I'm not sure."

52

"You could keep one of them here."

He didn't mention that Donnelly had voiced much the same solution. "Which one? And how do I explain why one should stay?"

Lucas's somber eyes turned thoughtful.

He watched the man closely. He had a keen mind, one that more often than not bordered on genius.

The overseer glanced up, a smile creasing his cheek. "Since you only planned on the whore in the first place, the best solution is to encourage the maid to stay."

"How?"

"There's only one thing I know of that tempts a woman to give up everything. Even employment."

Sin immediately caught his direction of thought. "A man."

"Exactly. All you have to do is push one of your men in the right direction. Get him to court her . . . with a little incentive, of course."

"What kind?"

"Depends on how homely she is."

"I see." He rose. "I think I know just the man for the job."

Lucas, too, came to his feet, his height equal to Sin's own. "Who's the poor sucker?"

"You."

The overseer didn't move. Sin didn't think he even breathed.

"Very funny."

"But necessary."

The man's eyes narrowed. "Sin—"

"With your looks and way with women, you shouldn't have any trouble at all."

"I see. And when you reached this decision, just what did you decide would be *my* incentive?"

"Nothing. You know I won't force you, Lucas. But I *am* asking for your help."

The overseer cursed softly. "I hate it when you do this. You know that, don't you?"

"Yes."

Still swearing, he pushed past Sin and stalked out into the hall. "If she looks like the sour end of a mop, you're going to owe me good for this one."

Deciding to let Lucas learn about Callie for himself, he merely nodded and closed the door. He leaned against the frame, smiling, and anticipating the expression on the overseer's face in the morning.

Then his thoughts drifted to the exquisitely beautiful woman who awaited him down the hall. Just the idea of possessing her sent a jolt of desire straight to his lower body. Making love to the woman hadn't been a part of his original plan. He'd only hired her to use as bait to catch the murderer. After a short time, he planned to send her to Nassau . . . and follow her. Sharing her bed hadn't even entered into his thoughts . . . until he'd seen her in that thin chemise. Touched her achingly beautiful body. Now, no matter how hard he tried, he couldn't dismiss the fact that he'd paid for her services and was within his rights to enjoy them.

Guilt pricked him. Even though she was a woman of profession, it didn't sit well with him to use her to lure a murderer and endanger her life. But, damn it, there wasn't an alternative.

Angry, and not sure at whom, he strode down the hall and opened the bedchamber door.

Moriah spun around, crossing her arms over her breasts. "W-What do you want?"

The man's dark gaze made a very thorough inspection of her towel-wrapped body as he walked toward her. "What I paid for."

Sweet heaven, what had she done? The heat smoldering in his eyes nearly buckled her knees. She held out one hand as if to ward him off—which was utterly ridiculous. "You can't."

He slid his fingers into her upswept hair, holding her captive. His deep, velvet voice caressed her tingling skin like a lover's kiss. "Oh, yes, princess, but I can."

"Please . . ." She felt panic threaten to choke her. "My s-side."

He dragged his gaze from her lips. "What?"

"I injured my side," she managed shakily.

"Which one?"

His concern eased her nerves. "The right."

He released her hand, then immediately lifted the edge of the large towel.

"What are you doing?"

He ignored her outburst and continued shoving the material upward until he'd exposed her thigh, hip, and entire side—and an indecent portion of the rest of her. He swore colorfully.

Knowing she would soon die of embarrassment, she turned away, hoping to use the ugly bruises to forestall his advances. She gave a small, if insincere, moan. "It hurts when you raise my arm."

He instantly let go of her. "Why the hell didn't you tell someone how badly you were injured?"

"It didn't hurt that much, earlier." Well, that was true, she thought guiltily as she pushed the towel into place. "I'm sure I'll be fine . . . in a few days."

He looked as if he wanted to strangle her. "Yes. I'm sure you will." He strode across the room and opened the double doors that connected to another bedchamber. Inside, he lit a lantern, revealing a large room decorated in masculine browns and rust. An enormous four-poster dominated one wall, while richly polished bookcases engulfed another. Sheer gold curtains moved with the lilac-scented breeze. At any other time, she might have admired the airy comfort of the room.

He yanked back the satin quilt, exposing crisp white sheets, then undid his breeches and shoved them down.

Her eyes grew wide at the sight of his sleek nakedness. Fire raced to her cheeks. Her breath clogged somewhere in her chest. Dear God in heaven.

"Come on," he rasped as he kicked aside the trousers and straightened.

She froze, her flesh quivering with terror. "But—"

"I may not be able to possess that lovely little body of yours yet," he conceded. "But I can damn sure share its warmth for the night. Now, get into bed."

Sara, her mind screamed. *This is for Sara.* Holding back her terror, and reassuring herself that her virtue was not really at stake, she moved on shaky legs toward the bed.

As she neared the edge, he reached out and touched her arm. "Stand still."

Much too aware of the heat radiating from his fingers, and of his naked body so close to her own, she couldn't speak.

"You need to get out of that wet towel. No. Put your arms down. I'll take it off. You'll only do more damage."

Too frightened to correct his mistaken assumption, she lowered her hands from where she'd clutched the front of the towel. Nausea rolled through her stomach. Why didn't she die? Why didn't the earth open and swallow her? She squeezed her eyes tightly shut in a desperate attempt to overcome the horrible humiliation of being disrobed by a virtual stranger.

Slowly, as if savoring each moment, he unwrapped the towel and let it slide away from her body. "You're beautiful," he said in a suddenly thick voice.

Shame made her dizzy. She wouldn't survive this.

"Get into bed, Moriah."

She couldn't move. Her legs wouldn't respond. No man had ever seen her like this . . . so naked . . . so vulnerable.

Suddenly strong arms swept her up to a hard chest, then laid her gently onto a feather tick.

Sara . . . Sara, her mind screamed again and again. Behind her eyelids, she saw the light turn to dark, then felt the bed dip as he climbed in beside her. *He won't do anything,* she told herself over and over. *He just wants to lie next to me.*

"Come here," he commanded in a seductive voice. "I want to hold you." His arm slipped around her lower waist, avoiding her ribs, and eased her spine to his chest. "Relax, princess. I'm not going to hurt you."

The heat from his chest burned into her back. The weight of his maleness pressed against her bottom, making her aware of its huge size. Numb with fear, she held herself still, not wanting to make any move he might consider enticement.

Through a fog, she became aware of the warmth of his breath near her ear, of the palm surrounding her breast. Horror and desire slammed together. *No. Oh, no.* Her mind replayed all she'd heard while in the closet at Madam Rossi's, the disgusting remarks, the sounds, Callie's whimpers. She trembled violently.

He sucked in his breath sharply, and his hand tightened. "Don't," he scolded gently. "I won't be able to restrain myself if you keep making those little sounds."

What sounds? she thought wildly. She held her breath, terrified that she'd do something else he might take as encouragement. Finally, after a long moment, the need for oxygen made her light-headed. Slowly, oh so slowly, she released the air from her lungs, then inhaled, trying desperately to ignore his presence. She failed miserably.

He nuzzled her neck. "You're too tense."

Rigid better described her bearing, she thought morosely, then willed her muscles to slacken.

"That's better," he murmured sleepily, his hand gently massaging her breast.

To her everlasting shame, she felt her nipple stiffen against his palm, something she knew her body had never, *ever* done except when cold . . . and she certainly wasn't that!

He released a long, deep sigh, his breath warm as it tickled over her neck. "How long did you say it would take for your side to heal?"

Too frightened to answer, she glanced anxiously about the dark room. A sliver of moonlight slipped through the veranda doors, and she focused on the tiny beam, willing her thoughts from the man beside her and the havoc his touch caused.

Within minutes, she heard his breathing deepen to a heavy, steady rhythm. Thank heavens. He had fallen asleep. Wanting more than anything to jump from the bed and run screaming from the room, yet knowing the slightest movement would awaken him, she quelled the urge, closed her eyes tightly . . . and prayed for morning.

CHAPTER
6

A warmth moved beneath her cheek, and she snuggled deeper into the comforting heat. Something brushed lightly over her jaw, her lips. She sighed contentedly.

A low masculine chuckle rumbled as a large hand slid down her back and cupped her bottom.

Her eyes shot open. Mere inches separated her face from Sin Masters's.

"Good morning," he whispered, his lips nearly touching hers, his breath feathery soft.

Too stunned to move, she could only stare.

He smiled, then leaned closer, brushing his mouth tenderly over hers. His fingers slid up her naked side and lightly traced the underswell of her breast.

She flinched in shock.

"Still sore?" he asked, stilling his hand.

Trying to slow her stampeding heart, she nodded vigorously.

He sighed, then gave her a quick, hard kiss and rose from the bed. "Maybe this evening." He stretched and strode to the wardrobe.

She tried not to look, but the power emanating from the sleek lines of his body held her immobile. Soft dark hairs curled riotously over a smooth, deeply tanned chest, then narrowed down across his tight stomach, only to widen out again at the apex of strong thighs. The all male part of him, which until two days ago she'd never had the slightest thought of even considering, appeared firm, and *large,* nothing like Clancy O'Toole.

Stunned by her brazen inspection, she snatched her gaze away, her cheeks flaming. "Sir, please. Clothe yourself."

He went deathly still. "What?"

Realizing her mistake, she quickly added, "I may be a woman of profession, but I abhor lewd displays."

With her lashes lowered, she couldn't see his expression, but the sarcasm in his words left little doubt to his reaction. "Oh, do forgive me, princess. I wouldn't want to shock your tender sensibilities."

Not daring to respond, she stared at the sheets in front of her, but she could hear clothing rustle, which hopefully meant he'd complied. Too, she was still upset over the fact that she'd awakened curled in his arms. What had ever possessed her?

"Now, if your ribs aren't too sore, I'd appreciate your presence in the dining room." Somehow he made the request sound like an order. "Breakfast will be served in half an hour. And I'm sure you'd like to see how your maid fares."

Callie! She glanced up just in time to see his white-clad form disappear through the door. Relieved to be alone and anxious to see her friend, not to mention very glad to be free of the man's distracting presence, she eased from the bed, dragging the sheet along with her. She must find some suitable clothing.

A quick inspection of the room revealed only the towel still lying on the floor, and men's garments hanging neatly in a closet.

Wrapping the sheet tightly around her, she sat on the edge of the bed, her hopes depleted. She couldn't leave.

"Miss Moriah?" a woman's voice called from the other side of the door, followed by a light rap. "I's brung you some things."

Hurriedly she opened the door leading out into the hall. "Thank heavens," she said, smiling at a plump Negress with a round grinning face.

The older woman held brightly flowered material cut in an odd shape. "I's Beula, the cook, and the massa, he said bring you this." She shoved the cloth into Moriah's hands.

"Master? I thought slavery had been abolished here in the Bahama Islands." She stared at the article, which looked like nothing more than a long piece of colorful silk.

"I's no slave, missy. But I been with the massa's family for as long as I can remember. My ma was 'afore me. I just calls him dat 'cause I respects him."

"I see," Moriah said offhandedly, still inspecting the unusual garment. "How do I wear this?"

Brilliant teeth flashed. "I shows you. The village girls wears them all the time." She took the material and shook it out. "Drop the sheet, chile, and lift your arms."

More comfortable *and* familiar with a servant helping her, she did as instructed.

Beula draped the fabric over Moriah's left breast and directed her to hold it there, then proceeded to wrap the material around her figure twice. Coming to the end of the cloth, the cheery maid tucked it into the valley between Moriah's breasts. "There. Dat does it."

Horrified, she stared down at the silky fabric clinging to her every curve and stopping just below her knees. Her arms and shoulders were totally naked. "I can't possibly wear this."

"It don't do no good to fuss, missy. Ain't nothin' else," the Negress explained calmly. "The village girls don't wear nothin' but these, and even if the men get your trunks up today, it's still gonna take a long time 'afore your own things dry. Now, sit down, chile. I'll help you brush out your hair." She motioned her to a gold-framed dressing table.

Realizing the entire situation was out of her hands, she complied, reluctantly.

The older woman pulled the pins out of the tangled topknot at the crown of Moriah's head, and the tumble of heavy hair fell free.

Beula gasped. "Lord-a-mercy, chile. I ain't never seed dat much hair on one person 'afore." Picking up the hairbrush, she drew it through the disheveled strands and clucked to herself. "The massa goin' to like this. Yes, suh, he is. The boy's got a weakness for long, silky hair."

Moriah's nerves vibrated. That's all she needed—*another* reason for him to pursue her. It seemed to take forever before Beula finished and Moriah could rise to follow the cook to the dining room.

For the last few minutes, Sin had enjoyed watching Lucas shift uncomfortably in the chair across the table from him. Knowing the overseer was on edge about this morning's meeting with the woman he planned to court, Sin tried hard not to tease. Of course, he thought mischievously, Lucas had no idea just how pretty the young mulatto was.

"I'll probably never forgive you for this," his friend mumbled, straightening the front of an open-neck shirt he'd worn for the occasion—though he hadn't conceded his cutoff breeches. He took a sip of coffee, then set the cup down.

"It was your idea," Sin reminded, trying unsuccessfully to stop a grin.

"You know damn well that I never meant to set myself up for this. You *know* I don't pursue women. I've never had to. Hell. I don't even think I know how."

Sin knew he wasn't boasting, just stating fact. The man had the looks of a finely sculpted mahogany god. "Maybe you won't have to this time, either," he consoled, if insincerely. "Hell, maybe—"

The soft patter of bare feet halted his words. He turned to see Beula and his barefooted mistress step into the room. For just an instant, he could have sworn his heart stopped.

He'd known that Moriah was lovely, but until this

moment, he'd never seen her in the daylight, seen the provocative shape of her deep violet eyes, seen her with that wealth of shimmering, straight black hair flowing down her back, or that delectable body wrapped seductively in flowered silk. It suddenly became hard to breathe.

The overseer rose. "If this is the maid, I'm a dead man."

"I's da maid, boy, and don't ya forget it," Callie snapped from directly behind Lucas, her hands on her shapely hips.

Dorothy, who stood next to the maid, retreated a step.

A look of fury crossed Lucas's face, and Sin recalled how much he hated to be called "boy." His eyes bright, ready for battle, the man spun around sharply. For a moment he froze in place, his body tight. Gray eyes met green, his surprised, hers cool. Then, inch by inch, Lucas relaxed, and a lazy, seductive smile slid into place. "I definitely won't forget."

"Humph," the pretty mulatto snorted, and hurried to her mistress. "Are you all right, chile?" Her eyes lowered to Moriah's clothing and grew wide. But she said nothing.

How could she? Sin mused. She wore virtually the same dress, only instead of peach and lime flowers like Moriah's, she was wrapped in oranges and yellows.

"I'm fine," Moriah said in a soft, quiet voice. Her glance moved to him, then quickly lowered to the tile floor.

He couldn't help wondering how a woman of her experience could be so shy. Or did her true personality only surface under the cover of darkness? Somehow, that thought felt ugly. In fact, everything about her profession suddenly rankled him.

Dorothy cleared her throat. "Sit down, Miss Morgan. Breakfast will be served shortly." She nodded at Callie. "You, girl, can eat in the kitchen with the rest of the help."

"No!" he and Moriah said in unison.

His housekeeper cocked a brow at the girl, and she blushed wildly.

Sin rose. "Callie may join us this morning."

"But it isn't prop—"

"That will be all, Dorothy." He glanced at Beula, who still stood under the archway. "And you might want to give Donnelly a hand . . . before he demolishes your kitchen."

The plump servant made a choking sound. "You let dat buzzard in *my* kitchen? Land sakes, Massa, what was you thinkin'?"

Punishment for his blunder, Sin barely stopped himself from saying.

"Lord-a-mercy, if there's anything left, it won't be fittin' to eat." Still mumbling, she stomped off toward the cookhouse.

Dorothy, her features a cool mask, retreated after the grumbling cook, her stiff gait giving evidence to her thoughts on his lack of decorum.

When everyone was seated at the table, he poured each of them a cup of coffee, then set the pot aside. "Lucas, I'd like you to meet Callie . . . ?"

"Malcom," the mulatto supplied.

Sin nodded. "And Moriah Morgan." He gestured to the woman with whom he'd spent a most enjoyable, if frustrating, night. "Ladies, may I present my overseer, Lucas Burke."

"How do you do," Moriah acknowledged primly.

The maid didn't respond.

If Lucas noticed, Sin couldn't tell.

Deciding to let those two take care of their own situation, he slid his gaze toward his mistress. With her head bent as she absently stirred her coffee, sunlight filtered in from the terrace and sparkled off her glossy, black hair, off the smooth slope of her bare shoulders. He studied her lowered lashes. They were long, and thick, making tiny crescents on her high, delicately carved cheekbones. The incredible flawlessness of her skin and length of her slender neck fascinated him. He knew he'd never seen such sweet perfection.

At the thought of how that smooth flesh had felt last night, his lower body grew warm. Damning his inability to stop staring, he curved a hand around his cup and continued his inspection.

Though he'd seen the flowered wraps on nearly all the island women, somehow they'd never looked like *that* on any of them. Moriah seemed much more exposed. The draped silk molded to her breasts like damp gauze, emphasizing their full, uplifted shape. The gentle curves recalled to mind the weight of her in his hand, the softness, the way her nipple had pressed tauntingly into his palm.

He took a drink of coffee.

The sound of breaking dishes jolted him to awareness.

"Don't you *ever* put your hands on me again," Moriah's maid hissed angrily, her eyes flashing at Lucas.

The overseer tried his damnedest to look innocent with pieces of broken china lying on the table in front of him—and clinging to the front of his wet, coffee-stained shirt. He glanced at Sin and shrugged. As gracefully as possible under the circumstances, he rose. "If you'll excuse me. I seem to have had an accident." Giving no further explanation, he strolled out.

"Callie," Moriah began, "I don't think—"

"Ain't no man goin' ta paw me," the mulatto interrupted. "Not behind no barn or *under no table.*" Rising, she lifted her chin. "I's goin' back ta my room ta rest." With her head held regally, her back stiff, she stalked away.

Sin bit back a grin. Under the table? Lucas was right. He *didn't* know how to court a woman.

"Sir, I don't find your man's behavior in the least bit amusing."

Checking his smile, he returned his attention to his coffee, trying to appear serious. "I'm sure he didn't mean any harm. He was just taken with your maid. She's a lovely woman. It won't happen again—" Something nudged his leg, and he looked down to see Achates, the black leopard, rubbing against his trousers.

"That still doesn't excuse—" She sucked in a sharp breath. "What *is* that thing?"

"A black leopard—or panther as he's sometimes called." He smiled and scratched the animal behind the ears. "Where have you been, Achates? I haven't seen you since yesterday."

"I—Is it dangerous?" she asked warily, shifting her legs to the side of her chair. Very shapely legs, he noted.

"I imagine some of its species are, but this one's just an overgrown kitten. I found him abandoned when he was only a few days old." He patted his knee. "Up, Achates. Meet Moriah."

The panther rose to its haunches and placed its paws on Sin's lap. Clear amber eyes stared curiously out of smooth black fur. It made a sound somewhere between a purr and a growl.

The girl edged over in her chair a few inches, away from the cat. "H-He's beautiful."

"He's a pest most of the time. Between stealing food from the kitchens and terrorizing the servants, he keeps the place in an uproar."

"Why don't you keep him outside?"

"I tried that. After I replaced the fourth broken window, I decided it was cheaper to let him have his own way. I installed a low, hinged door in my bedroom, so he can come and go as he pleases when everything's closed up."

The leopard, having lost interest in the conversation, climbed down, then padded to a rug in front of a cold fireplace and stretched out.

Beula bustled in the door with a harried-looking Donnelly in her wake. "I's managed to save some of the meal," the cook announced in a martyred tone, setting down dishes filled with steamed clams, fluffy eggs, and melon. She rolled her eyes at Donnelly.

The scowling man, his tumbled gray hair hanging in his eyes, didn't lift his head as he placed sweet bread and ham on the table.

After the servants departed, Moriah, between nervous glances at the panther, concentrated on her meal. When she'd finished and pushed away her plate, she noticed that her host, too, was done.

He set his napkin aside, then stood and extended his hand. "Would you like to take a walk?"

"Yes, I would." Still leery of the cat, she placed her hand in his and came to her feet, her eyes on the animal.

The leopard started to rise.

"Stay, Achates," Sin immediately ordered.

The panther stared for a moment, then plopped back down.

She felt overwhelming relief. She had never seen such a big, ferocious animal, yet his name intrigued her. "What does Achates mean?"

Drawing her hand through his arm, her host strode toward the terrace. "Friend."

She looked up at him, suddenly aware of his similarity to the panther. Glistening black hair, piercing eyes, powerful muscles. So wickedly beautiful. So frighteningly dangerous.

"Shall we see if the hands have been able to rescue your trunks?"

Ridding herself of the mental image, she nodded. "I'd like that very much." Yes, she thought with even more vehemence. Then she could regain her wardrobe and burn this thing she wore. Her step faltered. She couldn't go out like *this*. Pulling free of his hold, she stopped before the doors. "I can't be seen wearing this." Her hand swept down her front.

His eyes narrowed on her suspiciously, and she knew she'd made another mistake. Soiled doves were not modest. "I mean—"

"I know what you mean, princess. But I doubt the men will even notice. It *is* the normal dress here on Arcane."

Still unsure, yet helpless to correct the situation, she sighed and slipped her hand back through his arm. "Then by all means, lead on."

Walking through the coolness of the junglelike foilage and spongy grass on their way to the cove, she savored the alien sensation of cool turf cradling her feet. She'd never gone outside without her shoes. *Ladies* didn't do such, Mama had often told her. But Mama hadn't told her how wonderful it felt.

When they emerged from the trees onto the beach, she stopped and dug her toes into the warm sand. How utterly marvelous. Slowly she inhaled the fresh salt air and pushed her foot deeper into the fine granules.

He watched her curiously. "Haven't you ever gone barefoot in the sand?"

Embarrassed, and not even sure why, she shook her head.

"Where the hell were you raised, in a locked tower?"

"No. Boston."

"Just as bad." Taking her hand, he again started walking.

Up ahead, she heard men shouting and laughing as they pulled on ropes that stretched toward the water, then disappeared into its depths. Beside them, another vessel, obviously in the process of being built, was braced up by huge beams. For a moment she watched the commotion. "What are they doing?"

"Trying to bring up the sloop," her companion answered, taking off his shirt. "Wait here. I'll be right back." Racing across the white sand, he joined the men on the ropes.

With a mixture of embarrassment and awe, she observed the way his firm muscles flexed and strained as he sprinted across the beach, then made a place for himself in the line. Within minutes a fine sheen of moisture glistened off his healthy bronze skin and curled the hair near his neck. She experienced a heaviness in her chest when she recalled how solid his flesh felt to her touch.

Trying desperately to vanquish stirring thoughts of the previous night, she sat down on a nearby log. She didn't want to think about him. The man could be her sister's murderer, for goodness' sakes. Just because he was pleasant at times didn't mean he didn't have a dark side.

"Quite a sight, aren't they?" Callie said, walking up behind her.

Moriah clutched her chest to still the sudden leap that the girl's unannounced approach had caused. "Yes, they are." She faced her friend. "Did you get settled in all right?"

The woman didn't take her eyes off the men. Lucas in particular. "Yes. Donnelly gave me a fancy room on the upper level. I heard the housekeeper say that all the servants stayed on that floor."

"You're not a servant."

"As long as we're on this island, I am." She touched Moriah's hand, suddenly concerned. "Are you okay? Did you have any trouble last night? Did Sin try to—"

"No!" Heat surged to her cheeks. "I mean, I got bruised during the storm, and he saw the discoloration and he . . . well, he didn't force himself on me."

"Do you want me to move into your room? My presence might forestall his advances."

Her gaze returned to Sin, to the powerful muscles straining as he worked. Though he was frightening, somehow she trusted him. "I don't think that'll be necessary—at least, not yet. He's been a perfect gentleman. Even though he had the right, he didn't attempt to . . . well, you know. And by the time he's convinced I'm well, we'll surely have found out what we need to know and be ready to leave the island." She stared at the workers again. "Speaking of finding out what we need to know . . . it looks like they'll be at it awhile. Now might be a good time for us to explore on our own."

"I don't know, Moriah. If we were caught snooping around where we shouldn't, we'd be hard-pressed to explain ourselves."

"Then I'll do it by myself."

Callie's green eyes flashed. "That's not what I meant, and you know it."

"No. Listen. You don't understand. I think I should do the exploring. You can question the servants, keep them occupied, while I search for anything that might give me a clue to the identity of Sara's killer." She peeked at the struggling men just in time to see the leaning mast of the ship poke up out of the water. "But I think we'd better hurry."

CHAPTER
7

~~

Callie and Moriah separated near the front of the house, the mulatto heading for the kitchens, while Moriah went to find Sin's study or office, one she was quite certain he would have. Beula had mentioned that cane was the livelihood of the island, and it would be very difficult to run a plantation without one.

Walking slowly down various corridors on the east side of the manor, trying not to draw attention to herself and keeping a wary eye out for the panther, she casually opened first one door, then another. A spare bedchamber. A sitting room. A room stacked with linens. But no study.

Knowing his bedroom and the adjoining one were at the north end of the house, the parlor and dining room on the south, and the servants' quarters upstairs, she ventured to the east, her nerves tingling with each step. What if she was caught? How could she explain herself?

Vowing she'd think up some plausible tale if the need arose, she continued on. The first room she came to was darkly masculine and lined with books. Maps, charts, and papers were strewn across the top of a cherrywood desk.

With a quick glance behind her to make certain no one was about, she slipped inside and shut the door. Even with a slight breeze wafting in from the veranda, the lingering aroma of tobacco, spice, and musk moved over her senses. The room smelled like virile male . . . like Sin.

Now, why did that notion cause queer little flutters in her belly? Knowing she was being silly, she dismissed the sensation and inspected his private domain. She noticed a ladder-back chair by the open doors. The leather cushion was scorched as if something had burned the seat. How odd.

Moving to the desk, she gingerly lifted one of the papers. A map of the Bahamas leapt into view. If any of the seven hundred islands and twenty-three hundred islets were missing from the page, she couldn't tell. Every one of them appeared to be sketched on the parchment.

A line, dark and bold, started at Nassau and traced a curious, winding path through the islands until it came to one that was circled. Arcane? Studying it a moment longer, she shrugged and set the map aside.

The remaining papers were charts and shipping invoices that dealt mostly with sugarcane and rum. Recalling the docks in New Providence, she wondered if any of those crates she'd seen being loaded on a ship were Sin's. What did she care? she thought disgustedly, jerking open a drawer.

A drawstring pouch, tightly closed, sat amid neat stacks of blank paper. A piece of glistening gold chain protruded from one end of the secured bag.

Curious, she carefully untied it and peeked inside. An exquisite gold medallion carved with a figurehead rested atop numerous coins. Extracting the neckpiece, she lifted it to the light and instantly recognized the figure. She smiled. Sin was Catholic, too.

Replacing the coins and medallion, she continued her search—for what, she didn't know. When the contents of the desk didn't reveal anything to connect him to Sara's murder, she moved to the bookshelves.

In the beginning, her hunt was as fruitless as the first had been. Then she saw a page from a newspaper, folded much like a bookmark, sticking out of a volume.

She studied the article on the page. With each line she read, her eyes grew wider, and her hands began to shake. The story detailed—*very graphically*—Elizabeth Kirkland's killing, and she knew each word applied to her sister as well.

Trembling uncontrollably, she stared at the sketch of Miss Kirkland. So beautiful. So young. Just like Sara. Pain tore at her chest. Oh, God.

Tears blurred her vision, and she shoved the paper back into the book. Carver said both women were killed in the same way, but there was so much he hadn't told her. So much violence. So much she hadn't sensed when he demanded Sara's coffin remain closed at the funeral. A warm trickle slid down her cheek. How her sister must have suffered at the hands of that cruel, vicious monster. It hurt to breathe, to think.

In desperate need to escape the horror, she raced out across the veranda and ran for the cool serenity of the woods.

She ignored the sting of branches and thorns scraping her legs as she slapped her way through the undergrowth. Even the thick ivy branches covering the forest floor and stabbing her bare feet didn't matter. Nothing mattered but forgetting the horrifying words she'd read. Tortured. Mutilated. *Dissected.*

Moriah's stomach lurched, and she clamped a hand over her mouth. With her legs no longer able to support her, she dropped to the ground. Wracking sobs tore from her throat. Pain and tears spilled onto the ivy. What kind of insane demon could do such a thing?

Sin's image rose to mind, but she couldn't visualize him performing such sick barbarity. Yet he *had* the paper clipping. *Had* been the last person to spend time with both women.

She sat up and wiped the dampness from her cheeks. Could the sensitive, gentle man she met last night, in truth, turn into some savage beast? An animal capable of mutilation? But how could he have done the deed? Sara and the other woman had returned to Nassau from the island. And he never leaves Arcane.

Supposedly never leaves, she amended. But what if Madam Rossi and the others were lying to protect him? What if they knew of his duplicity and were covering for the man who generously supplemented their livelihood? Her heart cried no, but logic concluded it was a distinct possibility.

Suddenly a low growl tore through the silence.

Confused, she whipped around, searching for the source. Nothing. Not a single thing moved. Even the monkeys were silent. Still, the hairs on the nape of her neck began to prickle. Warily she scanned the underbrush, the thick matted foliage, the trees overhead.

Then she saw it.

Horrified, she screamed.

A giant white tiger lunged.

Moriah cried out again and threw up her hands to ward off the attack.

"No!" someone bellowed.

The tiger slammed to a halt in midair, then miraculously pitched backward and plummeted to the ground.

Shaking wildly, her mouth open in shock, she watched the animal rise on awkward legs and shake itself, then race away.

She twisted her head around in confusion.

Sin stood among the trees, his eyes fierce, so bright they were gold as he followed the cat's retreating form. Then he turned on her. Instantly the glow in his eyes diminished and they returned to their normal dark brown color. "Are you hurt?" he asked without moving, almost as if it frightened him to do so at the moment.

His voice sounded abrasive, like rough sand against rock; still she could have sworn she heard a slight quiver. "I don't think so." But inwardly she wasn't so sure. She could recall the way the cat had lunged at her, and how it had jerked to a stop and spiraled backward, then fallen.

How? And what about Sin's eyes? Why, or better yet, *how* had they changed color so drastically?

"I thought I told you to wait for me on the beach." The tenseness in his muscles uncoiled as he walked toward her.

What could she say? That she wanted to search his office? "I know. But you were so busy, I thought I'd walk for a bit. I, um, got lost."

"Moriah, when I give an order on this island, I expect it to be obeyed." He knelt down and touched her cheek, taking the bite out of his words. "I'm not saying that because I want to play the high-handed lord and master. There are dangers here. Especially in the woods. Unfortunately, most of which I created." He glanced toward the trees. "Like the tiger."

His touch unnerved her. "What are you talking about?"

Those deep brown eyes melted into hers. "I collect wild animals." His thumb traced her lower lip, his gaze moving over her face, almost as if she were one of the creatures he spoke about. "Their dangerous beauty intrigues me." He moved closer. "Their instincts for survival . . . for mating, are fiercely primitive, and magnificently unparalleled." His breath feathered her lips. "Their savage power stimulates the senses, while reminding a man of his own mortality. His own weaknesses."

Tremors of fear and excitement raced through her. Tingles tightened her skin. Crouched down beside her, he looked as savage and primitive as the animals he described. "I'm sorr—"

His mouth covered hers.

She gasped at his outrageous boldness. How dare he take such liberties. She wanted to pull away, deliver him a sound slap, but couldn't. A man's mistress did not box his ears for a kiss.

Shivers and heat chased through her body in turns as she forced herself to endure his sensual assault. But something was happening. She wasn't supposed to enjoy this. Yet she was, God help her, she *was*. His mouth tasted so good. Then she felt it, his tongue, moist and hot, pressing against her lips.

Horror and desire collided. One part of her demanded she stop this madness at once, while another begged her to continue, to embrace his volatile passion. She couldn't, her fear was too strong. She kept her lips tightly closed.

His hands slid around her, stroking gently, then tracing her spine until he reached the curve of her bottom. Long, slender fingers spread and captured the round flesh, pulling her to her knees, against his lower body, making her aware of the hardness between them.

Her moral upbringing soared away in a whirling mist, and unable to resist, she pressed into him.

He sucked in a breath, then crushed his lips down on hers again. He drew her closer . . . closer . . .

A discomfort moved through her bruised side. It didn't hurt, but the ache was enough to bring her to her senses. She pushed at his shoulder.

He drew away, confused.

"My s-side," she offered as explanation.

"Damn. I'm sorry," he said thickly, then released her. "I forgot about your injury. Are you okay?"

Still affected by his nearness, she could only nod.

"You're pale." Without warning, he scooped her up into his arms and started walking. "I'm taking you back to the house so you can lie down."

"But—"

"No arguments, woman. I'm the master here, and I say you'll rest."

Though he sounded serious enough, she didn't miss the light of humor in his eyes. His gentle teasing eased her concern, and she relaxed—just this once. "As well you should," she said, feigning reproach. "After all, I wouldn't be in such misery if it weren't for your fumbling advances."

His step faltered, and he glared down at her. *"What?"*

She grinned.

A chuckle vibrated in his big chest. "Why, you little

minx. Just for that I ought to toss your skirt up and take you here and now."

She sobered instantly. A quiver passed through her. "Please don't." Realizing how prim she sounded, she quickly added, "Not while I hurt."

"Princess, I was only baiting you. We have plenty of time for . . . you to heal." He explored her features, his eyes revealing a well of restraint before he looked away.

When they reached the manor, she saw Dorothy standing in the doorway, her face drawn, her hands fidgeting worriedly with a fold in her muslin skirt. "What happened? Is she all right?"

He nodded as he turned down the hall. "She's had a scare, and her ribs are giving her trouble, but she's fine."

The housekeeper let out her breath. "Thank goodness. I was so worried when she come up missing. I was afraid she met up with that woman—"

"Dorothy!" he snapped.

"All right. All right. You get her into bed. I'll fix some hot broth."

Met what woman? Moriah wanted to shout. Who lived in the woods who was so frightening, she had Sin worried and the housekeeper wringing her hands?

Donnelly stepped into view. He stared into Moriah's eyes, almost as if he were searching for something. After a moment, he nodded respectfully.

She was even more confused. "Sin, I don't think—"

"I know," he teased softly, shifting her weight in his arms. "So from now on, I'll do the thinking for you."

She bristled.

"At least," he continued, grinning, "until you're physically able to fend for yourself." He entered the room they'd shared the previous night and gently put her down on the bed.

Her thoughts were in a whirl over everything that had happened, but there was one thing she had to know. "How did you stop the tiger?"

He stiffened. "I didn't."

"Yes, you did. I may have been scared, but I know what

I saw. Without touching that animal, you halted it as surely as if you held it on a leash. How?"

He didn't move for the longest time, then very slowly, he turned away. "My presence frightened the tiger, Moriah. That's all." His expression completely unreadable, he quit the room.

Confused and a little scared, she stared at the closed door. He was lying. Damn it, she knew what she'd seen. She closed her eyes and rubbed tiredly at her temples. Or did she?

"Moriah?" Callie's voice followed a soft rap on the open veranda door as she entered. "What happened? Are you all right? I heard servants talking about you—"

"If one more person asks me that, I think I'll scream."

"Well, I guess that answers my last question." Her friend sat down on the bed. "But not the first."

"I was nearly breakfast for a white tiger."

Shock, then relief, flashed over the girl's features. "You sure know how to stop a person's heart." She stood up and paced to the empty fireplace. "How did you get away?"

"I'm not sure," she answered honestly. "But I know Sin had something to do with it." She pushed herself into a sitting position. "Did you learn anything from the servants about Sara?"

"A little."

"What?"

"I didn't learn anything about Sara and Sin's relationship. But I did find out some interesting things about the island and the people here."

"Such as?"

She sat down. "It seems that when the king of England granted this island to Sin's grandfather, it was inhabited by a group of mysterious natives called Howidaks. Islanders who were ruled by a voodoo priest named Mumdy. He has long since died, but from what I understand, his great-great-granddaughter, Mudanno, has taken up the roost."

"What has this to do with Sara?"

"I don't know." Callie lifted a shoulder. "Delta, the girl I spoke to, is the daughter of one of Beula's helpers. She sprained her ankle yesterday, and was down by the kitchens recuperating under her mother's watchful eye." She crossed her legs. "Delta said that everyone was afraid of Mudanno. Except Sin. I know it's going to sound strange, but Delta said he was the only one who had powers stronger than Mudanno's."

Moriah's throat went dry. "What kind of powers?"

"I don't know. And I'm not sure I want to. But one thing I do know for certain, your sister went to see Mudanno the day before she left the island."

Sin needed to vent his frustrations. The anger building inside him, mostly directed at himself, was wedging a crack in his control.

He topped the rise overlooking the cane fields and squinted in the sunlight toward a waving sea of yellowish red stalks surrounded on all sides by towering pines. Brushlike flowers topped the fifteen-foot canes of sugar and dwarfed the sweat-drenched, mostly Negro workers who moved through the rows like seasoned soldiers, attacking, destroying the weeds that threatened the life-blood of the island.

A small river that started at the cove, then meandered through the north woods, purifying itself, ran along the west edge of the fields, supplying additional water to the cane. The frequent rains and main well alone couldn't handle the job.

In need of strenuous exercise, and anxious to join the others, he pulled off the shirt he'd retrieved from the cove and tossed it over a nearby branch, then sprinted down the hillside and picked up a hoe.

No one said a word as he started in. His presence wasn't uncommon. Hard physical labor, he had concluded long ago, was a good outlet for frustration. Besides, the weeds in this fertile ground grew faster and wilder than the ivy covering the floor of the north forest.

At the end of a row nearly seven feet wide, he slammed

his hoe into the moist dirt. He shouldn't have stopped the tiger, he thought viciously, recalling the horrific mistake he'd made this morning. He shouldn't have shown Moriah even a hint of his capabilities.

The tool jabbed into the soil again. But what the hell was he supposed to have done? Let the animal kill her?

Moisture beaded on his brow as he assaulted a stubborn cluster of devil grass. No. He'd done the only thing he could have under the circumstances. He just wished she hadn't been quite so perceptive. Hadn't immediately associated the cat's unusual fall with him.

Damn this curse. He swung the hoe brutally. Damn *him* for not being able to control the beast.

"Leave some for the hands," Lucas said, strolling toward him.

Glancing up, he expected to see a grin on his friend's face. Instead, he found a concerned frown. "What's wrong?"

"You've got problems, boss."

Sin straightened and tossed the hoe aside. "What?"

"Mudanno."

A curse escaped before he could stop it. "What's she done now?"

"Nothing. But when I went up to the house for my courting debut, I stopped to talk to Delta. She was sitting outside the cookhouse with her foot all bandaged up. Anyway, she said Callie was asking a lot of questions about our not-so-dear voodoo priestess." He stared off into the distance. "And questions about Sara Winslow's visit to her."

Something inside Sin's gut knotted. "What the hell does she want to know about Sara?"

A shoulder rose in a gesture of uncertainty. "From what Delta said, Callie was curious about Sara's stay on Arcane, your relationship with her, and how Mudanno fit into the picture."

"Why?"

"Damned if I know. But I intend to find out. I just stopped by to keep you informed."

He watched Lucas's tall frame negotiate the hill toward the house, then disappear into the trees. How did Callie even know Sara? His eyes narrowed. Did Moriah know her, too?

He snatched up the hoe and slammed the tool into the ground. As soon as he calmed down, he would talk to Moriah and find out what this was all about.

In less than an hour, the hard work had settled him enough to confront his mistress, though, he had to admit, ever since he'd first seen her, he'd been at odds with himself. If she continued to test his control, he would be forced to keep his distance from her. And that notion didn't sit well at all.

He had just reached the corner of the house when a figure moved at the opposite end of the veranda. Stepping behind a lilac bush, he watched Moriah's maid dart quietly across the lawn and into the north woods.

Suspicious, he followed her.

She hesitated at the line of trees and scanned the upper branches, as if searching for something. The tiger, he decided, knowing Moriah must have told her of the danger. Evidently finding nothing threatening, she walked deeper into the shaded forest.

Birds squawked in protest to her presence. Monkeys chattered and scrambled from limb to limb. He used the sounds to mask his footsteps as he hurried after her.

There was something eerie about this part of the woods. It was too quiet. Too somber. The flesh along his arms began to tingle. He could *feel* a presence, feel eyes watching.

Callie must have experienced the same sensation. She stopped suddenly and warily glanced around. "Who's there?"

A twig snapped.

She whirled around, her eyes wide, searching.

His own gaze shot in the same direction. For a moment, he felt a tingle of apprehension, then he saw Lucas step from the trees.

"Where are you going?" the overseer asked her.

She grabbed for the trunk of a tree to steady herself. "My Lord. You nearly frightened the life out of me."

A curious expression crossed Lucas's face, and Sin knew why. The maid had spoken perfect English.

She herself must have realized the slip, because she quickly reverted. "Whatcha lookin' at, boy?"

He could almost feel the anger radiate from his overseer, and he wasn't surprised to hear Lucas say, "Call me 'boy' one more time, woman, and you'll be prying my foot off that sweet ass of yours."

Sin fought a smile and waited expectantly to see what the girl would say.

"You wouldn't dare—" she began.

"Try me," his friend interrupted.

She looked away, her manner uneasy. "Why ya followin' me?"

"The mock accent doesn't become you, woman. Now, what the hell's your game? Why are you asking questions about Sara? Why do you want to know about the witch, Mudanno?" His big hand caught her chin. "And why are you pretending to be something you're not?"

Sin arched a brow. He wouldn't mind knowing the answers to those questions.

The maid clenched her teeth together in a show of surprising calm. "Take your hands off of me, *boy.*"

Sin shook his head. The woman had guts, he'd give her that.

The muscles in Lucas's arms tightened. He gripped her by the shoulders and dug his fingers into her flesh. "You're pushing me."

Hoping his friend retained control, Sin watched the two of them glare at each other. Then something happened. Maybe it was the way their bodies were pressed so close, or something indefinable passing between them. But one moment Lucas was furious, and the next, he was kissing her.

Uneasy about watching the intimate scene, Sin started to leave. Just as he went to turn, he saw Lucas shove the girl from him, and order roughly, "Get back to the manor and stay there. And don't go near these woods again."

Evidently the low, threatening sound of his voice must have reached her. She retreated a step, then broke into a run.

Not wanting Lucas to know he'd witnessed their encounter, Sin, too, made for the house. But as he walked, he mulled over the day's events. His mistress had been prowling the woods when he saved her from the tiger. Her maid was prying into his and Sara's relationship, asking questions about Mudanno, and pretending to be someone she wasn't. Why?

He slapped a streamer of ivy out of his way. Something about his prim mistress and her nosy, *educated* maid just didn't add up.

MISTRESS OF SIN

CHAPTER

8

Moriah paced the bedchamber, trying to reason out the odd occurrence she'd experienced earlier. Some unseen force had stopped the tiger from attacking her. And it certainly looked like that force was Sin. Hadn't someone told Callie he had power stronger than a voodoo priestess's? And why had Dorothy been worried about her meeting someone in the woods? Donnelly, too? What did it all mean?

Knowing if she kept up these chaotic thoughts and pacing much longer, she'd be nothing but a tangle of nerves by evening, she hiked up the top of her skimpy wrap and headed for the door. She needed to do something to take her mind off the strangeness of the islanders.

Afraid to venture toward the woods again, she decided to see if the men had managed to drag the sloop up onto the shore, which she was certain they must have since Sin had come after her that morning.

Shoving her way through the dense underbrush, she heard voices long before she reached the beach and saw the huge, single-masted vessel she'd journeyed on lying on its side, resembling a huge whale she'd once seen stranded on a beach. Wondering how they managed to get the vessel ashore while still full of water, and supposing the gaping hole in its side had allowed drainage, she started forward.

Footsteps thudded off to the right.

She edged behind a fern.

Her host, his overseer, and one of the men she'd seen helping raise the sloop burst from another section of the trees, smiling broadly.

From her concealed position, she watched Sin's long, sure stride as he crossed the sand with the others. Again he wasn't wearing a shirt, and moisture glistened over his golden skin, sheathing his muscular arms and back. The flowing white britches he wore were damp, and clung shamelessly to his firm buttocks and thighs.

She rubbed her arms briskly to warm a sudden chill.

When he reached the wreckage, he walked slowly around the hull, stopping now and then to inspect the damage. Occasionally he shook his head and spoke to one of the other men. Then, barefooted, he climbed up onto the severely slanted deck and disappeared inside. Only moments had passed when he resurfaced, carrying her dripping trunk on one of his broad shoulders. He lowered the chest to a pair of workers standing below, then gestured toward the manor.

With difficulty, the men carried the waterlogged coffer between them and headed for the trees not far from where she stood.

To think that one of his first thoughts had been of her made her insides grow warm, but she didn't want to be discovered spying on him. She quickly returned to the house.

Once inside her bedroom, she shut the door and leaned against the jam, overjoyed that she'd soon have less revealing clothes to wear—even if they were the one's Callie had supplied. Anything would be better than the next-to-nothing wrap she wore now.

She dusted the sand from her feet, then crossed to the dressing table to get a hairbrush. Just as she touched the pearl-handled instrument, an object caught her eye.

A doll.

Curious, she picked up the small, stuffed toy. Who did that belong to? She hadn't noticed the novelty when she left a few minutes ago.

She examined the unusual workmanship closely. Material similar to the fabric she was wearing had been wrapped around the doll's body. And someone had sewn long, straight black hair to its head. The doll bore a striking resemblance to Moriah herself. That's absurd, she immediately scolded.

Certain that one of the maids must have brought a child with her to clean the room, she set the plaything aside, knowing she must have just missed seeing the toy earlier.

Pleased that she'd solved at least *this* mystery, she headed for the door. Surely the men from the beach had arrived with her chest, and she wanted to get the clothes rinsed in fresh water and hung out to dry.

Near the cookhouse, she found Dorothy standing in front of the open trunk, wagging her head and directing a pair of young island women. One sloshed items in a tub, while another wrung out the sodden garments, then hung them on a rope stretched between two trees.

She doubted they'd dry in a day, with the humidity so heavy in the air. But soon. She smiled and moved to join the women, but quickly halted. With the servants so busy, and the men down at the cove, now was the perfect chance for her to continue searching for clues to Sara's murder.

Unfortunately, she didn't know where to begin. Recalling how she'd left Sin's study in such a hurry after finding the newspaper, she decided to start there.

Having already searched the desk, she rifled through a stack of parchment on the sideboard, but found nothing of importance. The cupboard below held a variety of spirits, rum, sherry, whiskey, brandy, and bourbon, yet not one thing of interest. She was just about to close the door when a carved wooden box drew her attention. The small chest was nearly hidden behind the bottles. She lifted the small cubicle and raised the lid.

An exquisite ivory-handled dagger lay in a bed of blue velvet.

Carver's words screamed through her brain. *Each woman had a stab wound at the base of her throat, made by a knife or dagger of some sort.*

She slammed the lid shut, fighting tears, and vowing she would not go running from the room again. This time she was not going to fall apart. Besides, just because the man owned a knife didn't mean he was a killer.

Replacing the box, she pulled in a lung full of reviving air and rose. There was no place else to probe, at least, not in here.

Her gaze flicked to the book containing the newspaper article. She really should try to read the report on Miss Kirkland's murder again, but this time with more self-control. There might be something she missed.

After scanning the periodical for the third time, and fighting swells of nausea, she refolded the paper and closed the volume. Other than the fact that the bodies were found in different places, Sara's on the wharf and, according to the *Guardian,* Miss Kirkland's behind a church, she'd learned nothing new. Or had she? The commentary claimed that very little blood had been found at the Kirkland murder scene.

She rose to replace the book, trying to understand how the woman's body could have been so mutilated, with part of her organs missing, and there not be much blood. *Because the murders were committed somewhere else,* her logic shouted.

She clutched the volume to her chest as the importance of that fact struck her. The killings could have happened anywhere—and the bodies left on Nassau. Her heart began to hammer. They could have even taken place on any one of the islands . . . even here on Arcane—or on the sloop.

But the women returned alive.

The knot in her stomach eased some, lightened by that irrefutable detail. But just as quickly, her thoughts rebounded. Even though the women returned, that didn't mean they weren't followed. The killer could have been on the sloop with them. Or on another ship. Or . . .

Knowing the hundreds of possibilities would drive her crazy if she let them, she went to shove the volume into the shelf.

Then she noticed the title.

Horrified, she jerked her hand away.

The book toppled to the floor.

She stared at the bold lettering of the rare tome she'd once heard her mother's doctor discussing with a colleague. *Fabrica,* by Andreas Vesalius. The publication was reputed to be the first complete description of the human body . . . acquired by *dissection.*

"What are you doing in here?"

She jumped and spun around to find Sin standing in the doorway, his bare chest coated with perspiration, his expression suspicious.

Fear of the man tightened her lungs. "I . . . was t-trying to find a book to read."

His stared at the one on the floor. "You have an interest in anatomy?"

"No! I, um, mean, that's not the book I wanted. I was reaching for the one next to it, and that one fell out."

He glanced at the shelf behind her. "Oh, I see. You prefer reading about bricklaying." His gaze shifted. "Or was it forging iron?"

She swallowed a groan. "Um, bricks. I've always been intrigued with the fascinating creations masons are able to construct."

Moving toward her, he replaced Vesalius's work and handed her the volume in which she'd feigned interest. "There's an absorbing piece in there on Thomas Jefferson's design, the Serpentine Wall."

Though he sounded serious enough, she could have sworn she saw a flicker of amusement light his dark eyes. Of course, she must have been mistaken. "Thank you. I'm sure I'll enjoy the information." Gripping the book like a lifeline, she scurried from the room.

As she raced toward her chamber, thoughts of what

she'd discovered churned her stomach. Why would he have a book on dissection? Unless . . . No. She wouldn't allow her suspicions to run wild. Just because the man owned an old book about anatomy didn't prove he practiced the barbarity.

What she'd found was one of many books in his library. Certainly nothing to convict him. Besides, if he was anything like her, he may not have even read the blessed thing. Tired and discouraged, she headed for the veranda outside her bedchamber. Maybe reading, even if it was about bricklaying, might clear her head.

A sultry evening breeze tickled over her damp skin as the sun slipped low in the sky. She shifted in a cushioned wickerwork chair and closed the leather-bound volume, feeling thoroughly enlightened on masonry craftsmanship. Actually, she conceded, the information had been engrossing—and kept her occupied.

She swatted at another pesky mosquito and rose to go inside, knowing it was time to dress for supper, not that she had anything different to wear, but she could at least brush the tangles from her hair.

Something rustled the bushes behind her.

She spun around and nervously scanned the bordering foliage illuminated by oil lanterns lining the long patio, hoping she didn't fall prey to another tiger. Eerie shadows danced over the shiny leaves of rubber plants and spiky palms. But nothing moved.

Still, she could feel someone—or some*thing*—watching her. Easing toward the entrance, she kept her eyes on the undergrowth. She wasn't about to turn her back on whatever was out there.

Something pressed into her spine.

She whirled around.

The latch to the veranda door glistened in the lamplight.

An anxious laugh escaped her, and she reached for the handle.

"Leave this island," a voice whispered hauntingly.

Moriah whirled sharply. "Who's there?"

Silence.

"Y-You don't frighten me," she managed with only a slight catch in her voice.

Again nothing.

Trying to control her shaking hand, she opened the door and hurried inside, quickly closing it behind her. She pressed a palm to her pounding chest, but as she fought for composure, she couldn't help wondering if Sara had heard that same voice. That same command.

"Moriah?" Callie called as she walked into the bedchamber. "I was just coming to get you. Beula said supper will be ready in half an hour, and I knew you'd want to change first."

Into what? she thought grimly, then wondered if she should mention the voice she'd heard. Deciding to wait until later, she moved deeper into the room.

The green-eyed girl smiled, her teeth sparkling in her olive face. "I managed to dry out one of the dresses from the trunk."

"How?"

"The kitchen. I hung it near the oven. Kept Beula and the helpers in quite a state trying to avoid the gown and work at the same time."

"What about one for you?"

"Actually, I prefer the island wraps. They offer much more freedom."

Glancing down at her own flowered garment, she couldn't help but agree. She would miss the unencumbered feel once she'd replaced it with petticoats and a gown, however daringly cut. "But the island wear is hardly appropriate. Why, in Charleston, this—" she gestured to her attire "—would cause such a commotion, the authorities would lock me up for causing a public disturbance."

The mulatto ran a hand down her silk-draped hip. "But we're not in the city now." She motioned to Sin's chamber. "We'd better get you dressed soon or you *will* end up wearing the wrap during supper, too."

Moriah nodded, but she silently agreed with her friend. During the day, she'd found herself appreciating the sensuous feel of the silk hugging her body, not to mention the lack of bulky undergarments.

Knowing how her mother would react to her scandalous thoughts, she gave herself a mental scolding and followed Callie into the adjoining room.

She saw the dress Callie had taken such pains to dry lying on the bed—and she tried very hard not to swear out loud. It was the orchid dress she'd worn at the rendezvous house.

Uncomfortably she searched for the petticoats. They weren't anywhere in sight. "Where are the undergarments?"

"Didn't have room to dry them. Sorry."

Sorry? Wearing that clinging gown without undergarments was worse than what she had on. The front dipped so low, it barely covered the tips of her breasts.

She hesitated, then, reminding herself that it *was* a dress, at least, she moved to the basin to wash up before changing.

"Let me help," Callie offered, and began unwinding Moriah's wrap.

Catching the fabric before it fell away, she shook her head. "You don't have to—"

"It's all right. I prefer this to my other line of work."

She fought the urge to pull the girl into her arms and take away the pain she heard in that soft voice. Knowing Callie wouldn't appreciate pity, she tried for nonchalance. "Then when we return to New Providence, I'll pay you for your services."

"Don't be silly."

"I'm not. You've done so much for me . . . and for Sara. I want to do something for you."

The girl squeezed her hand. "Then just continue to be my friend."

Tears stung her eyes. Such small payment. So like

Callie. Willing herself not to cry, she dropped her hold on the island wear and reached for the orchid dress.

Silently the mulatto helped her into it, then did up the front lacings.

While Callie brushed out her hair, Moriah did her best to avoid the mirror, but the figure in the looking glass was impossible to ignore. The scantily clad reflection stared at her—taunted her with a wealth of white flesh that rose from the material, boldly displaying a part of her that, until a few days ago, had only been seen by her mother and maid.

Her thoughts returned to the previous night, when Sin had seen her completely unclothed. She burned with mortification, and for the first time since she'd begun the quest to find her sister's murderer, she wondered if seeing the killer behind bars was really worth the price she would ultimately pay.

Of course it was, she instantly admonished. Bringing Sara's murderer to justice was worth any expense . . . any amount of degradation. Sara would have done no less for her.

"All finished," Callie said, laying the brush aside.

She shook off thoughts of her sister and glanced again into the mirror. One side of her hair had been pulled back and secured with a white seashell comb. The rest hung loose, straight down, falling just below her waist, the blackness a stark contrast to her pale, bare shoulders. All in all, the effect was very unsettling.

"I don't think I've ever seen anyone as beautiful as you."

Embarrassed by the girl's praise, she shrugged. "Then you haven't looked in a mirror."

"Oh, posh. Come along. Supper's waiting."

She had serious reservations about appearing at the table in the gown. It had been bad enough when Donnelly saw her wearing the wretched thing. But short of donning the silk wrap or one of Dorothy's nightdresses, what could she do?

* * *

"Is there a problem, Lucas?" Sin asked, staring at his friend's somber face.

"No."

He arched a brow at the man's clipped answer and probed a little deeper. "Am I to assume, then, that you've had success with your 'Callie' endeavor?"

"No." The overseer's voice sounded like sandy grit. "But I will, don't worry."

He didn't doubt it, but never having seen his friend so ill at ease, he couldn't stop a smile. It wouldn't hurt the man to be taken down a peg or two. He was too confident by half. "Well, you have a little time. The sloop won't be fit to sail for a few weeks. I'm sure you can make the woman fall in love with you by then."

Lucas's eyes flashed with irritation, and Sin enjoyed the hell out of his consternation. This *courtin'* scheme was the best idea either of them had come up with in years.

"Good evening, gentlemen," Callie said as she and Moriah walked into the room.

Sin swung toward the women. His gaze moved briefly over the maid, then zeroed in on Moriah. When he saw what she wore, he felt as if a ship's boom had slammed into his chest. If he'd had any doubts as to her profession, he didn't now. The dress molding her enticing curves wreaked of seduction. Every line teased a man, daring him to touch the soft fabric, to slide that material off her shoulders and indulge in the sweetness beneath. To lift the satiny skirt and bury himself between silken thighs.

Moisture dampened his palms, and he felt himself grow heavy. He quickly looked away, and his gaze landed on Lucas. The overseer, too, stared at Moriah's dress, and Sin had to crush the urge to order him from the room. It was all he could do not to take off his own shirt and wrap it around the woman before beating her soundly. "Won't you join us," he said tightly, his glare returning to her face.

The surge of possessiveness surprised him. He'd never experienced the unnerving sensation with the other women he'd hired. Nor had he ever given much attention to their lack of attire.

When the women were seated, Beula set supper on the table, and he filled everyone's glass with white wine, determinedly keeping his gaze from his mistress.

His childhood friend, on the other hand, wallowed in the women's presence. His attention flitted between Moriah's charms and the maid's.

Sin seethed in silence, and by the time the majority of supper had passed, he was fighting for control. He had to put an end to the tension quickly, and Callie was a likely target. "I understand you were asking questions about Sara Winslow today."

The girl nearly choked on a slice of passion fruit. Her eyes darted to Moriah, then fluttered back. "I, well . . . yes."

"Why?"

Moriah grew pale. She set her fork down, her hand trembling, her gaze on the linen tablecloth.

He watched her closely, wondering at her sudden frailty. Was she sick?

The mulatto cleared her throat. "Miz Sara was my mistress 'afore she come ta your island."

He wanted to gnash his teeth at her use of illiterate dialect, but she didn't know he'd witnessed her and Lucas's confrontation. And what was this about Sara having a maid?

Callie met his eyes, then glanced away. "I was fond of da girl, and I just wanted ta know if she was happy in her last days."

The pain of Sara's death cut deeply, and he took a drink of wine to soothe the vicious ache. Yet even while hurting, he couldn't help the jolt of surprise at her having been Sara's maid. Or that Sara had employed a maid at all, for that matter. It was so unlike her. A companion, yes. But not a servant.

He set his glass down as visions of the exquisite blonde danced through his mind. He could see her childlike smile, her sparkling amber eyes, her enthusiasm for the beauty of Arcane. The back of his throat hurt when he remembered how she would snuggle up with Achates, the panther. She'd lie beside him on the rug, scratching his ears and chest, cooing softly, until they both fell asleep. He must have carried her to bed a dozen times. "Sara . . . was very happy here."

Moriah rose abruptly. "E-Excuse me," she said in a strained voice. "I'm not feeling well." Holding a hand to her stomach, she rushed from the room.

Concerned, he started to rise.

"I'll see to her," the maid blurted, springing to her feet. She ran after her mistress.

He shot Lucas a worried look. "Maybe I should—"

"I wouldn't," his friend countered, his gaze thoughtful as he stared in the direction the women had taken. "I've never known a female who appreciated a man's company when she was ailing."

Knowing he was probably correct in his assumption, Sin resumed his seat and nodded. But, damn it, he was still worried.

Lucas ran his finger around the rim of his glass. "Did Sara ever tell you about herself?"

Sin gaped at him, trying to conceal his surprise. The man never, *ever* pried. "Very little. I know she was recently widowed, and she once mentioned her strict mother and a willful sibling, but that's all."

"I see."

"See what?"

"Nothing much." The younger man downed his drink and stood up. "Think I'll turn in." He nodded. "Good night, boss."

Baffled, he watched him leave the room. What the hell was that all about?

CHAPTER
9

James Cunningham, owner of the Nassau Hotel, glanced up from the high front desk when he heard the main door open. Surprised to see a thin, robed priest enter the lobby, he greeted him warily. "Good afternoon, Father. What can I do for you?"

The clergyman smiled and approached the counter. "I'm Father Walter Crow." He nodded. "And I'd like to take a moment to ask you a few questions."

"About what?"

"Actually, my purpose is twofold. First, I'd like to ask you some questions about the dead woman found behind the church last year."

Recalling with vivid detail the woman he'd seen the coroner haul away, and wishing to hell he'd never ventured down the rear alley to see what the commotion was all about, he eyed the priest. "What do you want to know?"

"Is it true she was mutilated?"

"Whoever killed her did more than that. They sliced her open from chest to gullet. Cut out her female innards." He shuddered at the memory. "She looked like a gutted doe. Strange, though, there was hardly any blood."

The priest winced. "I see." He rested an arm on the counter. "Did you see anyone in the alley that night? Anyone at all?"

"No, I didn't. Besides, I've already told the sheriff everything I know. Haven't you talked to him?"

Thinning brown hair swayed as the man shook his head. "The authorities won't release any information." He leaned closer, his tone conspiritorial. "One of the deceased girl's close friends belongs to my parish, and they've asked me to check into this since the sheriff has evidently lost interest in the case. My parishioners were hoping folks might tell me something they were afraid to tell the constable."

"Well, I don't know nothing more," James defended. "If I had, I'd damn . . . er . . . I'd have told the authorities right away. Even if the gal was a whore, she didn't deserve to die like that. The maniac that done that to her belongs at the end of a noose."

Father Crow smiled indulgently. "I'm sure he does, my son." He brushed a finger over a page in the register book. "My second inquiry is about one of your guests, a Miss Moriah Morgan."

"She ain't a guest at the moment."

"You mean she's checked out?"

"Not exactly. She's away on a trip of some sort. Got her things stored in the attic till she returns."

"When will that be?"

James shrugged. "She wasn't sure." He regarded the priest suspiciously. "Does the Morgan woman have something to do with that gal's killing?"

"No. I've merely been asked to keep an eye on her. With a second murder just last month, well, her family is quite concerned about her welfare with her staying here alone and all."

"I can imagine they are," James agreed. He wouldn't want his daughter staying in a hotel without a chaperone.

The clergyman nodded as he withdrew his hand and slid it beneath the folds of the black robe. "Most certainly. That's why I'd like to impress upon you how important it is to notify me when the child returns."

"I'd be obliged, Father. Anything to keep the gal safe."

"Safe and alive," he added as he placed a card on the desk and strolled out.

Moriah clutched the folds of Dorothy's overlarge nightgown as she leaned against a pillar at the edge of the patio, trying to settle her jangled nerves. She hadn't expected to react so violently to Sin's mention of her sister's presence on Arcane. But when he'd asked Callie about Sara, visions of her beautiful sister held in his powerful arms had bombarded her. She didn't want to believe Sara had been his mistress. In the deepest part of her, she wanted to maintain that Sara had merely come for information about Buford's sister, and nothing more.

Tiredly she brushed her unbound hair out of her eyes and tried to concentrate on the beauty of the night. Stars winked in a velvet black sky, the scent of jasmine danced on a breeze, and the twitter of birds chanted in the stillness.

Sara was happy here, he had said, and she knew he spoke the truth. She'd heard it in the warmth of his voice, seen it in the look of tenderness on his face. Her sister had loved this island. And him?

She crossed her arms over her stomach, strangely unwilling to think about that possibility. Suddenly she knew she couldn't go on like this. The uncertainty of Sara's profession, her real motive for coming to Arcane, were driving her to distraction. Someway, somehow, she had to gain some ground. And by all that was holy, she'd do it tomorrow.

But there was still tonight.

Too agitated to stand still, she went back inside and grabbed for her hairbrush. And froze. She stared at the doll lying on the dressing table. A long needle had been jabbed into its right leg. A cold sensation moved over her, and she picked up the unusual toy to examine the pin more closely.

"Where the hell did you get that?"

She jumped and dropped the figure, then whirled around to face Sin. "H-Here, on the dresser."

He crossed the room in swift strides and snatched up the plaything. A muscle throbbed in his jaw. His eyes turned bright, and she thought she felt the floor vibrate. Suddenly, with a violent jerk of his arm, he threw the toy out the open door.

Anxiously she retreated a few steps.

For a long moment he just stood there, then he drew in a lengthy breath. "If you ever see another one of those," he said roughly, "bring it to me immediately."

She clutched the neckline of her gown together. "It's only a toy."

His gaze stabbed into hers. "That was no toy, Moriah. It's an effigy . . . a likeness used in witchcraft for curses. A malicious gift from our resident voodoo witch. Didn't you notice how the doll resembled you?"

"Well, yes, but—"

"And that needle in its leg," he continued, "represents a wound on your body that will occur in the near future."

Will occur? Not might? She gaped in disbelief. "You can't possibly believe in *curses.*"

He turned those dark eyes on her. Eyes clouded by pain. "Can't I?"

She stared at him, her thoughts tumbling over a hundred reasons for that remark. "Well, you shouldn't, anyway. Everyone knows that voodoo only works if the recipient believes in it. Which, I assure you, I do not."

His gaze slid over her curves. "I hope you're right," he said in a suddenly intimate tone. "I'd hate to see anything else happen to that lovely body of yours. And I certainly wouldn't want you to suffer another injury that might keep you from my bed."

Her mouth went dry. She didn't dare respond to that. Gripping the front of the gown tighter, she moved toward the veranda, never taking her eyes from the man across the room. "Um, how do you think the doll got here? Mudanno didn't bring the thing herself, did she?"

He went very still. "How did you know her name?"

"I, er, heard one of the servants mention her." Well, that *was* the truth. Sort of. Callie had spoken of the priestess, and he thought Callie was a servant. "And I believe I heard Mudanno speak to me earlier, from the undergrowth. At least it sounded like a woman, and I assume the voice belonged to her."

He was beside her in an instant, gripping her shoulders, his expression fierce. "What did she say?"

"F-For me to leave the island."

"Son of a bitch." He stepped away, his features strained as he shoved a hand into his pocket and stared into the growing darkness. He was silent for a span of time, then appeared to come to grips with himself and glanced up. "Don't leave this room until I return. Not for any reason." He left abruptly.

She stared at the closed door, feeling as if she'd just survived another shipwreck. How could he be so gentle one moment, talking seductively and filled with concern, then in the next instant be so arrogant and high-handed? And where was he going?

The answer came in an instant. Mudanno.

Stay here, my foot! Hurrying across the veranda and around the side of the house, she stopped to see which way he'd gone. Through the trees she caught a glimpse of his white shirt disappearing into the woods.

Holding her loose robe together and running to keep up with his brisk pace, she kept him in her sights at all times, when she wasn't watching for tigers. She didn't dare lose him. She might never find her way out again.

Twice she fell, and once she ran into a low broken branch. The sharp point tore her gown and scraped her thigh, but she couldn't let the discomfort slow her down, not even when she felt a warm wetness slide down her leg.

When he finally drew to a stop at the edge of a stream lined with crudely carved canoes, he stared toward a fire barely visible through the trees. Beyond that, she could make out a clearing lined with thatch huts.

She leaned into a pine, catching her breath, rubbing

her stinging thigh, and waiting to see what he would do next. A sudden throbbing of drums nearly startled the life out of her. Her gaze flew to the glen.

A dark silhouette swayed across the firelight, blocking the glow, then moving past. Someone was dancing around the flames.

She held her breath and watched anxiously as he forded the creek and walked toward the village. Fear skittered through her belly, but she didn't know if it was for herself or for him. Lifting the hem of her gown, she edged closer, slipping from one tree to the next until she could see the entire encampment.

He slowly approached the most beautiful woman she had ever seen. She was barely eighteen, by the looks of her, and her satiny skin resembled coffee lightened with cream. Her naked breasts jiggled slightly in the fluttering light, their dark tips hard, thrusting.

Heat rushed to her face, and she whipped her gaze upward.

A gold chain encircled the dancer's head, and a medallion hung in the center of her forehead. Flowing hair, the color of cocoa, tumbled over smooth shoulders and down to her slender hips; the ends brushed a long flowered skirt that wrapped her lower body. One slim leg peeked through a slit at the side of the material where it was tied together low on her hip. A ring of white flowers banded a delicate ankle.

"Mudanno," she whispered. It had to be.

The woman walked toward him, her movements languid, sensuous, her arms raised in invitation.

He didn't move.

Those long, sleek brown limbs encircled his neck as she pressed her body to his. She slid her fingers through his thick hair and pulled his head down until their lips met.

Something ugly clawed through Moriah's midsection.

Still he didn't move, nor did he resist.

The woman stepped back, her features clouded with disappointment. "You will mate with me someday, powerful one. You will give Mudanno your seed." She trailed her hand over his flat stomach and traced the waistband of his breeches. "And I will grow our child. A child who will possess my powers . . . and yours."

His voice was so low, she barely heard his words. "We'll never share a bed, woman. Nor will you bear my babe. Understand that, and stop these foolish games."

She chuckled throatily. "Your will is great, but in the end, we'll see which of us is strongest."

He released a frustrated breath. "Stay away from my house, Mudanno. And stay the hell away from Moriah."

The priestess flicked a graceful hand. "Ah, the woman who shares your bed. She is not as the fair-haired one. She is spineless. I want her gone."

Moriah gritted her teeth. *Spineless? Why, you . . . witch.* She inched closer.

In a movement so quick she hardly saw it, Sin gripped the woman's throat. "Because of my respect for your father, rest his soul, I tolerate your presence here, but if you harm her, so help me, you *will* leave this island."

Several men wearing skirts similar to Mudanno's appeared out of the darkness between the huts, clubs and lances in hand.

Moriah clamped a hand over her mouth to keep from crying out her fear for Sin.

"Release me," the dancer ordered.

"Do you really think your men could hurt me?" he asked softly. Without taking his hand from her throat, he lowered his gaze to the fire.

A low rumble shook the ground. Flames exploded in a shower of sparks.

Moriah choked on a gasp.

The men turned and ran.

"I meant what I said, witch. No more dolls. No more threats. Leave my woman alone." He shoved her from him, then, like an apparition, he faded into the trees.

Still in shock, Moriah huddled behind a large trunk until he'd passed her by, then, her thoughts churning, she followed him as he headed for the manor. He had jerked an immovable piece of metal from a bulkhead to save her life. He had stopped the tiger's attack without touching the animal. And now he'd caused the fire to explode by simply looking into the flames. How, damn it? How?

A trick, her logic resolved. It had to be. Besides, hadn't she once seen a similar maneuver performed in a magic show? Of course, she thought with relief, he'd probably held a fistful of gunpowder and tossed it in at just the right moment. Too, as for the metal frame he'd ripped from the bulkhead . . . well, he was a very powerful man. And, no doubt, extremely strong. Though her summation still didn't explain the tiger, she felt much better.

When she reached the edge of the yard, she waited until he turned for the main foyer, then raced around the other side and entered by way of the veranda.

She hurried through her room to his and snatched up the book on masonry, then started to climb into the smaller bed in the adjoining room. The tear in her nightgown, red with dried blood, halted her actions. She'd forgotten all about the injury. Knowing there wasn't time to change, she crawled under the covers and pulled them up to her chest.

Hearing his footsteps in the hall, she quickly selected a page in the book and settled into the pillows. If only her pounding heart wouldn't give her away.

A door opened and closed in the next room. She heard him moving around, then he appeared in the doorway between their chambers. For a breathless moment, he didn't say anything. He just stood there, staring.

Had he seen her? Did he know she'd followed him? She tightened her fingers on the leather binding.

He watched her a moment longer, then ordered, "Get up, Moriah. You're in the wrong bed."

She went numb. He expected her to . . . She dug her nails into the book's cover. "Please. My side . . ."

A sardonic smile twisted his mouth. "You should have thought of that *before* you followed me through the woods."

"How did you—"

"I saw you running when I crossed the yard. Now, get

up. We have some things to discuss." His gaze went to her lips. "And do."

Panic gripped her. The time had come. She had no more excuses to avoid the *thing* he expected her to do. She couldn't move.

"Get up," he commanded, harshly.

Terrified, she scrambled over the other side of the bed and stood, dragging the covers with her, holding them clutched to her breast.

The floor dipped crazily. She blinked and tried to focus in a suddenly foggy room.

"What the hell?" someone exclaimed an instant before arms closed around her . . . before the darkness came. . . .

Something cool brushed her brow, bringing her slowly, sluggishly, to awareness. She lifted her lashes, and found herself lying in bed, staring into Sin's concerned brown eyes. "What happened?" The last thing she remembered, he was walking toward her. . . .

"You collapsed, princess."

"Why would I do that?" And since when had she started swooning like her mother always did?

He placed a warm palm on her bare thigh. "You ran into a monkey fiddle tree, that's why."

She stared at him blankly.

His fingers slid over the outer edge of her thigh, sending delicious tingles along her flesh. "The tree's pointed branches are filled with a poisonous white sap. When you hit the limb, a piece broke off in your leg. That alone wouldn't have made you ill, but when you combine the poison with your body's aversion to the bark, an allergy, so to speak, it caused an abrupt reaction. Your body handled the jolt the only way it could, by shutting down."

"Will it happen again?"

Strands of silky dark hair moved as he shook his head. "Probably not." He drew his thumb over a tender spot on her leg. "I cleaned the wound, applied some healing herbs, and wrapped it in gauze. If you don't get an infection, you should be fine by tomorrow."

For the first time, she noticed the constriction around her upper thigh, and tried not to visualize how much of her he'd seen while tying the bandage there.

"Why did you follow me?"

The question didn't surprise her, and she answered truthfully. "I thought you would go to Mudanno, and I wanted to see her for myself."

"Why?"

"Just curious, I guess."

His eyes flashed with anger. "Curious enough to damn near get yourself killed?"

"I didn't do it on purpose. Besides, how was I to know you had poisonous trees in the woods?" She glared at him. "You could have warned me."

"I warned you not to follow me!" He closed his eyes and clenched his teeth as if to control his outburst. "You may not believe in voodoo, princess," he said in a calmer voice, "but it's a very real force. Damn it, woman. Look at your leg. You're *right* leg."

Knowing he referred to where the doll had been stabbed, she shook her head. "A coincidence."

He pushed off the bed. "Well, if it's all the same to you, I'd prefer you didn't have any more *coincidences*. The next one might kill you."

"Don't be absurd. I can't believe you actually put any store in that magic gibberish. You strike me as much too intelligent."

He shoved a hand into his pocket. "I have my doubts about magic. But I know there's a force stronger than any of us. A force so powerful, it's frightening."

Praying he was referring to nature's strength, she reluctantly nodded in agreement. "I'm sure there is, but voodoo isn't part of that formidable energy."

"Then how do you explain this, aside from coincidence?" He gestured to her thigh.

He had a point, she conceded. "Carelessness combined

with the seed that had been planted by the appearance of the doll. I could have unconsciously expected it to happen, and by doing so, caused the accident myself."

A glimmer of admiration lit his ebony eyes. "You're an amazing woman."

"No. Just logical."

He brushed the backs of his fingers over her cheek. "Rationale becomes you. A man has to keep on his toes in your presence."

Basking in his approval, she lifted her eyes to his.

The squawk of a distant parrot drifted on a hot, sultry breeze as he eased onto the side of the bed and leaned over her, their gazes still locked. "Very amazing."

Her breath became shallow and thin, as if his potent masculinity extracted the very air from the room. She could smell his spicy scent mingle with the aroma of jasmine. The combination was both intoxicating and arousing. Her whole world centered on only him.

He slid his thumb along her jaw and bent his head. Slowly, gently, he took her lips.

Sweet shivers raced around in her midsection. If only he'd tried to force her, she thought in self-defense, she might have been able to resist. But this tender, erotic persuasion wasn't fair, and it was her undoing. Like sugar mixed in hot tea, she helplessly dissolved beneath his scalding kiss.

The pressure of his mouth increased, crushing her into the bed pillow. She felt the heat of his chest warm the tips of her breasts, then caress the stiff peaks with masculine skill as he moved over her. Desire flashed through her most intimate region, and she helplessly arched into him in an urgent need to experience more of the fiery sensation.

A tremor vibrated through him, and his fingers encircled her upper arms, pulling her closer. The kiss became more demanding, and he hungrily ground against the tender flesh of her mouth, forcing her lips apart to receive the insistent thrust of his tongue.

Startled, she tried to push him away, but the attempt was feeble at best. This thing he was doing to her drained her strength . . . her willpower. Uncaring of the consequences, she slid her fingers into his silky hair and opened her mouth to him.

A violent shudder moved through his body.

Glass exploded.

He tore away from her and lunged to his feet. For a heartbeat, he didn't move. He just stared at her as if she'd grown horns. Confusion marred his handsome features, and he raised a hand to the nape of his neck. "I'm sorry, princess. I shouldn't have pressed you like that. You're not up to my brand of passion at the moment."

She watched him warily. His brand of passion? What did that mean? That there was more than one kind? And what broke? She glanced around.

His gaze, too, drifted over the room, then settled on a shattered windowpane in the open veranda door. A low curse rumbled from his chest.

"How did that happen?" she asked in bewilderment.

He hesitated, then avoided her eyes and mumbled something about Achates probably being the cause of the mishap. He went to the door. "I'll be back in a few minutes."

Certain he must be the strangest man she'd ever known, and extremely thankful for Achates' interference at the most opportune moment, she shoved away the covers and started to rise.

The room dipped and rolled.

She grabbed the mattress to steady herself. He said she'd be well tomorrow, *not today*. But she wanted to find a dressing robe—and be cocooned by the concealing garment before he returned.

When the room righted again, she slowly pushed to her feet. Her legs trembled. Shaking off her weakness, she focused on the wardrobe and very gingerly edged her way toward the finely built cabinet, holding to the basin next to the bed for as long as she could. Finally, her arm stretched to the limit, she let go and stumbled shakily to the closet.

Inside, she found what she sought, and quickly pulled on the satin jacket. Even tightly belted, the unfastened front gaped open all the way to her navel, as did the huge nightgown she wore. Embarrassed by the display, she clutched the lapels together and started back to bed.

Suddenly an eerie voice drifted in from the veranda. *"You will die, whore—just like the others."*

She spun around.

No one was there.

Tingling with fear, she stumbled to the doors and quickly closed them. After securing the lock, she leaned her head on the wood frame, trying to slow her raging heartbeat. Who was doing this? Why?

Only one answer came to mind . . . the killer. She shuddered at the horrifying significance of that possibility.

The murderer could be right here on Arcane.

CHAPTER

10

"What the hell are you doing out of bed?"

Moriah nearly leapt out of her skin.

Sin glared at her from the open door. "Well?"

"I-I just wanted to put on a dressing robe."

His gaze lowered to the gaping front. "It doesn't help much."

She snatched the material together, her cheeks flaming. "W-Where were you?" She retreated a step, recalling that both times she'd heard that awful voice, *he* had appeared shortly afterwards.

"I went to summon one of the maids to clean up the broken glass." He glanced at the closed doors. "Why'd you shut them?"

Not about to let him know how frightened she was, in case he was the culprit, she sought another cause. "Bugs."

Someone knocked on the door.

"Enter," he commanded.

Assuming it was the girl he'd summoned, she was surprised to see Dorothy lumber into the room, carrying a supper tray. She set the meal on the table next to the bed. "Here we are, child. Sin figured you'd like some hot herb broth and sweet bread to fill the empty spot in your belly."

As if on command, her stomach gave a small groan. Embarrassed, she glanced at her host, but he seemed to have found something of interest outside the glass doors. Unsure about this man who could be so terrifying in one instant, then so thoughtful the next, she climbed onto the bed, then nodded to the housekeeper. "Thank you."

After Dorothy left, Sin sat in a chair beside the bed and watched her while she nibbled on the bread.

Very uncomfortable with his silent perusal, she lowered her lashes. "Am I keeping you from something?"

His gaze moved over her figure. "Yes. But it can't be helped."

Fire singed her cheeks. "Oh." She took a quick sip of the beefy soup, and struggled to find a safer topic. "Um, were you born here on Arcane?"

A flicker of a smile touched his lips. "No. Savannah, Georgia. I moved my household to the island five years ago."

Wondering what he was like before he decided on a life of seclusion, and why he'd done so, she pressed on. "Why? Couldn't you grow sugarcane in Georgia?"

His gaze drifted away from hers. "Possibly, but that's not why I came here."

"Then what is the reason?"

He rose and strode to the fireplace, then shoved a hand into his pocket. "I needed privacy."

The word spilled out before she could stop it. "Why?"

Someone knocked softly.

With an expression of relief, he opened the door.

Callie stood on the other side. "How is she?"

He flung the panel wide, then gestured toward the bed. "See for yourself." With a brisk nod to Moriah, he left the room.

She wanted to gnash her teeth at the man's adept ability to avoid her question.

Callie hurried to the bed and grabbed her hand. "Oh, thank the Lord. You're all right." The mulatto's fingers trembled. "When he told us about the accident, I was so worried."

She squeezed the girl's hand. "Well, as you can see, I'm perfectly fine. Just a little weak." *And irritated.* She edged up higher on the pillow. "Have you learned anything more about Sara?"

"Just that everyone liked her. She made a good impression on folks around here."

"She did that everywhere she went."

"Yes."

Moriah picked at the quilt. "You know, I think that's one of the reasons it's so hard for me to imagine someone wanting to kill her." She dug her fingers into the satin. "Unless they weren't in their right mind."

"I still think our 'friend,' Mudanno, might give us some answers. I'm going to pay her a visit."

"No. There's something scary about that woman. I don't want you to go near her. Besides, she's got an army of men at her disposal who, I'm sure, are capable of extreme violence."

Callie straightened and smoothed down the flowered wrap she wore. "Moriah, when are you going to learn that *men* are the least of my worries? Believe me, I know how to handle them."

"I'm sure you do. I saw an example of that at breakfast. Incidentally, what did Lucas do that made you throw coffee at him?"

"Trailed his finger up my leg." Her solemn eyes drifted to the carpet. "No man does that anymore unless he pays for the privilege." She walked out into the hallway. "And now that I know you're okay, I think I'll do a little nosing around. I'll see you tomorrow."

"Callie, please, don't go to Mudanno's."

The pretty mulatto didn't respond, she merely flashed a smile and shut the door.

Praying her friend didn't do anything foolish, she leaned into the pillows and closed her eyes, feeling as if she were losing control of her entire life. Too many things were happening that she didn't understand: the aura of mystery that surrounded Sin; the voice that might, or might not, belong to the killer—or the witch; the prospect that one of the gentle people she'd met on Arcane could be a maniacal killer.

A half growl, half purr echoed in the room.

Her eyes sprang open.

Achates stood on the veranda, looking in through the broken window.

"Shoo. Go away," she whispered urgently, waving her hand at the animal.

The panther poked its head through the paneless square.

Horrified, she looked wildly about for something to throw. Other than the supper tray, nothing was within reach. "Please go," she begged.

He made another purring sound, then edged his sleek body through the opening.

Her heart began to pound savagely.

In a lumbering gait, the cat approached the bed, then sat on his haunches and plopped his paws on the quilt.

She scrambled backward, away from the leopard, and nearly fell off the other side of the bed.

He sprang up onto the mattress.

"No!" She closed her eyes and threw out a hand to ward off an attack.

A warm tongue gently licked her fingers.

Surprised, yet wary, she peeked through the fringe of her lowered lashes.

The animal purred roughly, then lay down, nuzzling her hand with his head.

He wanted to be petted, she noted with a mixture of shock and relief. "Why, you big pussy cat." She gave a nervous chuckle and gingerly scratched its head.

The panther rolled onto his side and stretched out his long black body.

She smiled, again reminded of the animal's master and the way *he* had stretched earlier that morning. She flicked a black ear. "Get comfortable, by all means."

Soon soft snoring told her the cat had done exactly that.

Moving slowly, not wanting to disturb him, she eased

down and put her head on the far pillow, strangely comforted by the leopard's presence. Then another presence intruded on her thoughts. Sin. Her flesh warmed at the mere thought of his name.

She closed her eyes, recalling the way he'd kissed her. Remembered tingles skipped through her veins. No one had ever taken such liberties with her. Even Carver had only been permitted a light brushing of lips. Once. And, truth to tell, the action hadn't affected her in the least.

Echoing shivers centered on her breasts when she recounted how Sin's chest had felt touching her own. *Arousing* was the only word that accurately described the sensation. Well, that or *wonderful.*

She sighed and stroked the panther's fur, wishing there weren't so many hurdles between her and her magnificent host. . . .

As Sin strolled toward the bedchamber, he wondered again at his lack of control. Over the last few years, he must have brought a dozen women to his island, and not once had he lost his composure. Hell, not even at the most crucial moment. Yet with Moriah, a simple kiss had set him off.

Why? he demanded as he gripped the door latch. Why her?

If there were such a thing as traveling back in time, he knew he experienced it the moment he opened her door. Seeing her curled on her side, sound asleep, with her arm looped over the slumbering panther, he thought he'd stepped into the past. Thought he was again seeing Sara.

But he'd never felt this way around Sara, he realized with sudden clarity. He'd never felt this scorching heat in his loins, this uncontrollable urge to possess . . . and protect. Everything about Moriah fired his blood.

Startled by the unfamiliar sensation, he strode to the chair and sat down. Since when had he become prone to fantasizing?

Achates lifted his head, his amber eyes fixed on the terrace. He gave a low, menacing growl.

Surprised at the animal's behavior—and curious—

Sin rose and unlocked the doors. Moonlight bathed the patio and lawns in silver, but he didn't see anything out of the ordinary. He was about to close the panels when a figure darted across the lawn.

A woman.

Without a sound, he slipped out and followed her.

When he got close enough to identify the roaming female, he was more suspicious than inquisitive. Why would Moriah's maid be traipsing through the forest at this time of night? And for the second time in the space of a day?

Not wanting to alert her to his presence, he kept to the shadows and watched as she moved silently through the woods, her gaze again darting frequently to scan the overhead trees, then down to watch for protruding branches.

He tailed her for nearly an hour, but couldn't decide where she was going. She kept veering around in circles. Hell, they'd passed the same orchid plant three times. Then the reason hit him.

She was lost.

Shaking his head, he started to make his presence known, give her a sound order not to enter the woods again, and take her to the manor.

A silhouette moved behind her.

Sin darted behind a pine, then parted the branches so he could see.

Callie whirled around.

One of Mudanno's men stepped from the darkness, a lance held in his thick brown hand. The expression on his face was one of cruel satisfaction, as if he'd just received his bounty from the spoils of war.

He expected her to scream or try to run, but she did neither. She held her ground and simply stared.

The native appeared both surprised and confused. He lifted the lance and pressed its tip to the center of her chest.

Instinctively Sin took a step forward, but froze when the woman spoke without a trace of fear.

"Take me to Mudanno."

Mudanno's man curled his lip in a feral snarl, and roughly gripped the maid's arm.

"No!" She tried to pull free.

Sin had seen enough. He started toward them.

Something hard slammed into the back of his head. Pain exploded. The ground rolled . . . tilted . . . then dropped away. . . .

Callie's heart knocked into her ribs as she tried again to jerk her arm out of the half-dressed man's brutal grip. "Let me go!"

Another native appeared at her side, holding a heavy club. He latched on to her other arm.

Her flesh tightened with fear. Why hadn't she listened to Moriah? "Please, take me to your priestess." She tried to keep her voice steady, but didn't succeed. Her words came out sounding like a child's whimper.

The man with the lance raised the blunt end of the weapon and poked it between her legs. He slid the wood upward, pressing the handle to her private region.

She twisted wildly, trying to dislodge the object.

Her captor's hold strengthened. He spoke to his partner in a language she didn't understand, and they both laughed.

The other native pinched the tip of her breast through her wrap, his mouth curved into a malicious smile.

Pain and fear erupted. She kicked the lance away and screamed.

An open palm struck her cheek. Then another. Ears ringing, she shook her head. "Leave me alone, you bastards!"

One of them viciously twisted her arm behind her back and shoved upward, until she thought her bones would snap. The excruciating pain was too much. She slumped in defeat. It wouldn't do any good to fight. With a single, powerful blow, either one of them could end her life.

Lowering her head, she walked between her captors. No matter how much she resisted, she knew she wouldn't be able to stop the violation they would surely inflict. Her only hope was to detach herself from the horror when the time came . . . just as she'd always done.

When they forded a creek, she saw a yellow glow on the ground. At the same moment, she heard soft chants. Warily she lifted her head and shook the hair out of her eyes.

She was at the edge of a circular clearing surrounded by thatch huts. A fire blazed in the center, its eerie light flowing over a nearly naked woman who stood close to the flames with her hands raised to the heavens, her head back, her long hair almost touching the ground.

She knew this had to be Mudanno. But she hadn't expected her to be so young. Or so beautiful.

The men shoved Callie forward, and she stumbled into the clearing.

The chants stopped.

Mudanno lowered her arms. Without glancing at Callie, she spoke. "Why do you trespass in my sacred forest?"

The woman's hollow voice was just plain spooky—and how was she supposed to have known the forest was sacred? "I wanted to see you about Sara Winslow."

The voodoo priestess snapped her head around. Her black eyes sparked—or was it the light reflecting off the medallion centering her forehead? "The fair-haired one breathes the air of the dead. There is nothing to tell."

"Why did she come to see you?"

"She sought help for the powerful one."

Did she mean Sin? "How?"

Those obsidian eyes drew into slits. "It is the custom of the Howidak, my people, to take before they give."

Though relieved to be free of the men, she couldn't comprehend the woman's demand. "Take what? I don't have anything of value." Even the wrap she wore was the most expensive material to ever touch her flesh.

A slow, mysterious smile widened the witch's mouth. "You will share *tom-coo* drink. Talk."

She couldn't stop the ripple of apprehension about

sharing anything this woman offered. "Listen, maybe this isn't such a good time. I'll come back later."

A hand gripped the back of her neck and shoved her to her knees at Mudanno's feet. She jerked her head up just in time to see the woman's naked breasts quiver with laughter. "You will talk now."

The priestess clapped her hands twice, and an old woman scurried out of one of the huts, carrying a small wooden bowl filled with inky fluid.

Callie instantly recognized the heavy scent of opium, and she'd seen what the despicable drug had done to several of her friends. She sprang to her feet in a desperate attempt to run, only to find herself surrounded by towering men.

Mudanno rapped out a stream of words in a foreign language.

Thick hands latched on to Callie's arms and dragged her up to stand face-to-face with the witch.

Fear sliced through her.

The priestess took the bowl from the old woman and held it up to Callie's mouth. "Drink."

"Like hell, I will."

Someone grabbed a handful of her hair and yanked her head back.

"No!" she cried, struggling frantically, twisting her head from side to side.

One of the men clamped a hand on her chin, digging his thumb and finger into her cheeks, forcing her mouth open.

Mudanno poured the black potion between her lips.

She tried desperately to spit it out, but with her head back and mouth held open, she choked, and was finally forced to swallow.

A cheer went up from the onlookers, and the men released her.

Her knees buckled, and she dropped to the ground. Knowing she couldn't fight all of them, she just sat there, catching her breath and trying to think of a way to escape.

The witch began to dance in front of her in a swaying taunt. Oddly, Callie was drawn to the movements . . . and to the gleaming gold disk on the woman's forehead as the metal flickered in the firelight. Entranced, she watched the brilliant disk undulate, swirl, twinkle. It reminded her of a carnival act she'd once seen in Nassau. The entertainer had used a similar medal to hypnotize volunteers from the audience.

Drums began a slow, lazy beat.

Strange, Callie thought. She could feel them pulsing inside her.

Voices chanted softly, low. The disk claimed her entire vision. An odd warmth slithered through her limbs, making them difficult to move. She fixed her gaze on Mudanno's face, trying to avoid the medal. Funny, she hadn't noticed earlier how queenlike the woman appeared. Callie's eyelids grew heavy.

Mudanno held out her hand. "Come. We talk."

Wanting to resist, but strangely unable to do so, she put her fingers in the priestess's palm, and a surge of excitement rushed through her body—as if she'd touched something holy.

Smiling, Mudanno led her to a large hut where a mat had been spread out in the center of the room. "Sit."

Callie wanted to say something, but the thought fled before it even formed. Her head felt queer. Clouded. She sat down.

"You belong to Mudanno," the woman began in a soft, haunting voice. "You want only to please." She moved her head slowly, from side to side, blinding Callie with the luminous radiance of the medallion. She lifted her hand and stroked Callie's hair. "Mudanno will tell you how to please."

She tried desperately to clear her thoughts. She shook her head, but it only made her dizzy. When her gaze focused again, the witch was smiling with satisfaction.

"You will return to the big house and bring me the one called Moriah."

"I can't."

Mudanno's eyes flared. "You disobey my command?"

Callie felt the movement of her hair and realized she was shaking her head. "Moriah's sick. Her leg . . . the monkey fiddle tree . . ."

A knowing smile curved the priestess's mouth. "I see." She tapped a long, slender finger against her lower lip. Finally she raised her lashes. "You will return to your queen tomorrow night, and each night, until you bring the powerful one's whore."

Something inside Callie screamed in refusal, but the sensation grew weaker . . . and weaker. . . . Holding her head up was getting harder, and the words that came out of her throat sounded as if they belonged to someone else. "Yes, my queen."

Mudanno rose. "Now, tell me why you have come— and why you want to know of the fair-haired woman."

"To find her murderer," Callie slurred, strangely unable to attempt a lie. "She was Moriah's sister."

Mudanno threw her head back and laughed.

Oddly, Callie felt warmed by the sound. In fact, she felt warm all over . . . and sleepy.

The witch clapped her hands, and two men rushed into the hut.

"Take her. She will return again tomorrow."

CHAPTER

11

~

Still unsteady from her recent injury, Moriah stumbled over another ivy vine in her attempt to locate Sin. When Achates' low growl had awakened her, she'd raised her lashes just in time to see her host race out across the lawn, apparently in pursuit of someone, and disregarding her wound and dress, she'd hurried after him.

Unfortunately, at her slower pace, she'd lost sight of him immediately. Now she feared she was lost. Which way had he gone? Where was the manor?

A rustling of underbrush sent a coil of fear down her spine, and she clutched her leg, scrambling for the shelter of a low-branched pine. Not five yards away, leaves parted, and she saw Lucas amble across a small glen—completely naked.

Stunned, she clamped a hand over her mouth to stop a gasp, then instantly turned to leave. Her gaze landed on a large pond, barely visible through the dense foliage. So that's where he was going—for a moonlight swim.

A figure moved, and she glanced up to see a woman standing on the opposite bank.

Callie.

And the overseer?

The second Lucas recognized the girl, Moriah saw his

serene expression turn furious, then he stalked around the bank toward her.

The anger on his face frightened her, and she worried that he might hurt Callie. Whether he was naked or not, she would not allow her friend to be abused by another man. Concern urging her on, she crept quietly toward the concealing trees at the edge of the pool.

He stopped in front of the young mulatto. "What are you doing out here?"

Callie's eyes studied the movement of his mouth. "Searching for you."

The muscles across his shoulders tensed, and his voice sounded rough. "What did you want to see me about?"

To Moriah's astonishment, Callie placed her hand on the man's bare chest, and trailed her fingers down over his stomach. "I want you," she murmured.

Shocked to the center of her moral fiber, Moriah quickly glanced away, torn between running and staying. She didn't want to watch the private encounter, but she didn't know how to get back to the manor.

"You want me?" the man asked sarcastically. "Since when?"

Flabbergasted, Moriah watched her friend's gaze move slowly over his body. "Since the first moment I saw you."

"Is that why you threw a cup of coffee on me?"

She slid her hand lower. "It wasn't the proper time or place."

Lucas sucked in a shocked breath.

Moriah held hers.

"And now the time is right?" the overseer asked, his voice uneven.

"Yes."

Exhibiting an unshakable will, he snatched her hand away and held it a good distance from his flesh. "I think you've been drinking."

Moriah thought so, too. Why else would Callie behave in such a wanton manner?

The girl frowned as if trying to recall, then smiled seductively. "Yes, I have."

He dropped her hand. "Go back to the house."

Shaking her head, she reached for the end of the wrap tucked between her breasts.

"Damn it, don't do that!" Lucas roared. "Just get the hell away from me." He whirled abruptly and dove into the pool. Fleetingly Moriah wondered if the action was meant to escape Callie or cool his own ardor. Or both.

She watched him swim the pond's width in swift, angry strokes, then climb out on the other side. Without a backward glance, he stormed off into the trees.

Still embarrassed by his nudity, she returned her attention to her friend.

Callie was gone.

Gone. "Oh, no," Moriah whispered as a sudden realization hit her. She'd have to catch Lucas to find the way home. Knowing she had no time to waste, she hurried after him.

Just ahead, she saw him disappear around a thick fern. "Lucas, wait!" She broke into a full run. Her foot tangled in ivy at the same instant she saw him step into her path. She shot forward—straight into his arms.

Startled, he gripped her shoulders. "What—"

"What the hell's going on here?"

The grating sound of Sin's voice nearly stopped her heart. Where had he come from? She warily glanced in his direction to see him standing amid the underbrush, a hand massaging the back of his head.

"What are you doing here?" Lucas asked.

"Trying to find Moriah's maid." He glared at her with such distaste, she fought the urge to hide behind the overseer.

"Callie's on her way to the manor. I just saw her not two minutes ago."

"I see," he said in a tone that implied he didn't *see* at all. "You dismiss one to sample the charms of another. What's wrong, Lucas? Wasn't the maid cooperative enough?"

She felt the naked man tense. *Naked.*

"Sin, it's not what you think."

The ground started to rumble.

"Goddamn it, Sin!"

Coconuts erupted from a nearby palm, barely missing them.

The heavens opened up in a torrential downpour.

Lucas shoved Moriah behind him. "Calm down, damn it. I told you, it's not what you think."

The alarm in the overseer's voice must have reached him. His bright eyes grew dark, and he stared in wonder at the coconuts lying all around. He closed his eyes, letting the rain plaster his clothes to his body and drip hair into his eyes, but he didn't move.

Lucas touched his arm. "Sin? Are you all right?"

He immediately stepped away. "If you wanted to try her out, all you had to do was tell me." He stared at her with such loathing, she cringed. "I'd have gladly shared."

"You don't know what you're saying."

"Oh, yes, *friend,* I do." He curled a lip in disgust. "Other than being accident-prone, she's no different than any of the other whores I've hired in the past. I can take her or leave her. And since you're obviously intrigued, you can have her." His eyes bored into hers. "I no longer desire her."

Feeling as if a giant fist had closed over her heart, she watched him walk away. *Damn him. Damn him to hell.* Tears rolled down her cheeks, mingling with the warm raindrops, yet she didn't know why she was crying. She brushed rivulets of hair from her eyes. "Lucas, I . . ."

"Come on, woman. I'm going to get dressed, then we'll talk."

She clamped her lips together and followed him, wondering why she was so upset over Sin's dismissal. That's what she wanted, wasn't it? To be free of his advances? Free to search for clues to her sister's murderer? But, damn it, why did it hurt so much?

"Wait here a second," Lucas said, startling her.

Blinking through the sheet of rain, she watched him

disappear inside a thatch hut nestled in the pines. He returned a moment later wearing his cutoff breeches and motioning her indoors.

"I'll make some tea while you start explaining what you and Callie were doing out at this time of night." He lit a candle, illuminating the neat interior of his cozy home. From palm fans to bamboo curtains, the hut flaunted its tropical decor.

Taking a seat at a small, elegantly carved table, she tried to decide just how much to tell Sin's friend. She watched him light a potbellied stove and place a kettle on its surface. Woodsmoke clung to the moist air as heat radiated through the dampness. Observing him as he worked, she realized with sudden clarity that she trusted Lucas. She wasn't sure why. But there was an honor about him that reached out to her.

"Well?" he asked as he sat down. "What's the reason you're here instead of in bed?"

"I was following Sin, but I lost him."

"Why?"

She traced the outline of a fern carved into the smooth tabletop. "I saw him running into the woods. I thought he was chasing someone."

His expression hardened. "Callie."

"Yes. But, I never found him. Although I did manage to get lost until I stumbled across you and Callie." The moment the words were out, she blushed profusely. She hadn't meant to acknowledge *that*.

He twisted his mouth into a knowing smile. "I see. Tell me, do you know why she was in the woods?"

She took a breath, praying she wasn't wrong about Lucas. "I think she was going to see Mudanno."

All humor left him. "What for?"

Unable to sit still, she rose and crossed her arms over her stomach. "She's trying to find out who killed Sara."

"Sara Winslow?"

She nodded numbly, unsure she made the right decision.

"Why?" he demanded. "What was she to you and Callie?"

"Sara was Callie's friend . . . and my sister."

Lucas let out a slow whistle. "So that's what this is all about." The kettle rumbled to a boil, and he snatched it off the stove, but he didn't seem surprised at her disclosure as he set the steaming pot on a metal tray. "What has Mudanno got to do with the murder?"

"Sara went to see the priestess the day before she left the island. If she and Sara had a disagreement, it's possible Mudanno or her men followed my sister to Nassau and . . ."

He handed her a cup and returned to his seat. "Killed her? I guess that is a possibility, but why would she want to?"

Haltingly she explained about her previous jaunt into the woods and how she'd learned of Mudanno's determination to bear Sin's child. "I haven't been able to prove my theory, but I think she's eliminating his mistresses in hopes that he'll be afraid to bring another woman to the island. Eventually he'd have to go to her for . . . well . . ." She floundered helplessly.

Lucas smiled. "So you've decided the boss's urges are so great that he'd bed any woman—even one he detested—just to satisfy his need?" He shook his curly head. "Woman, you've got a lot to learn about Sin."

"I've learned enough to know he can't keep his hands off a woman if she's within ten feet of him."

"Not any woman," he countered softly. "Just you."

Fury shook her voice. "Of course me. After all, I *am* bought and paid for, aren't I?"

His gray eyes moved over her. "Yes. You are that." He rose. "And before we get any deeper into this conversation, I'm going to see Sin. He misunderstood the situation a few minutes ago, and I'm going to set him straight."

"You don't have to do that for me. What he thinks about me doesn't matter. I'm only here to find Sara's killer, nothing more."

His eyes narrowed. "I'm not doing it for you. Sin is my friend, and I'll be damned if I'll let something I haven't even *considered* get in the way of that friendship."

Knowing Lucas would know the answer to the question that had been plaguing her, she watched him walk toward the doorless entrance before hitting him with the query. "Lucas? Did Sin make those coconuts fall?"

He stopped and very slowly turned around. Their eyes met, his wary, then resigned. "Yes."

"How?"

"You'll have to ask him."

"Doesn't it bother you that he could have killed us?"

"Could have," the overseer agreed. "But he didn't."

Not in the least mollified, she pointed out, "Perhaps he will . . . next time."

"You've got a lot of misconceptions about my friend. He's not an ogre, Moriah. And he'd never hurt anyone. He's simply a man, a very frightened one at the moment. Instead of fearing this thing that surrounds him, maybe you should consider helping him."

"How? By letting him use me for target practice? Besides, what makes you think I could do anything, anyway?"

Lucas smiled. "Because you're the first person Sin's ever come in contact with that makes him lose control. Until you came along, he had a will of steel. But something about you affects him, cracks that rigid barrier. Woman, you can reach him like no one else."

Certain he was putting too much store in her capabilities, and just a little scared—well, perhaps a lot scared—she pulled the damp robe she wore closer together. She still couldn't rationalize how a man could make such things happen without using a mechanical device of some sort. Too, how would he react when he found out the truth about her? "Are you going to tell him who I am?"

"No. That has no bearing on what he witnessed between us tonight. But you might think about telling him yourself. If I'm not mistaken, you're not one of

Madam Rossi's women, and if that's the case, you'd better inform Sin. If not, it won't be long before he has you in his bed. Remember, he believes he's fully within his rights to possess you, and that won't change until you tell him different." He started out the door, then stopped. "Can I trust you to stay here until I return?"

"Where would I go? Mudanno's? Not hardly. Besides, if you recall, I belong to you now, and I'm not welcome in the main house."

"If you were mine, you'd already be in that bed." He nodded toward the straw tick, then grinned and stepped outside. "But you're not, and neither of us wish you to be." He winked. "I'll be back soon."

Embarrassed and pleased by his mild acceptance of the ghastly situation, she watched him leave, offhandedly noticing that the downpour of moments ago had ceased altogether. These tropical rainstorms were odd indeed, she concluded. She remembered one torrent she'd seen the first day she went to Nassau. Rain had ruthlessly hammered one side of a street while the other remained sunny and dry.

Yes, weather was strange here in the tropics . . . and so were the people. Sin in particular. Wondering how he'd truly accomplished the remarkable feat she'd seen earlier, she strolled outside. Wet ivy cushioned her feet and damp earth sharpened the air as she walked to where the coconuts were scattered. She picked one up and examined the hard-shelled object closely.

Nothing.

Too tired to try to figure out how he'd caused the melee, she tossed the hairy brown ball on the ground. She had a more pressing problem to deal with—where she would stay. She certainly couldn't remain with the overseer. And what about Mudanno? She still needed to talk to that witch.

Then there was Sin. He would be angry when he found out she'd duped him. Probably insist she reimburse him. Briefly she wondered how much he'd paid.

And what about Callie? He'd probably throw her out,

also. Damn, she'd gotten herself and her friend into a fine pickle.

Disgusted and wondering if there were any caves she and Callie could live in until the sloop was ready, she flounced toward Lucas's hut.

A white-garbed figure stood in her path.

Her heart jumped, then raced wildly.

Still damp, his shirt and breeches molded his broad shoulders, narrow waist, and muscular thighs. A wealth of midnight hair curled over his brow, shimmering in the moonlight with tiny droplets.

The very air grew thicker, hotter, as she gazed into Sin's magnificent dark eyes.

He smiled slowly. "I believe I owe you an apology, princess."

CHAPTER

12

When they returned from the woods, she found the doors to his chamber were closed, the curtains drawn, and in the center of the room stood a huge, steaming tub.

Sin touched her spine with his palm, urging her forward.

She hesitated. "How did you have a bath prepared so quickly? And keep it so hot?"

"I ordered it for you earlier, when I sent for a maid to clean up the broken glass." He motioned to the square pane visible through the connecting doors and now covered with cheesecloth. "As for why the water's still hot, I imagine the pots were on the stove until Dorothy saw us coming across the lawn. Having been my mother's personal servant for many years, she's very adept at timing."

Pleased by his thoughtfulness, and anxious for a long soak, but nervous in his overpowering presence, she struggled for something to say. "Um, where's your mother now?"

"She died of dysentery eight years ago."

"I'm so sorry."

"So am I," he agreed a little roughly. "Now, quit

talking, woman. It's time for your bath." He turned her around and reached for the belt at her waist.

She jumped back. "What are you doing?"

He advanced and pulled the tie free. "I've wronged you and Lucas, princess. And I intend to make amends. I'm going to be your servant for this night." He pushed the robe off her shoulders, allowing the garment to slip to the floor. "And to start off, I'm going to bathe you."

Her heart toppled over at the prospect, but quickly righted. "You can't."

He parted the gaping neckline of Dorothy's gown and eased it over the tops of her shoulders. "Sure I can."

Clutching the material close to her breasts, she retreated a step. "Wait." *Tell him the truth,* her mind screamed. She opened her mouth, but the words refused to come. "I, um, can't bathe just yet. The bandage."

Evidently not put off by the reminder, he lowered himself to one knee and ran his palm up her leg, raising the hem of the gown as he did so.

Fiery tingles raced through her limbs.

Slowly, patiently, he undid the gauze and eased it away, then traced the wound with a gentle finger. "Looks good."

It feels even better. Aghast at her own wayward thoughts, she tried to sidestep his touch.

His large, warm hand encircled her thigh. "No, princess. Stand still. I'll put you in the tub." He reluctantly removed his hand, then rose ever so slowly.

Their eyes met . . . and held.

The air thickened, making her light-headed. Drowning in those shimmering onyx pools, she couldn't breathe—didn't want to. Delicious shivers raced over her flesh as he eased the nightgown off and let it drop to the carpet. Cool air from the veranda whispered through the room to stroke her bare flesh.

Still holding her shoulders, he lowered his gaze and released a low, hissing breath. "You *are* exquisite."

Her mouth went dry. The sound of his husky voice sent spears of desire straight to her woman's center.

In slow motion he drew his fingers along her collarbone, over the slope of her breasts, then down to trail erotically over the centering tips. He paused, tracing the sensitive nubs.

She tightened unbearably. Her lungs strained for oxygen.

After an eternity, he lowered his hands to encircle her waist, allowing a ripple of air to filter into her chest. But it wasn't enough to clear her head, and when he lifted her into the tub, her limbs were as responsive as a freshly cooked noodle. Closing her eyes, she leaned her head on the rim, allowing the heat to absorb her reason, and offering him liberties she'd never given to another.

"That's right, princess. Relax. Let me take care of you."

A thought of protest entered her mind, but fled the instant a warm, soapy cloth touched her throat. The intoxicating scent of honeysuckle drifted up with the steam, numbing her reason.

At first his ministrations seemed impersonal as he carefully washed her neck and shoulders, her arms, wrists, and each separate finger. Still, he left a trail of shivers.

Every inch of her body came alive, tuned and expectant, anxiously awaiting the next contact. But when his bare hands closed over her breasts, the unexpected jolt of pleasure that streaked through her body tightened her spine into an arch. She pressed urgently into his palms.

He inhaled sharply and a slight tremor passed through his fingers. "Ah, God, princess. You're setting fire to my blood."

The tub rocked and shuddered.

He quickly snatched his hands away.

Stunned by the loss, she opened her eyes to find him standing with his back to her, breathing heavily.

"Sin?"

"Get out of the water," he said hoarsely. "We'll sit on the veranda for a while."

Quick to comply, she stood and grabbed a towel from a stack on the floor. "I need my clothes."

He faced her . . . explored her. "There's no one back there to see you."

You are, she thought, holding the towel closer to her wet body. "If you'll hand me that gown and step out of the room, I'll get dressed."

His gaze touched every inch of her exposed flesh. "It's probably for the best." But he didn't retrieve the over-large gown; instead, he tossed her one of the island wraps. Nor did he leave the room. However, he did turn around long enough for her to drop the towel and hurriedly wind the silk about her nakedness. And none too soon.

A second later, he faced her. "All set?"

Feeling at least partially clothed, and guilty as a thief over her shameless behavior just moments ago, she nodded and started for the glass doors.

He was beside her in an instant. "No. I'll carry you."

"That isn't necess—"

"Yes it is." He scooped her up into his arms and carried her out to the patio, then eased her into a thickly padded chair.

Flushed from her close contact with him, she averted her gaze and examined the surroundings. From his veranda she could see dense foliage growing along the outer edge of the flagstones. Beyond that sprawled the beautifully manicured lawn, surrounded by woods and undergrowth.

She shivered. How well she remembered that lawn and those trees—and what lay beyond. Not wanting to think about her infamous journey—either one of them—or the resulting consequences, she focused on the white stone portico.

A low wrought-iron table sat between her seat and an equally comfortable-looking chair cushioned in soft mint green. Stoneware pots filled with exotic plants, most of which she didn't recognize, hung or sat in strategic places along the stone, their mixed fragrances a heady blend of light floral and rich earthiness. The latter reminded her of her host, and she glanced up at him.

He just stood there, staring at her with an odd expression on his face.

What now? She expected him to say something. *Do* something. When she couldn't stand his scrutiny any longer, she met his gaze. "Is something wrong?"

"Yes."

She waited for him to elaborate.

He didn't.

"Well? *What's* wrong?"

"You take my breath away."

Self-consciously she placed a hand over her naked skin above the wrap, unsure how to respond.

He sighed and shoved his fingers through his hair. "I'm sorry, princess. I didn't mean to make you uncomfortable." He sat down in the opposite chair and stretched his long legs out in front of him. "There's just something about you that makes it impossible for me to keep my thoughts out of the bedchamber when I'm around you."

"I wish I knew what it was." *So I could stop it,* she added silently.

He slid his eyes lazily toward her. "Oh, I think you already know." He gave a wry snort. "It must be a great asset in your profession."

Did she detect an underlying note of distaste? Why? He was the one who'd hired her. In his mind she was exactly what he'd wanted. Incapable of understanding this complex man, she sought a different topic. "You said you were born in Georgia. Were you also raised there?"

"I lived on Sunfield Plantation for twenty-six years."

"Sunfield? I've heard of that place. Isn't it one of the largest tobacco plantations in Georgia?"

He shrugged. "I guess. My father and Lucas ran Sunfield and the other two estates. I was more interested in shipbuilding and shipping."

She recalled the huge ship under construction at the cove. "Is that why you're building one here?"

"No. Usually the freighters are built at our dry dock in

Savannah. But when we lost one in a storm off the English coast a few months ago, the crew wanted to stay on Arcane until they could build another one. I didn't see any problem with that, so I sent Lucas after the supplies and had them brought to the island." He stared up at the beamed overhang supporting the upper balcony. "It's worked out well. The men are content, and the freighter's progressing at a respectable rate."

"Are you going to send for more supplies to repair the sloop?"

He shook his head, causing silky, blue-black strands to shimmer beneath the lamplight. "With both vessels down, there's no way to get word to Savannah. Fortunately, I had extra lumber brought in with the last shipment." He smiled lazily. "It was actually meant for a gazebo down by the healing pool, but it'll have to wait awhile."

"Healing pool?"

"The pond by Lucas's hut. The water is supposed to have mystical powers capable of curing all ills." He grinned. "Actually, I think there's a mineral spring at the bottom, comparable to the ones in Bath."

Though she was intrigued by the pool, she couldn't focus on anything beyond the fact that, with the ships under repair, she was completely stranded on this island. Thank goodness she hadn't told him of her duplicity. She ran her thumbs over the smooth wood arms of the chair. "Do you have enough wood to restore both vessels?"

"More than enough."

"What about food supplies?"

He sent her a drowsy look beneath lowered lashes. "We normally keep extra on hand. With all the tropical storms in this area, frequent travel isn't always possible." Yawning, he closed his eyes and pressed his head into the chair cushion. A quietness settled over him.

Moments later, his deep, even breathing drifted on the silent breeze, and she realized he'd fallen asleep.

She studied his relaxed features, knowing that, no matter how she might wish to deny it, he was beyond a doubt the most attractive man she'd ever seen. Every feature on his face shouted masculine perfection, from the thick black lashes that a woman would kill for, to the arrogant jut of his square, bronze chin that any other man would give a fortune to possess. Yet he accepted his exceptional appearance with complete indifference. Just as he did his sensual appeal to women.

Uneasy with her thoughts, she glanced away. It would be better to concentrate on how she would go about learning more about Sara's stay here. And this aura of mystery that surrounds her host.

"What are you thinking?" Sin said softly, startling her.

Her mind raced for an answer. "I was just wondering if there were any other poisonous plants around here I should be aware of."

Appearing refreshed, he leaned forward and braced his forearms on his knees. "Well, let's see. There's the pencil tree, milkbush, Indian tree spurge, and Malabar tree."

"Good heavens."

"I'm teasing, princess. Those are just different names for the monkey fiddle tree. Most of the plants on this island are harmless if they're not ingested."

"Well, I'm certainly glad to hear that. With all those threats outdoors, I'd have been afraid to leave the house."

Humor lit his ebony eyes. "Speaking of being housebound, do you know how to play any games?"

"Like what?"

"Cribbage?"

She shook her head.

"Dominoes?"

"No."

He rubbed his jaw. "Chess?"

"Sorry."

"How about checkers?"

"No again."

He slumped back in the chair. "This is going to be a long night."

"You could always go to bed."

The impact of those eyes colliding with hers rattled her senses.

"Is that what you want?" he asked softly.

She swallowed. "No. I'm not sleepy." She fought frantically to regain her balance. "And I do know how to play one game. Poker." *If* she could remember all Callie taught her.

He studied her for a few seconds, then, resigned, he came lithely to his feet. "I'll get the cards."

She smiled as she awaited his return. He really wasn't a bad sort. If you discounted the fact that he hired mistresses.

The scent of jasmine and honeysuckle trickled in on the moist breeze, and she inhaled the sweet aromas, remembering the wonderful smell of Mama's gardens behind their house.

"Still wondering about poisonous plants?" he teased as he returned to her side.

"No. Gardens and swings."

He sat down, his brow arched. "Would you care to elaborate?"

"I'm just being silly. The scent of the flowers around here reminds me of the fragrant gardens my mother used to have in Boston."

"And the swings?"

"They were there, too. Father built one for each of us—right in the center of Mama's pansies. He cleared a path through the flowers and a big circle beneath a magnolia tree." She grinned. "Mama was furious for days—not that Papa minded. He enjoyed the hell out of unraveling her."

"Each of us?"

Realizing her slip, she invented, "Me and my brother." Then, recalling her own experiences, she continued. "I loved that swing more than anything Father ever gave me. I would glide so high, my toes would nearly touch the sky." She smiled sadly. "I don't think I've ever known such freedom since. Such peace."

Sin was curiously silent for a moment. "What does your father do?"

"He died in a wagon accident when I was twelve." Leaving only Sara to brighten her life. And now she was gone, too. "We moved to Charleston after that to be near my mother's folks."

"It's my turn to be sorry."

She shoved aside her melancholy. "Did you say we were going to play poker?"

He watched her a second longer, then held up his hand. "Here we go. A brand-new pack of cards and poker chips."

She stared at the box of brightly colored disks. Callie never said anything about those. They'd used beans to make their wagers. She could only assume that these were used in the same way. "I like the blue ones."

"The five-dollar chips?"

She nearly choked. When she could at last speak, she did so vehemently. "I can't possibly wager that kind of money."

"We don't *have* to play for money."

"Thank heavens."

"We could always play for favors."

She eyed him suspiciously. "What kind of favors?"

He set the chips aside. "Oh, you know, the usual. Fetch me a drink. Light my cigar. Whatever the winner chooses."

That didn't sound too bad. "All right. One favor per game?"

"Done." He began to shuffle the cards.

Four hours later, she wasn't so sure this had been such a good idea. He owed her three favors . . . and she owed him sixteen.

He started to deal the cards again.

"No." She touched his hands to stop him. "I don't think I can afford any more losses."

"If we quit now, we'll have to start paying up."

"Might as well get it over with."

A smile pulled at the corner of his mouth. "You go first, then. As I recall, I owe you three favors."

Enjoying the victory, however slight, she dramatically drew her hand across her brow. "I could use a tall, cool drink."

He rose and bowed. "Right away, princess." With a jaunty bounce to his step, he sauntered indoors.

She was still flushed from the way he called her princess and made the word sound so intimate when he returned with a large, slender glass filled with pink liquid.

"Mmm," she crooned as she sipped the delicious fruit punch.

"Next?" he prompted.

"I think a pillow for my head would be nice."

He chuckled softly, then disappeared inside. A moment later, he came out fluffing a plump, feathery square. He slid his hand behind her neck and eased her forward, then gently stuffed the pillow behind her and pressed her head into its softness.

Then, lowering himself to one knee, he asked with mock seriousness, "And the last favor?"

She burrowed comfortably into the downy cushion, savoring the game. "Oh, I think I might like to wait for the last one. You know, give it more thought."

His eyes sparkled with amusement. "Smart girl."

"I know." Lowering her lashes, she sighed in contentment. "I do love the game of poker."

"So do I," he murmured softly, his breath suddenly close to her cheek.

Her eyes sprang open.

His crinkled with humor. "Because now it's your turn to pay up."

Relaxing, she nodded. "Of course. But do take into consideration my injury." She grinned, knowing what he must think of that remark after the way she'd traipsed through the woods after him. "What's the first favor?"

Amusement left him, and his gaze turned serious. "I want a kiss."

"What? That's not a favor. You said—"

"Fetch me a drink, light my cigar, or . . . *whatever* the winner chooses."

Oh, sweet heaven. Now she'd done it. "But—"

"A kiss, princess." He touched a finger to his mouth. "Right here." He placed his hands on the arms of her chair and moved closer, so close their noses nearly touched. "And you won't even have to exert yourself to do it."

She was already *over*exerted with the way her heart was pounding. Realizing she didn't actually have a choice, she gingerly touched his cheek. "A kiss it is, then." Very lightly she set her mouth against his.

His lips felt warm and sweet, and oh, so soft, she decided, knowing she really could get to like this. Sighing, and with a tinge of regret, she started to pull away.

His hand came up behind her neck, holding her in place. The pressure of his mouth increased. He tilted his head to the side and molded his lips over hers.

Heat shot through her body.

He pressed her back into the pillow, his lips sliding slowly, sensually, across hers.

She gasped at the intimate gesture, then groaned when his tongue slipped between her lips to brush gently against her own.

Nothing, but *nothing* could have prepared her for the streak of fire that flashed through her belly, or the tremors that followed the searing blaze.

Real tremors that rocked her chair.

He released her abruptly and rose, his expression at first incredulous, then angry. "Son of a bitch."

"What?" She looked around anxiously. "Is it an earthquake?"

That made him even angrier. He clenched his fists and sucked in a deep breath. It took him a long time to settle enough to answer her question. "This area has been known to suffer occasional tremors."

Unsure of his temperament, she asked timidly, "Is there a volcano nearby?"

He stared at her for a few seconds, then a sardonic smile twisted his lips. "Yes, I guess there is at that. Much closer than you think." He gestured indoors. "I believe your earlier suggestion is now applicable."

"What suggestion?"

"That we go to bed."

Her heart stopped in the middle of a beat. He didn't mean . . .

"It's been a long day, princess, and we're both ready to drop." He extended his hand. "Do you walk or do I carry you again?"

She rose quickly. "I can walk, thank you." Being held in his arms was an unnerving experience she'd prefer to forgo.

As she started through the door, he put an arm out to halt her. "I want to collect another favor."

Her senses vibrated. She'd never survive another kiss tonight. "Sin—"

"Promise me you won't go near the north woods again."

Though relieved, she was also suspicious. "Why?"

"In case you haven't already noticed, it's damned dangerous. Much more than you realize. I'm asking as a favor, Moriah, but I can make it an order."

She didn't know what urged her to test him, but she couldn't stop the impulse. "What makes you think I'd follow your orders?"

He gripped her by the shoulders, his eyes bright with anger. "Because the last person who disobeyed that command ended up facedown in the healing pool."

Was he saying he'd drowned someone for flouting a command? Or was he recounting what happened *because* of the person's noncompliance? She explored the taut lines of his face and saw his genuine concern for her safety.

He shook her. "Swear to me, damn it."

Irritated at his high-handed attitude, she wrenched free. "All right! All right! I promise."

CHAPTER
13

Blanche stared at the plate in front of her, wishing she'd never sent a note announcing her untimely visit. But damnation, she needed to know if Walt had learned anything about the killings. Any slight clue that could help put the maniac behind bars before Sin's mistress returned.

Still, her stomach rolled at the idea of eating raw oysters, unseasoned cabbage, half-cooked beans, and bread with suspicious pinched-off places on the sides.

She watched her brother slosh sour lemonade in her glass. "It looks delicious," she lied politely.

"I thought you'd approve. Lemonade always was one of your favorite drinks."

Sweet lemonade, she silently corrected. Trying not to make a face, she sipped the tart liquid, then set the glass down. "Well, have you talked to anyone about the murders?"

He sucked an oyster into his mouth and swallowed it. "Yes, as a matter of fact, I've spoken to several people."

Her spirits brightened. "Did you learn anything new?"

"I believe so." He ate a spoonful of beans. "The proprietor of the Nassau Hotel said he saw the Kirkland woman's body, and even though she'd been mutilated, there wasn't much blood. At least, not as much as there should have been. A dockworker said the same about the Winslow woman."

That made absolutely no sense to her. "I don't understand."

He set his fork down. "Sister mine, think for a moment what that indicates."

She tried, she really did, but was still at a loss.

He sighed. "It means, love, that the murders were obviously committed somewhere else."

"I still don't understand."

Nibbling a piece of bread, he watched her. "Didn't you say you never saw Miss Kirkland leave Bliss Island?"

"Well, yes."

"Yet her body was found on Nassau, which, of course, led everyone to believe the killing took place here."

Blanche nearly choked on a piece of cabbage. "You mean that maniac could be on *my* island?" She shook her head. "No. It couldn't be. I know everyone there. Besides, when Sara Winslow returned, I watched her leave on the ferry to Nassau."

He chased a bean around an oyster shell. "That doesn't mean the culprit wasn't about." He met her eyes. "Do you recall anyone leaving Bliss on the same ferry as Mrs. Winslow? Or perhaps the following one?"

She searched her memory. "No. Only Brandy Wiles, one of the other whores. She'd gone to visit her ailing mother. Besides her, there wasn't anyone else that I can remember."

"Wiles? I believe I heard you mention her before. Wasn't she also one of Sin Masters's lady friends?"

"Yes. She was the last one that came back alive . . . and stayed that way. You remember. I introduced her to you when you brought my birthday present last year. The day you lugged back that gunny sack full of fruit for the poor. Anyway, she retired from the business a couple months ago and went to live with her mother. But she wouldn't—"

"No," he agreed instantly. "She couldn't be the killer. I'm certain of that. But I do believe I'll have a talk with her mother."

"Why her mother? Why not Brandy herself?"

He patted her hand. "Because, sister mine, last night Miss Wiles's body was discovered hanging among sides of beef in Mr. Buckley's cellar. She'd been dead for several weeks."

Blanche closed her eyes in a moment's distress. "If that bastard isn't caught soon, he's going to ruin my business." She set down her fork. "I'm going to see Brandy's ma. Maybe she knows who the girl was last seen with, then I'm going to stop by your church on my way home and see if they've heard anything new."

"There's no need. I've already talked to them. They haven't."

She shrugged. "It's on my way, and it won't hurt to ask."

"Sister mine. You haven't been in a church since you were a child. No offense, my dear. But the Almighty might not look kindly on your presence . . . considering your occupation. I'd rather you wouldn't."

She chuckled. "Don't worry. I'll leave if the walls start crumbling."

He sighed and returned to his meal. "As you wish."

Sunshine had settled over the bedchamber when Moriah awoke the next morning. Rubbing the sleep from her eyes, she sat up—and instantly scanned the room for Sin. After last night's battle of wills, and her hasty retreat to the adjoining bedchamber, she'd heard him leave his room, but to her knowledge, he hadn't returned.

When she saw only Callie standing before the clothes closet hanging up a pile of gowns, she wasn't sure whether to be pleased or annoyed that he wasn't there. Don't be foolish, she mentally scolded. Of course she was pleased. Then she recalled her friend's escapade with Lucas last night, and felt her neck grow warm. "What time is it?"

"Not long until breakfast. I was just getting your things ready now." She glanced at Moriah. "How are you feeling?"

"Fine." Wanting to ask why she'd been in the forest, but knowing she couldn't without revealing what she'd witnessed, she tried another approach. "I think I'll go for a walk in the woods after I eat." She smiled. "Hopefully without encountering any tigers or poison trees."

"And break your word?" a masculine voice asked from the veranda. Sin stepped into the room, his features taut, a muscle pulsing in his temple. "Is that how you keep your promises?"

She met his gaze head-on. "I *did not* say I wouldn't go into the forest. Only the north woods."

Callie lowered the gown she was holding, her manner stiff.

"If you want to walk," he said to Moriah, "then I or one of my men will gladly escort you. Just don't go traipsing off again without a companion—*anywhere.*" He sent her a malevolent smile. "Besides, tonight you'll get all the walking you'll be able to handle."

Callie hung up the last dress and headed for the door. "When ya need me, Miz Morgan, jist call." She quickly closed the panel behind her.

Moriah frowned at the girl's unusual behavior, then turned on her host. "What do you mean I'll be walking tonight?"

"We've been invited to Woosak's birthday party."

"Who's Woosak?"

"Our resident doctor . . . more or less. She lives in the cane workers' village on the south end of Arcane." His eyes lit with amusement. "It's nearly three miles. So you might want to save your strength for this evening."

Infuriated at the bossy male, she barely kept herself from telling him to eat worms. Instead, she demurely lowered her lashes to hide her anger. "All right, Sin."

She heard him shift uneasily. "Moriah . . ."

"I agreed. What more do you want?"

"A little more sincerity," he shot back, then spun on his heels and stalked out.

Left to her own devices, and not wanting to bother her friend, she climbed from the bed and explored the garments hanging in the wardrobe. Nothing she selected would be conservative, she decided, so why concern herself?

Grabbing a dark blue satin gown, she tossed it on the bed.

Unfortunately, she couldn't find a chemise. Releasing a frustrated sigh, she wiggled into the blue satin and buttoned the front to a spot below her breasts. The rest was secured by silver ties.

She inspected herself in the mirror and shook her head. Another off-the-shoulder style, the gown fit extremely snug around her midriff, then dipped into a wide vee between her breasts. Only the thin silver laces, which left a two-inch, *very revealing* gap, held the front together above the row of pearl buttons. "Damn."

Disgusted, she flounced toward the dining room. After breakfast, she really was going for a walk. Perhaps to the outer finger of the cove. She needed a little peace and quiet . . . and time to consider her next course of action.

When she entered the dining room, Sin and Lucas were already seated and talking quietly.

Sin's words trailed off midsentence when he looked up. His eyes locked on the front of her dress.

Resisting the urge to cross her arms over her exposed flesh, she lifted her chin. It didn't do any good to show modesty around this man. "Do I take it you like the dress?"

"In the bedchamber, perhaps." The last word hissed between his straight teeth. "Not the breakfast table."

"Oh, I don't know," the overseer offered, "it sure sharpens my appetite."

Sin glared at the curly-headed man. "Don't you have some work to do?"

"Sure thing, boss. Soon as I eat." Grinning, he shoved

a wedge of peach in his mouth. "By the way," he asked around the fruit, "where's the maid? Isn't she going to join us this morning?"

Moriah blushed, recalling the confrontation she'd seen between Lucas and Callie. "I don't think so." The girl was probably too embarrassed to face the overseer.

Lucas smirked. "Had a rough night, did she?"

Sin set his fork down with a firm thud. "How's the sloop coming along?"

The younger man shrugged. "Haven't had time to check. The fields needed tending."

Glistening black hair moved as her host nodded his head in agreement. "I noticed yesterday that the south twenty looked . . ."

She lowered her lashes, not wanting to watch him. He did queer things to her insides. Stubbornly she shut out the men's conversation and indulged in her meal, not realizing until that moment just how hungry she was. The fish was marvelous. The eggs. The salt pork. Everything. Guiltily she thought of how Mama always scorned her for eating like a sow—even though she never gained an ounce. Not wanting to resemble the pig her mother accused her of being, she chose not to ask for seconds and regretfully pushed her plate away. When she looked up, she found both men watching her. "What?"

Sin's lips quirked. "I asked you to pass the salt."

"Oh." Her cheeks warmed as she handed him the saltcellar.

"Now that I have your attention," he continued, "I thought you might like to see the cane fields when Lucas and I go there this morning."

Although the offer seemed genuine enough, she wasn't fooled. He wanted her where he could keep an eye on her. Too bad. She smiled sweetly. "No, thank you. I'll just laze around here today." Her gaze challenged his. "And rest up for the long walk tonight. I wouldn't want to overexert myself."

She thought she saw a flicker of admiration in his eyes before he glanced away. "You're right, of course. You do need plenty of rest." His stare pinned hers in retaliation, and his voice lowered to a seductive drawl. "This evening is going to be thoroughly exhausting . . . in many ways."

The innuendo behind that remark sent tingles racing through her limbs. Hating the way his erotic undertones turned her bones to mush, she pushed back the chair and stood. "If you'll excuse me, I believe I'll relax on the patio . . . with my favorite masonry book."

Sin's laughter followed her from the room as he and Lucas headed outdoors.

Well, at least one thing was in her favor, she mused as she stalked through the entry. With both men gone for the day, she was free to search for clues. Her steps slowed as a realization hit her. She no longer believed that Sin had anything to do with her sister's death. Not even after the anger she'd witnessed in him last night when she'd nearly been struck by coconuts—something she still wanted him to explain, when she got up the nerve to ask. Too, there was a tenderness about him, a gentleness, that was completely at odds with the type of man who butchered women. No. He hadn't done the deed. She was fairly certain. But that didn't mean someone else on Arcane wasn't responsible.

She stopped in the hallway. Perhaps that's where she'd gone wrong so far. She'd been concerned with Sin, finding something incriminating in the house, and with Mudanno, yet not the rest of the island and its inhabitants.

With Sin occupied, perhaps now was the time to talk to some of the crewmen who made frequent trips to Nassau. Yes, she decided. It most certainly was.

In a whirl of blue satin, she hurried to the cove.

Half-dressed men sawed and hammered as they worked to repair the sloop. They'd managed to brace the craft on stilts, much like the freighter beside it, enabling them better access to the gaping hole in the ship's side.

The man she was introduced to when she boarded on Bliss Island, Captain Jonas, saw her and came over.

"Miss Morgan. It's good to see ye again, lass. But I'm

afraid Master Sin ain't here. I figure he's down in the fields about now."

"I didn't come here to find him. I just wanted to see how the repairs were coming along."

A gnarled hand swept a damp strand of gray hair off his brow. "Pretty slow, lass. That crater in the side's gonna take some fixin'."

The aroma of salt water, fish, and warm sand wafted on a light breeze. She dug her toes into the hot granules beneath her bare feet, trying to think of a way to approach the subject of Nassau. "Doesn't it bother you to be dry-docked, so to speak? I mean, you must be used to making quite a few trips to the main island instead of staying in one place so long."

He smiled, showing mature, wide-spaced teeth. "I do at that, miss. Sure enough." He flicked a wrinkled hand toward the ocean. "That lady there, she's me whole life."

Compassion rolled through her for the man who looked as if he should have retired years ago. "Do all these other men make the voyages with you, too?"

"Nay, only me sloop's crew. Most o' these boys was on the freighter that went down. They won't sail under me again till the new one's built."

"You mean you haven't always captained the sloop?"

"Nay. Davie Waller did."

She scanned the crowd of men, wanting to talk to the former captain. "Which one is Mr. Waller?"

"Davie's dead, lass. He drowned in the healin' pool a few months ago."

So that's the man Sin had spoken about. "I'm sorry to hear that." She eyed the men again. "I imagine when you journey to New Providence your sailors enjoy spending time in Nassau, with so much to do and all."

The tail of his red knit cap wobbled as he shook his head. "Nay, lass. There's only three men on me crew now, and it takes all of them to man me sloop in them restless waters while Donnelly goes ashore for supplies." His aging eyes twinkled. "Or whatever."

Knowing he referred to the women the servant often

brought back for Sin, she fought a surge of humiliation. "You mean Donnelly's the only one who leaves the ship?"

"Aye."

"But don't your men *ever* disembark for entertainment?"

Captain Jonas smiled. "Ah, sweet lass, there's more *entertainment* here on Arcane than anywhere else." He winked. "Best rum in the South Seas and prettiest women. What more could a man want?"

Flustered, she glanced away, but an option she'd never considered grew. Donnelly hired the women. And he returned them. He was the only one who went ashore. The only one who had full access to Sin's mistresses.

Dear God, *Donnelly*.

Horrified by her summation, she rambled an excuse to Captain Jonas about getting back to the house and bid him good day.

Inside the entry, she stood for a full minute, trying to decide what to do. Should she search Donnelly's room? Question him? Make inquiries of the other servants?

She shook her head. Questioning him directly was out. If he was the killer, he'd catch on immediately. No. Her best course of action would be to search his chamber.

Her gaze moved to the wide staircase that led to the second level. All the servants' quarters were on the top floor, she remembered Callie saying. But she didn't dare go up *there* until she knew the manservant's whereabouts.

Scurrying to the cookhouse, where she was sure the servants would be, she looked for someone familiar.

Beula's sweat-streaked face poked out of the doorway. "Why, missy. What you doin' down here? Is you hungry, chile? Is dat it?"

"No. No. I was just searching for Donnelly. I wanted to ask him about—" she glanced at her bare feet "—my shoes."

The cook's scarf-draped head wagged from side to side. "Dat ole buzzard's restin' in his room. Don't 'spect to see him till supper. Don't know why the massa don't put dat one out to pasture and get him outa my hair." She grumbled on as she waddled back inside. "Ain't good for nothin' no more. A body oughta be fittin' for somethin'. Yes sir, least a chore now and then, or a . . ."

Moriah stared at the vacant door, knowing she'd just come to a temporary standstill. She would have to wait to search Donnelly's room.

She brightened. But that didn't mean she couldn't question Sin about him at the affair this evening. Surely he knew the servant better than anyone. Perhaps he could even, inadvertently, give her a possible motive to link Donnelly to the murders.

CHAPTER
14

Callie didn't want to return to Mudanno's, but something inside her, like an invisible chain, pulled her through the dark recess of the north woods. Though she tried to resist, her struggles were useless. Her limbs moved of their own volition, responding only to Mudanno's command of the previous night.

When she was again given the *tom-coo* potion, she attempted to fight, but was once more forced to swallow the black liquid. In a matter of minutes, a glow spread through her body, arresting any desire to protest. A lethargic haze encompassed her as she stared at Mudanno and her ever-present gold disk.

"Come," the priestess urged, moving toward the fire centering her village. "Join the others."

Wondering at her own submissiveness, Callie followed obediently.

Bare-chested men and women danced around the flames, their dark bodies undulating to the somber rhythm of the drums.

She felt the beat move deliciously through her and began to sway to the lazy sound. Time stood still. There was no dark, no light. Only music.

One of the men, big and muscular, came to stand in

front of her, drawing her out of her misty peace. He held a length of fabric in one hand and began unwinding her wrap with the other.

A cry of protest tried to climb her throat, but the words never emerged. Her feet wouldn't move to step away, her hands wouldn't rise to stop him. Through a fog, she felt a tingling sensation ripple over her flesh when he pulled the silky material slowly away from her body.

She met his eyes and saw unbridled lust shimmering in their depths. It frightened her, yet she couldn't seem to voice her objection.

The man dropped her wrap, then put his arms around her waist and tied a skirt low on her hips, while his gaze roamed her naked breasts. At last he stepped away, his wide nostrils flaring, his eyes bright, hot. With a flick of his hand, he gestured for her to join the dancers.

As she numbly walked toward them, she watched their figures maneuver in a lumbering, sidestepping gait around the center flames, their mahogany bodies glistening in the wavering glow.

Without even realizing she'd moved, she found herself among them, swaying to the drum beat, her body's rhythm sensual, erotic.

A woman laughed softly from somewhere nearby and said something in a strange language, then clapped her hands twice.

People started circling Callie. She tried to focus on the steadily shifting dancers, but couldn't. After a time, she became aware of the other women retreating from the sphere—leaving her surrounded by only men.

A hand touched her breast.

She wanted to jerk away, to strike out, but her limbs wouldn't function.

More hands moved over her. They were everywhere, pinching her nipples, sliding over her stomach, her legs, her buttocks . . . shoving up under her skirt.

She forced a whimper past her dry lips. "Nooo."

"Enough!"

At Mudanno's command, the hands fell away.

Callie was so grateful to the young priestess, she wanted to fall at her feet and kiss them. "Thank you," she sobbed. "Oh, thank you."

"You are welcome." An evil little smile widened the woman's voluptuous mouth. "But always remember, only *I* can protect you—and I will . . . as long as I am pleased with you."

Gold sparkled from her medallion, capturing Callie's whole attention. "I will never displease you, my queen."

The witch laughed. "I know. Now, come, little breed. We will drink and dance."

Moriah sat on the veranda watching a tiny hummingbird dart from blossom to blossom on a bordering honeysuckle shrub, and enjoying the cool evening breeze rustling through the pines. She'd been dressed for an hour, wondering where Callie had disappeared to and waiting for Sin to come and escort her to Woosak's village.

Still, even in the serenity of dusk, she couldn't dismiss thoughts of Donnelly. Why hadn't she seen before that only *he* had the opportunity to commit the murders on Nassau? A sadness touched her soul. How could anyone appear to be so gentle, and in truth be savagely inhuman? And why would he perform such barbarity?

Hoping she'd learn the answers tonight, she shifted her legs and straightened the short skirt of the pink and white wrap she wore. The silk fabric slipped through her fingers, and she wished again that she hadn't allowed Dorothy to convince her to wear the skimpy garment. What did she care if she looked out of place in a gown, or that her defiance might reflect on Sin?

Thinking of her host, she smiled. He was such a mixture of contrasts. One moment the domineering master, the next mischievous, so tender at times, then sensual and passionate.

She shivered, though it wasn't cold. His passion frightened her. Made her feel things she had no business feeling. He made her forget she was engaged—however temporarily—and that she'd never see him again after she left the island.

Saddened by the thought, and strangely unwilling to consider her departure, she rose and folded her arms over her stomach, staring out at the shadows dancing over the moonlit lawn.

"All set?" Sin asked quietly from behind her.

She swung around to find him in the open doorway, his arms crossed, his broad shoulder propped against the jam. An unruly wave of midnight hair rested lazily on his brow, and for the first time, he wasn't wearing his loose white shirt and pants. Snug buff breeches clung to some very interesting, *very male,* contours, while a silvery blue shirt of fine silk flowed over his powerful arms and chest. He was absolutely breathtaking. She swallowed. "Yes, I'm ready."

He straightened and took her hand. "Come on, then."

The contact was staggering. Fire licked up her arm. Startled, she withdrew, then embarrassed by the hasty action, she became defensive. "You don't have to hold my hand. I'm not a child."

He narrowed those entrancing black eyes. "No, you're not. But you are stubborn, independent, reckless, and accident-prone as hell."

"And you're bossy, arrogant, and *strange.*"

He went deathly still.

She could have bitten off her tongue. What had she done?

"Strange?" he returned in a dangerously soft tone.

Frightened by his tense manner, she didn't dare mention the coconuts or tiger. She grasped for an explanation. "W-What else would you call a man who collects wild animals?"

A weight seemed to lift from his shoulders, and his mouth tilted in a smile. "A zoologist?"

"Or an eccentric."

He threw his head back and laughed deeply. *"Touché."*

She preferred him like this, she thought fondly. When he laughed, he was so approachable, so human, and she couldn't help returning his smile.

Gently he brushed a finger down her cheek. "You bring light to my world, princess. Bright shimmering rays that make me feel alive." He traced her upper lip. "And stimulated."

The abrupt change in his manner made her nervous. This sensual side of him scared her to death. "W-Why do you collect them? The animals, I mean."

He traced her jaw with his thumb. "I told you, I'm attracted to the exotic, the dangerously beautiful creatures who arouse this otherwise unresponsive world." He drew little circles over the pulsing hollow at the base of her throat. "A lot like you."

She tried not to tremble. "I'm not an animal."

"No, you're not," he agreed in that flesh-melting tone. "You're a woman." He lowered his gaze to her lips. "My woman."

She couldn't move. His voice and touch held her spellbound. Her lips parted to drag air into her suddenly empty lungs.

His eyes darkened. The hand at her throat slipped behind her neck, pulling her forward until their lips met, then merged.

The world dropped from beneath her, and she floated in a dark abyss. His mouth, his earthy scent, and the heat of his body pressed to hers were her only holds on reality.

Her feet left the floor, and she realized he'd lifted her into his arms without their lips breaking contact. Lingeringly, erotically, his mouth tasted hers as he walked, toward the bed. The thought of where he was taking her both frightened and excited her . . . until the sheets touched her spine. Panic erupted. She twisted her head to the side. "Please, I—"

"Shh," he murmured, brushing his lips back and forth across hers. "I just want to enjoy your sweetness for a minute." Smoldering eyes explored the exposed flesh above her wrap. "As much as I might wish it otherwise, we don't have time for anything more."

Thank heavens, she thought gratefully. Succumbing to this man's charms would be much too easy.

Knowing she had nothing to fear, she didn't protest when he again lowered his mouth over hers. For the first time in her life, she was free to explore her own sensuality without consequence.

Tentatively she slid her hands into his thick hair, reveling in the feel of vibrant strands gliding through her fingers. She tested the shape of his head, the corded muscles in the back of his neck, the width of his commanding shoulders. Awed by his immense power, yet no longer afraid, she raked her nails down his taut back.

His flesh rippled, and a low groan rumbled through his chest. "Jesus," he whispered, recapturing her mouth with carnal purpose. Slowly, deliberately, he pressed his tongue between her lips.

Instead of rejecting the intrusion, she embraced the gentle thrust, the hungry exploration. He tasted of rum and mint . . . and male. The combination took her breath away, and she dissolved beneath his amorous invasion, tightening her arms around his back, arching into him.

A shudder moved through his body.

"Sin? Sin, are you in there?" Lucas's voice boomed from the other side of the door. "Come on. Donnelly and the others have already gone. We're late."

Sin cursed as he pushed off the bed and pulled her up with him. "I'm coming, damn it." He flung open the door and glared at his friend.

Lucas grinned unabashedly.

Sin swore again.

"I brought what you asked for, boss," the overseer said, still smiling.

"Where is it?"

"Right here." He gestured toward something lying on the floor.

She glanced at the peculiar device. It appeared to be a piece of sail tied between two long poles, making a sort of hammock in the middle, then piled high with pillows. "What is it?"

"A litter," Sin advised, then motioned her to sit on the contraption.

Each taking an end, they lifted the conveyance to hip level.

She stared at the thing as if it were alive. She wasn't about to let them lug her around on that. "Don't be silly. You can't carry me."

"I just did, princess," her host reminded.

A surge of heat stung her cheeks. "Why are you doing this?"

"It's a long walk," Sin reminded, "and you don't have any shoes. Now, get on."

Recalling how she'd mentioned the lack of footwear to Beula earlier, she wondered if Sin had spoken to the woman. She glanced up into the stern lines of his face, and decided not to argue. "This is ridiculous," she grumbled as she gingerly perched her bottom on the flimsy thing.

"Heavy, too," Lucas added with a chuckle.

She shot him a quelling look.

Sin, holding the front half, made a groaning sound. "My arms are being ripped from their sockets."

"Oh, do stop teasing," she pleaded, knowing she didn't weigh *that* much. "I feel bad enough as it is."

"You should," Lucas jibed, then pretended to drop his end.

Moriah gasped, grabbing the sides. When it righted again she demanded, "Put me down this instant. I'll walk."

"Too late," Sin countered, and began striding forward.

Still holding the sides for balance, she became aware of the uncomfortable position he'd put her in. Oh, not that the litter itself was disagreeable. It wasn't. But from where she sat, she had an unobstructed view of his broad back and tight rear end. An intriguing sight that held her completely entranced . . . and soon made her grow warm all over.

So engrossed was she that the three-mile jaunt passed without her notice until the smell of roasting meat and the sound of banjo music filtered into her wandering brain. She glanced up to see they'd just left the woods and entered a wide valley ripe with sugarcane. At the edge of the field, in an immense circular clearing, a large warehouse stood behind a series of white brick houses. The entire village and crops were surrounded by dense pines, and smoke rose from a wide center pit.

Curiously she stared at the dwellings built similar to Sin's home. "Why are the walls so thick?"

"Protection from storms," he answered over his shoulder, then hoisted his end of the litter higher. "We get a lot of wind and rain in this area. Besides, the density helps the insides stay cooler and prevents deterioration in this humid climate."

"Hey, boss!" someone called out.

Captain Jonas and a hairy man wearing loose breeches walked toward them. She recognized Jonas's companion as one of the crewmen she'd seen at the cove.

"Whatcha got there?" the captain taunted Sin fondly, then shot her a wink.

"A whale, by the feel of it."

"Oh, stop," she scolded with mock seriousness, then spoiled it all by laughing.

Several more crewmen and some others who she assumed were field hands approached Sin. They teased him familiarly as two of them took his end of the litter, while others relieved Lucas of his burden. It wasn't hard to tell that Sin was well liked by his workers and friends.

Feeling extraordinarily shy, she kept her gaze downcast as the strangers carried her to the center of the festivities, near a table between the houses and field. It had been decorated with flowers and streamers of shiny green vines. An enormous cake with white frosting dominated the center.

Two large chairs cushioned with pillows sat nearby.

One stood empty, while the other was occupied by an aging Negress wearing a flowered dressing robe that belted at the waist. She was nothing more than bone and thin flesh.

The men carrying Moriah stopped in front of the old woman, while Sin went to her and kissed her wrinkled cheek. "Happy Birthday, beautiful."

A smile widened the woman's mouth, revealing her scarce teeth. "Only you would see beauty in this old face." She glanced at Moriah. "Your woman, she is good?"

"Thanks to you," he returned.

She waved a gaunt hand. "The Great One make herbs for healing woman's leg. Not Woosak."

"I'm still grateful." He rose and withdrew a small wrapped package, then handed it to the old woman. "And this is from both of us."

Surprised to learn he'd sought herbs from the old woman on her behalf, she gave him a curious glance, then returned her attention to the gift.

Woosak's shaky hands pulled at the ribbon, then peeled the paper away.

Moriah stared at the object. It was a male doll carved out of polished teakwood.

A low cackling sound erupted from the woman's throat. "What Woosak do with *tee sha?* This old body not want another lover." She looked at Moriah. "Better Sin's woman have."

"She doesn't need it," he proclaimed. "She already has all the lovers she can handle." His gaze touched hers. "All the lovers she's going to need for quite some time."

Oh, hell. Why didn't she just die and get it over with? Anything would be better than this public humiliation.

Woosak laughed. "Then I keep. Someday the Great One give Woosak homely granddaughter who could use."

"He wouldn't dare." Sin's husky laugh sent ripples up her spine. The others standing around joined him, then, as the merriment died down, he moved next to Moriah. "Come on, princess. Give these poor men a rest." He

lifted her off the litter and sat her in the chair beside the aging islander.

Having forgotten all about the men who held her, she could only burn with embarrassment.

"Where's the rum?" he called to no one in particular.

Lucas seconded the request.

When one of the crewmen pointed to a small wood shelter near the warehouse, Sin and Lucas strode in the indicated direction, followed by several others.

Suddenly Sin stopped and swung his hand toward her. "That's Moriah, everyone!" Grinning, he continued on.

Shame rippled through her in waves. What was the matter with him? Men don't introduce their *mistresses*.

"The boss, he good man," Woosak said, startling her.

"The boss?" She composed herself and turned to the woman, knowing it wouldn't do any good to dwell on her hated position.

The old Negress nodded. "He bring Woosak and others from big plantations. Make all happy."

Savannah, Moriah recalled. Her gaze moved over the many, many workers, realizing just how vast the plantations must have been. "Didn't you like Savannah?"

"Savannah, white folk say. Woosak say evil devil village."

"Why?"

Her thin shoulders lifted in a shrug. "Old master, sire to Sin, he make all unhappy. Only to boss and Lucas he be kind." She stared at the ground. "It good the old one die."

"Sin's father died? How?"

Woosak's weathered cheeks creased in a smile. "The Great One take." Her gaze moved to Sin, who stood with the others, passing around a bottle. "But He bring young master much sadness." She caressed the teak doll. "Give boss heavy burden."

"What kind of burden?"

Woosak lowered her gaze to her lap. "The curse."

"Curse?" The word nearly lodged in her throat. First voodoo witches and now curses?

"Woosak no talk of boss to others before you. But is good to tell one who take burden away." A bony hand closed over Moriah's. "Boss's power is strong, sometimes makes Woosak shiver, but inside, young master is good. You must believe. Must help."

Her gaze shot to Sin's tall form towering above the other men. An uneasiness slithered through her. Did Sin's *curse* have anything to do with the strange occurrences she'd experienced since she'd been on Arcane? Her heart picked up speed as she recalled the incident with the tiger . . . and coconuts . . . and quivering ground . . . and exploding fire . . . and broken window.

A hundred thoughts whirled through her brain, but only one settled into some semblance of order. Mudanno's declaration. . . . *a child who will possess my powers . . . and yours.*

"Dear God," she whispered, not sure whether to be frightened *for* him . . . or *of* him. But there was one thing she did know for certain.

She couldn't help him.

CHAPTER

15

The woman had no idea how lovely she was, Sin thought as he strolled toward Moriah. Light from several lanterns hanging around the village danced in her violet eyes and over her bare shoulders. Her long, straight hair shimmered like black silk in the soft glow.

He could almost feel the texture slipping through his fingers. Feel the sweet softness of her skin, of her full, lush lips. He could vividly recall her scent and taste. Wild sensations pulsed through every inch of him, tightening his body even as he walked.

Certain the fullness in his breeches wouldn't be missed by Woosak's sharp eye—and probably not Moriah's either—he turned abruptly and stopped in front of the table, pretending to steal a piece of fruit.

He had to quit thinking about her, that was all there was to it. At thirty-one, he was too damned old to go around in this half-aroused state all the time. Shoving a piece of banana into his mouth, he chewed vigorously. He hadn't had this much trouble with a mistress since he first came to Arcane.

Recalling those early months, when he'd thought to use the island women's services, he shook his head. Lucas had tried to warn him not to mess with the girls he'd watch grow up. They knew him too well and would easily become involved. But he hadn't listened, and in the end, his stupidity broke Tonna's heart and cost him a damned good field hand—her father.

Vowing to never let that happen again, he'd sent Donnelly to Nassau to find him a mistress. One of the freighter's crewmen told of the rendezvous house. Up to now, Sin had liked the arrangement. When he tired of a woman, he simply returned her to Bliss Island and hired another.

And not one of them had caused him to lose control. Never had his passion—or theirs—roused the beast in him. Only Moriah did that.

Turning slightly so he could view her without being noticed, he studied her, wondering at this strange hold she had on him. Okay, he conceded, so she was the most beautiful one he'd ever encountered, and the most modest, the most headstrong, the most entertaining, the most . . . Damn. He was doing it again.

Stuffing in another bite, this time guava, he sighed. If he didn't take her soon, he wouldn't live through the ordeal when it finally did happen.

But when he looked at her, he saw so much more than just those sweet curves and tempting mouth. He saw her intelligence, her quick wit, and her unending curiosity. She challenged him, defied him, and kept him running to keep up with her vigorous escapades. Everything about the woman exhilarated him.

Except her profession.

Not wanting thoughts of that particular subject to ruin his evening, he pushed them to the corner of his mind and again headed for his lady.

Near the edge of the cane fields, he caught a glimpse of Lucas arguing with Callie. Fleetingly he wondered where she'd been earlier when Moriah asked for her. Assuming Lucas had kept the woman occupied, he dismissed the couple and continued on toward the women.

Lazy drums joined the banjo in a lumbering waltz as he approached.

Moriah glanced up and smiled in welcome.

"You come to dance," Woosak remarked with uncanny certainty—a habit that annoyed the hell out of him most of the time.

"You know me too well," he teased, then lifted a palm to the old lady.

She slapped his hand away. "Young fool. You no dance Woosak." She nudged Moriah. "Go, child. It is your arms he seeks."

Bright pink stained his mistress's cheeks.

He pulled her up into his arms. "She's right, you know," he whispered for her ears only. "But, then, the old gal usually is." He winked at the aging Negress. "I'll pretend she's you, beautiful."

Woosak's shrill cackle echoed behind him as he led his woman to a circle of other dancers.

"She's very nice," Moriah said as he slipped his arm around her waist.

"She's shrewd as hell," he corrected. "And nosy, and interfering, and manipulative." He glanced at the old lady. "And I absolutely adore her."

"Certainly sounds like it."

He grinned. "Our mock insults don't mean a thing. It's a game we've played since I was in swaddlings."

She peeked over his shoulder at Donnelly and Dorothy, who were dancing nearby. "Have you known all these people since you were a child?"

"All except the natives in the north woods." God, she smelled good, just like a summer flower garden. He nuzzled her hair.

"Donnelly, too?" she asked a little breathlessly.

He pressed her closer, enjoying the feel of those enticing curves. "He was my father's manservant before I was born." The drumbeat slowed, and so did their movements.

"Has he been happy in your employ?"

"What's all this interest in my servants?"

She didn't meet his eyes. "It's just Donnelly, mostly. I

don't know for sure, but I get the impression he's unhappy. I thought you might know why."

That gave him pause. He, too, had noticed the man's increasingly distant manner. He glanced at the older man. "I think he's worried I'll retire him."

"Will you?"

He traced a finger along her spine, wishing he could touch her naked flesh. "Yes. He's been a faithful companion and deserves the rest. Besides, he's been isolated on Arcane for half a decade now. When he's relieved of his duties, he can travel, visit his daughter in England, or simply take life easy however he chooses."

"Have you mentioned this to him?"

"No. But I've hinted to both him and Jonas."

Her smooth brow crinkled. "The sloop's captain?"

"Former captain," he corrected. "This is the second vessel he's lost in the last four months. And the last. Like Donnelly, Jonas is nearing seventy, and it's time to terminate his responsibilities."

"Have you told *him?*"

"No. But I will. I have to." He trailed a palm over her silk-covered bottom and pressed her into the heaviness growing between them. "I can't wait until this party is over."

A tremor moved through her body, heightening his male instincts. "To hell with waiting. Come on, let's get something to eat for appearance' sake, then I'm taking you home." Wishing they didn't have to eat at all, but knowing their immediate departure would insult Woosak's family, he led her to the table and seated her on one of the long benches.

Moriah inhaled the delicious aroma of roasted meat, steaming potatoes, baked bread, and coconut as she watched him fill two plates from the mounds of food spread over one end of the table. Though she was worried about what would transpire once they were alone at the manor, and still mulling over her talk with the old Negress earlier, it didn't lessen her appetite. As mother would say, *nothing did that.* "What kind of meat is this?" she asked when he set the fare in front of her.

"Wild boar. We have quite a few of them here on Arcane."

Gingerly she sampled a piece of meat. "Tastes like pork."

"That's because it *is* pork. The boar is an ancestor to the domestic hog." Digging into his own meal, he nodded to a half-shell coconut filled with white liquid. "Try some of that."

She did—and most everything else within reach. Full and content, she shoved her plate away. "That was superb."

Having already finished his own meal, he wrapped an arm around her shoulders. "Let's say our good-byes to Woosak."

The warmth in his voice and the feel of his long fingers on her bare flesh sent tingles up her spine. "Maybe we should stay. I wouldn't want to offend her by leaving too soon."

He leaned close, his warm, moist breath caressing her ear. "She won't be. She knows what I want before I do." He traced her lobe with his tongue. "Besides, by eating, we fulfilled our obligation. And . . . I have a surprise for you."

Fire streaked through her midsection. The longing in his voice melted over her. "A surprise?"

"Mmm, a pleasing one, I hope." He nibbled her neck. "Come on, princess. Let's go."

She couldn't fight the inevitable. She'd known what would happen when she made the decision to come to Arcane, and now was the moment of truth. Sin Masters would make love to her. But no matter what the consequences, she knew her virtue was a small price to pay to see her sister's killer at the end of a hangman's noose.

There is another alternative, her logic reminded. *You can tell him the truth.*

As they approached Woosak, the idea became more and more promising.

The old Negress took one look at Moriah, and instantly shooed away a group of people surrounding her. Then she eyed Sin. "You go, too, boss. Woosak speak to woman. Important female talk."

Stunned by her abrupt dismissal, Moriah suppressed a twinge of nervousness as she watched her host shrug and join a crowd of men.

The old woman caught her hand. "Why you think you no help boss?"

She stared at the thin Negress. How had she known Moriah's thoughts? This island got stranger by the minute. "It's not that I don't want to help him. I can't. The only one who can rescue him from this curse, or power, or whatever, is himself. Only him."

Her frizzy gray head bobbed up and down. "Yes. Very wise. Woosak see now." She met Moriah's gaze. "But I also see more. I see innocence—and your need to tell boss." She shook her head. "Is not good. He will feel betrayed. Will be angry. Hurt. Is not good, you do this now. Give more time."

She stared in astonishment. Good God, what *else* did she know? "If I don't tell him, how do I stop him from . . ."

Woosak squeezed her hand. "If this be your wish, you will find way."

But what if it wasn't her wish? "How can you be sure?"

"The Great One, He talk to this old woman. He say it be so."

Moriah gaped, wondering if Woosak truly expected her to believe that. The aged eyes crinkled with understanding. "Sin's woman must learn trust."

Sin's woman must be insane! She eased her fingers from the bony ones. "What if you're wrong?"

"Great One is never wrong."

"But—"

She lifted a hand and motioned to Sin. "You come now. Take woman home."

Moriah clamped her teeth together. The old woman was certainly sure of herself.

Sin slipped his arm around her, his palm resting just below her breast, and chasing away thoughts of Woosak. Did the man realize how easily his touch unnerved her? How his scent mingled with the damp air to stroke her senses and test her perseverance? Even the sound of his sensual voice slid over her flesh like warm oil.

With a minimum of salutations to the birthday girl, Sin whisked her away, leading her into the woods with long strides that had her trotting to keep up.

Once inside the moonlit forest, he laced his fingers through hers and slowed. "I think Woosak's taken a shine to you," he said matter-of-factly.

Heat from his large hand rippled up her arm. "She's a . . . unique woman."

"No longer nice?"

"Well, that too."

He chuckled. "She has me vacillating all the time, wanting to strangle her in one instant and hug her in the next."

A broken branch crunched beneath her bare foot. Pain shot up her leg. "Ow!" She grabbed her toes, hopping.

"Sit down," he ordered, easing her onto a log. "Here, let me see." He brushed her hands away and lifted her stinging foot. A tiny drop of blood shone in the moonlight. "Damn it. I knew I should have carried you."

"Don't be silly. The pain's already gone." The feel of his fingers encircling her ankle bothered her more than the little nick.

He brushed the crimson droplet away with his thumb and inspected the wound. "It's only a scratch, but in this humid region, infection sets in quickly." He scooped her up in his arms and started weaving his way through thick stands of gardenias tangled with ferns.

"Sin," she protested. "This isn't necessary. I'm quite capable of walking. Put me down."

"Why? I happen to like the feel of you in my arms." He kissed the exposed slope of her breast. "In fact, I like the feel of you . . . anywhere, anytime, or anyplace."

Wanting to hide her face in humiliation—and punch

his nose at the same time—she conceded to his high-handedness and gingerly encircled his neck for balance. "Did anyone ever mention how bossy you are?"

"Never."

"Liar."

After a few stops, they finally reached the manor, then he strode in through the veranda door and sat her on the edge of his bed. "Sit still. I want to clean that scratch."

Realizing they were completely alone, she shifted uneasily as he gathered a damp cloth, gauze, and salve, then returned to kneel in front of her. "Lift your foot."

"You're making too much of this."

Not in the mood for resistance, he gripped her ankle and raised her leg. Gently he cleaned the cut and massaged in a dab of salve, then wrapped her foot. After he tied the fabric in place, he didn't rise as she'd expected; instead, he just knelt there, cradling her heel in his warm palm.

As surely as if he'd moved, she felt the change in him. The air became still. His breathing grew uneven. His fingers closed around her ankle as his gaze explored her bare leg, the hem of her skirt, her hips, her barely covered breasts, her naked shoulders, then finally met her eyes.

A flare of desire glowed in the dark depths. "I want you, princess."

Those four little words had the effect of an explosion. Her pulse erupted in a frenzied burst of speed. "Sin . . ."

He lowered his head to plant nibbling kisses on her calf, then higher, tasting the sensitive inner flesh of her knee.

Shimmering waves of desire rippled through her liquid limbs. Oh, damn. Where was her willpower?

His long fingers traced the tingling skin on her opposite thigh, inching upward with each tiny, intoxicating circle he drew while his mouth and tongue continued their erotic assault.

Fire licked through her belly. "Sin, please . . ."

The bed shifted.

Those marauding fingers edged higher, slowly trailing

up her inner thigh beneath her wrap. His lips followed a like path on her opposite leg.

It was becoming hard to breathe, and her lungs fought for air. Heat and shivers took turns pulsing through her woman's mound. Her body grew tense, expectant.

A door slammed.

The tips of his fingers lightly brushed her feminine curls, sending stabs of desire straight to her core. She sucked in a breath. *"Sin!"*

His head shot up. "What?"

She scooted her legs out of his reach. "Y-You said you had a s-surprise for me. Where is it?" Anything to stop the torment.

"Woman, are you trying to kill me?" A long sigh left him, and he rose. "It should be on your bed. I'll get the damned thing." In stiff strides, he disappeared into the adjoining chamber.

The instant he was out of sight, she pulled her skirt down and tucked it tightly beneath her now-closed knees. That had been close. Dragging in a few stabling breaths, she waited for his return, trying to think of a way to avoid his unnerving sensuality.

He emerged a moment later, carrying a linen-wrapped bundle. "These weren't done in time for Woosak's party, or I'd have given them to you earlier. Beula's daughter stayed behind to finish them." He placed the linen on her lap.

"You mean she missed the celebration because of me?"

"No. I saw her arrive while we were eating."

Relieved, she unfolded the material.

A pair of intricately stitched leather sandals sat amid the white fabric.

"Oh, Sin. They're beautiful." Warmth rushed over her at his thoughtfulness.

He traced the leather with a long finger. "I should have had them made sooner." He motioned toward her bandaged foot. "If I had, that would have been prevented."

Hating the way he blamed himself for her mishap, she

covered his fingers with hers. "It's not your fault. If I hadn't been so clumsy . . ."

Their eyes met. Locked.

Tension filled the hot, flower-scented room.

Slowly he turned his hand over, lacing his fingers through hers. "Your touch unmans me, princess. Everything about you jars my senses." Holding her gaze, he bent closer, closer, until at long last he closed his eyes and captured her lips.

The maelstrom of emotions she'd experienced just minutes ago rushed in to claim her, and she didn't resist when he brushed the shoes aside to give him access to her bare knees. Lifting her legs to loosen their hold on the fabric, he inched her skirt up, lovingly caressing her thigh, the tingling flesh between.

Her resistance crumbled. His masculine skill was just too much for her.

He pushed the material higher, leaving her fully exposed to his hot gaze, but she couldn't force a word of protest past her dry throat. She could only watch . . . and feel.

His eyes grew bright, and a curtain toppled from its brackets as he encircled her thigh with his warm fingers. The contrast of his dark hand against her pale flesh was so erotic, she shivered.

Then she felt his hand gliding upward, his fingers fluttering over her most intimate region. "Oh, God." Her arms wouldn't support her, and she fell back on her elbows.

His mouth sought hers with a hunger that left her weak.

A windowpane shattered, but she barely noticed. Her whole world was centered on the erotic movement of his hand, on the sweet torture of his breathtaking kiss. She collapsed back on the bed, taking him with her, her limbs useless, her body trembling uncontrollably. Desperate for stability in her spiraling world, she gripped the quilt beneath her.

He became merciless in his carnal assault. His mouth

left hers to tug at the top of her wrap. The material loosened, then slid from her flesh. A breeze tightened her nipple. "Oh, princess." He claimed the feast with ravenous hunger.

A flash of heat shot through her breast, and she arched her spine, mindlessly seeking more.

He swirled his tongue over the bud, then he nipped gently with his teeth. At the same time, his fingers parted her.

She dug her nails into the quilt.

While he continued to nurse greedily, he found the center of her fire and stroked delicately.

Sweet flames consumed her.

She couldn't stand any more. The coil in her belly had grown unbearable. She arched her hips, giving him better access. He covered her fully with his hand, sliding his finger urgently over her need. His mouth tightened on her breasts.

The headboard cracked.

She tried to focus on the destruction, but desire engulfed her. The coil snapped. An earth-shattering explosion burst through her core. She cried out, but it didn't stop the wild convulsions. Pleasure, so intense it hurt, ripped into her soul. "Sin! Oh, God, Sin!" A whirlpool of fire sucked her down until she feared she'd drown in the blazing depths.

Distantly she felt his finger press into her. "Open for me, princess. Let me show you another side of heaven."

A wave of renewed passion sprang to life, and nothing could have stopped her from blindly offering what he sought. She lifted her hips, urgently seeking that intense, wondrous sensation she'd known just moments before.

"Sweet Christ," he groaned.

A loud crash exploded in the room.

He leapt from the bed as if she'd shot him.

She, too, sprang to her feet and frantically glanced around.

The wardrobe closet lay in a splintered heap amid silk and linen garments.

"Goddamn it!" Sin roared.

She retreated a step, suddenly frightened.

Her reaction made him even angrier. With quick, jerky movements, he kicked the sandals across the chamber and stalked out of the room, vowing to have every damned thing in the house nailed down.

She scanned the devastation in the room and recalled what had caused the destruction. Her face burned. How had things gotten so out of hand? And what was the matter with her? Why hadn't she tried to stop him?

Straightening her wrap, she walked out onto the patio. Rain splattered against the edges of the flagstones.

Achates sat by a chair, his sleek black fur damp and glistening, his amber eyes knowing.

"Don't give me that look," she ordered, no longer afraid of the beast. "What happened in there wasn't my fault."

The panther made a guttural noise that sounded like a snort.

Irritated, she stalked inside and made for the adjoining room. Males. They're all alike. Disgusted with the lot, she peeled off her wrap and climbed into bed, knowing Sin wouldn't return to her tonight. Thank God. The liberties she'd allowed him—*and what she'd nearly done*—scared the hell out of her. Even memories of Clancy O'Toole didn't interfere when Sin touched her. Nothing did.

She glanced at the carnage in the next room. Well, *almost* nothing.

Shaking her head, she closed her eyes, wondering if Sara had experienced the same devastation with Sin.

The thought hurt.

CHAPTER
16

Sin was still in a foul mood the next morning as he stood next to Lucas, staring at the freighter. Moriah was driving him crazy, and if that weren't enough, his crops were ready, but his freighter wasn't. All because the crew had stopped construction to work on the damaged sloop. They were a full week behind schedule.

"The cane isn't going to wait." Lucas voiced his thoughts. "Looks like we're going to have to store it in the warehouse."

Jamming his fingers into his pocket and closing them around the crystal, Sin nodded. "I hate to, though. We won't get as high a price for cane that's been sitting that long." He had built a reputation for superior-quality produce, and he wouldn't try to pass off a lesser grade for the same price. Sighing, he withdrew his hand. "Gather the men; it's time to get to work."

As Lucas walked off, he noticed that the younger man had a satisfied look about him. Wondering if Moriah's maid was responsible, he sprinted off toward the fields. He needed to work off some frustration.

By nine o'clock that evening, he knew he'd succeeded. He was so tired, he fell asleep in the bathtub, then could barely hold his head up at supper.

Moriah, he noticed during their meal, seemed distant. Praying the incident she'd witnessed last night hadn't upset her as much as him, he ate quickly and retired.

A few minutes later, she joined him long enough to announce her intentions.

He narrowed his eyes on his mistress. "What do you mean you aren't sleeping in the same bed with me again?"

She flicked a long strand of hair over her bare shoulder. "I can't sleep properly with you beside me. You snore and toss your arms all night. Why, I'm nothing but bruises when I wake up in the mornings."

He rubbed his tired neck. "I've never had any complaints before. Nor have I seen your bruises." Weariness dragging him down, he shrugged and continued undressing. "But suit yourself." Too exhausted to argue, he practically fell into bed.

Moriah glared at his comatose form sprawled across the mattress. She'd worked all day to get up the nerve to bring up the topic of her duplicity, and had planned to do so when he contested her choice of beds—then the idiot not only agrees but falls asleep!

Wanting to kick him, she tromped into the adjoining room, then snatched off her wrap and flounced into bed. With a last scathing look at the sleeping man, she blew out the lantern. At least she didn't have to worry about being mauled tonight.

Still, somewhere in the deepest part of her, she knew she would miss his security and warmth.

She punched her pillow. "I won't miss it one bit, I tell you." Flopping over, she jerked the covers up to her ear. "And tomorrow I'll tell him. Damn it, I will."

Unfortunately, the next day—and the next—followed the same pattern. Sin spent all of his time harvesting cane or working on the freighter.

And it was nearly impossible to catch up with Callie

anymore. Praying the woman was investigating during her many disappearances and would soon fill her in, Moriah decided to go for a walk, anything to rid herself of this awful boredom. After searching Donnelly's room —and finding nothing incriminating—she'd found herself at loose ends.

She ventured out across the lawn toward a flower garden she'd discovered. The rock-lined grounds sat among the trees on the west side of the house, completely secluded. As she grew near, the delicious scent of roses, lilac, and carnations wafted toward her.

She breathed deeply, enjoying the delicate aromas, and smiling as she stepped into the garden. She stopped short. Someone had cut a neat path through the flowers, then widened it out into a bare circle beneath a large overhanging branch.

And from the branch hung a swing.

Her insides warmed. Sin had done this.

Trembling with emotion, she eased onto the seat and gripped the ropes on either side, then set the swing into motion.

"Uh-oh," a barely audible voice muttered.

She glanced up to see Donnelly standing at the edge of the trees, and quickly jumped from the still-moving swing. Being in such a secluded area with him sent a sliver of apprehension along her nerve endings. She cleared her throat. "I'm not supposed to be here, am I?"

"No, missy. You're not." He moved toward her.

She retreated a step.

"Sin was saving this for a surprise," the old man continued. "They'll be finished with the fields early today, and he planned on showing it to you after supper."

Warmth for Sin replaced her misgivings. "I see." She glanced at the swing, then to Donnelly. "Then perhaps this could be our little secret?" She smiled lamely. "I-I wouldn't want to spoil his surprise."

He gave a short bow. "If you wish."

"I do wish."

The thin man nodded and started to turn.

"Donnelly? Do you remember Sara Winslow?"

He was uncertain how to respond at first, then dipped his head. "I remember the lass well."

How well? she wondered. "I understand she was very happy here."

He started walking, and Moriah followed. "Yes, she was."

"Then why did she leave?"

He turned on her. "What was Sara to you?"

Frightened, yet hoping to force him into revealing his true nature, she lifted her chin. "She was my sister."

His eyes searched her face, possibly for some resemblance, but his expression didn't change. And she had the strangest notion that her confession hadn't surprised him. "I don't mean to pry, miss, and you can certainly tell me if I'm out of line, but it's my impression that you're not a . . . er . . . well, that is, a woman of indiscretion."

She shifted uncomfortably. "If you mean am I a woman of profession, then the answer is no. I only posed as such because there wasn't any other way to get to Sin's island."

Aged eyes lit with warm satisfaction. "After coming to know you, I had hoped as much." He glanced away. "The thought of you in such circumstances didn't sit well. You weren't like the others. You never stopped being a true lady. You didn't demand things even when you were ill. You were always so gentle and kind. . . ."

A surge of pride and embarrassment swept through her. Her face grew hot. "Thank you." She brushed a mosquito off her cheek. "But you didn't answer my question. If Sara was happy here, why did she leave?"

He sidestepped a shrub. "She found out what she wanted to know."

A dozen possibilities raced through her thoughts. "What?"

"She thought Sin killed Elizabeth Kirkland."

Though she'd considered the same possibility, hearing him voice Sara's belief still shocked her.

"That's why she came here. She told Sin so. The boy was pretty upset with her at first, but after a while, he understood her need."

Sara had confronted Sin and told him she thought he'd killed his former mistress? Is *that* what caused her death? Had he or someone else murdered her to silence her? Moriah's heart screamed in denial. Forcing down the rising alarm, she prompted, "What do you mean he understood? Understood what? And why would Sara try to find out who killed some prostitute she didn't even know?"

Gray brows rose. "But Sara did know her. Elizabeth Kirkland was Sara's sister-in-law. Surely you knew that."

The ground tilted beneath her feet, and she grabbed on to his arm. "Sister-in-law? I thought Buford's little sister was a young girl who'd run away from home. I had no idea. . . . My God!"

Visions of the newspaper article wavered into view. Tortured. Mutilated. Dissected. "Why would Sara pursue this? Why not Buford?" she demanded.

"It's my understanding that the lass's husband disowned the girl when he learned of her profession, even though she'd been married and widowed, but Sara kept in touch with her. When Elizabeth disappeared, Sara was all set to start looking for her, but Winslow wouldn't allow it. Then they found the Kirkland girl's body. Sara was devastated and determined to find the one responsible. Unfortunately, Sara's husband wouldn't permit her inquiries. Still, she secretly investigated the murder . . . and all points led to Sin. When the lass's husband died, she assumed pretty much the same role you did in order to reach the lad."

"Then she never . . . ? She wasn't his . . . ?"

Donnelly shrugged his thin shoulders. "I wouldn't know, miss."

But Moriah did. She *hadn't* been wrong about her

sister. Sara was not a tainted woman. Everything she'd done had been for a reason. Oh, Sara.

Sin sank down in the brass bathtub and let his muscles absorb the welcoming heat of the water. The harvest was in, the freighter nearly finished, and he felt terrific. The laborious work had honed his body and heightened his need for Moriah—if he could get past the beast.

Just the thought of possessing her sent a rush of fire to his loins. He sighed and leaned his head on the rim. Tonight, princess, he thought contentedly, closing his eyes. Maybe tonight.

"Sin? Can I talk to you?"

He raised his lashes to see Lucas stroll into the room. "What is it?" he asked, sitting up.

"I just spoke to Beula. She said Callie's been acting peculiar. And she disappears every day for a few hours."

"Does Beula know where the girl goes?"

"She's seen her slipping out of the house. Nothing more. I've tried to question the little witch myself, but she won't talk to me."

Sin rose, and Lucas handed him a towel. Draping it around his waist, he stepped from the tub. "I don't know what to think."

The overseer crossed to the bed and sat down while Sin pulled on his breeches. "I'm beginning to. She admitted she'd been drinking once. I figure she's been into your private stock."

Shrugging into his shirt, he considered his friend's words. But he'd fixed himself a drink from the liquor cabinet just prior to his bath. None of the stock had been missing that he could tell. "I don't think so, Lucas. I'd have noticed."

"Then that leaves Mudanno."

Sin felt the blood leave his face. "You don't think—"

"No. Damn it, Callie wouldn't . . ." Lucas's fists tightened. "But, then, I didn't think Davie Waller would either."

Recalling the way they'd found Davie, the former

captain of the sloop, sent a stab of fury through Sin's gut. Mudanno had supplied the man with her drug potion as long as he'd given her gifts. When the gifts ran out, the potion stopped. Addicted and suffering, Davie had drowned himself in the healing pool. Mudanno claimed she hadn't forced the man to take the drug. Still . . . "We'd better find out," he said bitterly.

"You're damn right. But *I* will," his friend snapped, just before he slammed out of the room.

Moriah couldn't stop trembling. When she'd first decided to tell Sin the truth, it had sounded like a good idea. Now that the time was growing closer, she wasn't so sure.

Stop it, she scolded herself. "It won't be so bad."

"What won't be so bad, Miss Morgan?"

Gasping, she whirled around.

Dorothy stood in the doorway holding a clean towel and soap, her head tilted in question.

Not as comfortable with the older woman as she was with Beula, she shrugged. "Nothing. I was just talking out loud to myself about . . ." She struggled for something to say. "About . . . the approaching storm I heard the maids discussing." Well, she *had* heard that on her way in from the garden.

The plump woman smiled gently, her first real show of warmth. "Don't worry, miss. This house was built to withstand a hurricane—and most else, for that matter."

"Hurricane?"

Setting the towel down near a recently filled tub, Dorothy nodded. "That's the storm the help's been talking about. There's one headed this way. One of the seamen noticed a warning swirl of dark clouds on the horizon about an hour ago. They figure it'll hit just after dark."

Having experienced the force of a hurricane, she stifled a groan. Why tonight? Didn't she have enough to worry about? "I see. Well, thank you, Dorothy, for reassuring me, that is."

"You're welcome. Now, let me help you out of that wrap. Supper'll be ready soon."

Unnerved about the coming storm *and* her inevitable talk with Sin, she quietly complied.

Flushed and warm after her bath, she chose to wear one of Callie's gowns for the evening meal. Surely there was *one* that would cover enough of her to boost her courage and supply the composure she needed to confront Sin.

But there wasn't.

She eventually settled on a shimmering aqua gown that changed colors in the light. All in all, the dress wasn't bad, and if the bodice hadn't been so low, she might have admired the cut and style. The clinging fabric fit her waist and midriff to perfection, then, with the support of a bottom hoop in the hem, flared out like a lace-covered umbrella.

The back collar was high, she gave it that much. But the front. That was horrible. The skimpy amount of material clearly exposed her nipples and just barely covered the darker centers. Too, the little puffy sleeves looked as if they were only held on by a thread at the sides of her bosom.

She would never get used to this.

Grabbing the hairbrush, she pulled the bristles through her tangled strands, then set off to join her host.

He was already seated at the dining table when she entered. As he rose, his gaze moved over her, then stopped at her breasts. Desire lit his eyes, but he quickly raised his head. "Good evening, princess."

His voice sounded unusually husky, she noticed as she took her seat . . . with his help. "Where's Lucas tonight?"

Resuming his place, he lifted a platter of roasted chicken. "He ate earlier, then went out to help the men secure the house and grounds against the coming storm. I'm going out, too, after . . . well, later."

She accepted the platter he passed to her. "Will the storm be a bad one?" She tried not to sound nervous.

He stabbed an ear of corn and plopped it onto his plate, then reached for a bowl of sautéed mushrooms. "I hope not. But at least the cane is in."

Watching his relaxed manner made her feel slightly better. In fact, if the storm were her only worry this evening, she'd be quite content. But it wasn't. Distractedly she picked up her fork.

Sin, too, began to eat. But after a few moments, his eyes drifted to her nearly naked chest.

She wished he wouldn't do that. He made her feel all hot and funny. Made her recall the night of Woosak's party, and what had happened afterwards. Lowering her gaze, she tried to concentrate again on her own meal.

It passed too swiftly for her, and she knew the time had come for her to tell him her true reason for being here. She eased her plate away and folded her hands on the table. "Sin—"

"It's about time," he grated. "I've waited all day to show you something. I was afraid the hurricane might hit before you finished."

Hoping beyond hope that she could feign surprise, she rose when he extended his hand and allowed him to lead her toward the secluded garden.

As she walked, her continuing deception began to wear. She was so sick of the masquerade. He had saved her from drowning, and she had repaid him by constantly lying to him.

He had been so kind, so considerate.

Still she had lied.

He'd saved her from the tiger. At every turn, he'd cared for her, pampered her, withheld himself from what he believed was his right.

She repaid him with deception.

He'd carried her from Woosak's village, and shown her a glimpse of heaven.

She had done nothing but pile one tale upon another. Tears stung her eyes. Shame and remorse twisted her insides.

"Oh, princess. Don't cry. I only meant to make you happy."

She blinked and glanced up.

They were standing in front of the swing.

Her watery gaze met his. "Oh, Sin."

He brushed her cheek with the backs of his fingers, his eyes soft, warm. "Come on, you sit. I'll push."

She couldn't do it. She couldn't take any more from him. Shaking her head, she pulled back out of his loose grasp. "I can't. Sin, there's something I have to tell you."

Wariness darkened his eyes. "What?"

Dying inside, she uttered the words that would change their relationship. "Sara Winslow was my sister."

CHAPTER

17

The very air crackled around her, but Sin didn't move. Didn't speak. Only the tightening of his features revealed that he'd even heard her words. Moriah wanted to throw her arms around him. Beg him not to be angry. "Don't glare at me like that. Let me explain."

His eyes brightened dangerously, and the swing began to rock.

"Please," she said gently, trying to soothe him before his anger got out of hand. "Let me explain."

"Explain what? That you came to this island because you assumed I killed your sister *and* Beth Kirkland, and you needed proof? That every word you've said to me has been a lie? That you took my money under false pretenses?" His frigid gaze raked her. "With no intention of delivering the goods?"

Knowing he was right hurt all the more. "Sara did the same thing, and you forgave her. Am I any different?"

"Different!" he roared. "You're about as different as water and sand. Damn you, I wasn't in love with Sara!"

Her heart jumped with happiness at his volatile admission, but was quickly subdued by his increasing fury.

"I've been such a fool," he snarled. "Instead of being

184

taken in by your sweet curves and sensuous smile, I should have known you were up to something. When I think of the times I wondered at your modesty, I could kick myself. I should have seen through your game. Damn it, I should have known better than to fall for your little scheme."

Everything he said was true. Her heart grew heavy. "Sin, please . . ."

He brushed past her, then spun back around, his eyes hard. "Just to set the record straight, I did *not* kill Beth. And I did *not* kill Sara. She was my friend, and I enjoyed her company. Nothing more." He laughed harshly. "But you, on the other hand, I *could* kill." He clenched his hands as if to keep from doing just that. "I want you off my island, Moriah. As soon as humanly possible." With a last frozen glower, he walked away.

Oh, God. She could feel his pain, the betrayal, and she knew she deserved everything he'd said. Shattered and sick inside, she fought to hold back the tears stinging her eyes. She had no one to blame but herself. If only she'd told him the truth when she first arrived . . . But she couldn't have. She didn't know him then. Didn't know the sensitive, gentle man, the caring one.

Feeling as if her heart were a weight too heavy to bear, she glanced at the surprise he'd gone to so much trouble to give her.

The swing lay on the ground, the seat broken, the ropes smoking where they'd burned in two.

Her tears fell. He had done that to hurt her . . . and oh, God, how he'd succeeded. Unable to stand, she dropped to her knees and clutched her stomach. Racking sobs shook her shoulders. Her heart. She hated him. Damn it, she *hated him.*

When her tears were at last spent, she became aware of the damp wind whipping her hair across her face. But she didn't want to go back to the manor. She couldn't bear to see the condemnation in his eyes, or worse, nothing at all.

Though he'd implied he loved her, she doubted that

still held true. Rising, she brushed off her skirt and ducked her head against the wind. She wouldn't go into the north woods because she'd given Sin her word, but that didn't mean she couldn't go to the beach beyond the cove.

She made her way past the house unnoticed, then hurried to the beach. Finding a large piece of driftwood, she sat down, digging her toes into the sand and staring out at the dark, churning ocean. If Dorothy hadn't told her the storm wasn't expected until later, she would have been concerned.

She brushed a damp strand of hair off her cheek as Sin's face stole into her thoughts. She could see him as she had that first time in his bedchamber—so devastatingly handsome, so male—and how entranced she'd been. If only there hadn't been her deception between them.

Inhaling a strained breath, she recalled his anger over the voodoo doll, then his gentle care when she was injured, his genuine affection for his servants, his wit, his intelligence. The way he walked, how he gestured with his hands when he spoke, the way he could melt her with a single look, or singe her insides with just a touch.

He was everything she wanted.

Well, if you discounted his unusual power. But even that didn't frighten her anymore. Lucas had been right. Sin wouldn't harm anyone. Even as angry and hurt as he'd been over her deception, he hadn't taken his fury out on her. At least, not physically.

She knew he feared his loss of control, but she doubted he'd ever considered the so-called curse as a gift. But he would, she vowed. Before she left Arcane, she'd make him see that.

A sudden wind slammed into her, bringing with it a torrent of water. Through the raging downpour she saw a wave rise to a monstrous height.

Dear God. The hurricane! Scrambling to her feet, she raced frantically toward the manor. Rain blinded her, battered her head and shoulders mercilessly, whipped her skirts until they tangled around her legs.

With both hands she gathered the yards of material to her waist and ran wildly for the trees.

She slammed into solid flesh.

"Moriah . . ." His voice died on the wind. He didn't waste time trying to speak again. He swung her up into his arms and ran like a madman, twisting and turning in an attempt to outrun the storm.

The world erupted around them in a whirling fury.

She buried her face in the warmth of his neck.

Suddenly the rain stopped. The wind howled angrily, but she couldn't feel it anymore.

Then her feet touched a cool flagstone floor.

Relief nearly buckled her knees. They'd made it indoors. She opened her eyes to find herself standing just inside the entryway.

Sin towered over her, staring down in an expression that matched the fury of the storm outside. "You little fool! You damned near got yourself killed! Damned near got us *both* killed." The ground began to quiver, and he clamped his mouth shut. Gripping her arm, he shoved her in the direction of her room. "The doors to your chamber have been boarded. See if you can manage to stay inside them."

Knowing full well that she was to blame for what just happened, and unable to argue over her own stupidity, she clutched her shivering arms and hurried down the hall.

Dorothy met her at her door. The housekeeper's gray hair hung in damp strands beneath a white mobcap, her fleshy cheeks at first drawn down with concern, then smoothing with relief. "Oh, child. When you came up missing, we thought we'd find you dead. Sin was nearly out of his mind. Even Lucas couldn't stop him from charging out into that devil wind to find you." She wrapped a blanket around Moriah's shoulders and led her into the room. "I never saw anyone so crazed—and I hope I never see it again. I thought his mind had snapped."

Moriah felt as if her own had. She couldn't stop shaking. Her jaws hurt from clenching her teeth. Never in her life had she witnessed such violence, such horrific destruction . . . or such fury in one man.

Anger that wouldn't soften soon, she was certain.

Allowing Dorothy to help her disrobe, she climbed into a tub and sank into its soapy heat for the second time that night. But the welcoming warmth didn't take away the chill that surrounded her heart.

Sin despised her.

When she was at last ensconced in bed, she slept fitfully, her thoughts returning again and again to the man who had come to mean so much to her. By morning, she felt as if she'd slept on a bed of nails.

He didn't make an appearance at breakfast, and she assumed he was outside with the men, unboarding the house. But when he didn't show up for dinner, and Beula informed her he'd eaten in his study, she knew he was avoiding her, and would probably continue to do so until she left.

His rejection hurt. She never realized how much she'd come to enjoy his presence until he withheld it. She missed him.

But he wanted her out of his life. She'd heard the servants talking about how fiercely he was pushing his men—and himself—in an effort to rectify damage done by the hurricane, finish the freighter, and repair the sloop all at the same time.

She plunked down on the bed and cast an exasperated look through the connecting door to Sin's room. She hadn't even heard him come in last night. *And his bed was still made when I awoke this morning.*

Just the thought of where he might have slept—and with whom—boiled her insides. She could almost envision him in the arms of one of those lovely island girls, some of whom, according to Dorothy, had taken shelter in the manor.

She balled her hands into fists. Fine. What did she care? They had no hold on each other. Why should she care one whit what Mr. Valsin Masters did?

The trouble was, she cared very much, and his continued scorn was tearing her apart.

Well, by God, this was going to stop. Getting up, she strode briskly to the dressing table and drew the brush through her hair. Moping around wasn't helping one bit. What she needed was fresh air and sunshine, anything to clear her head.

She spied Achates stretched out on the flagstones. "Hello, fella. I see you managed to survive the hurricane."

The panther sat up, and she scratched its ears. "How would you like to go for a walk? I'll let you be my protector."

He made his purring noise, and she smiled fondly.

"Okay, come on, then."

Certain that Sin was down at the cove and not wanting to go anywhere near him, she headed for the healing pool.

Under the heat of the sun, steam rose from the damp earth as she picked her way though the wind-tangled underbrush. The hurricane had left uprooted trees, twisted vines, and broken shutters, and the surge of showers that followed had created a stifling, humid heat. Thank God the brunt of the storm hadn't hit the island. The fury of the hurricane's outer edges had been volatile enough.

Stopping beside the pool, she made a quick survey of the area to make sure she was alone. Not that she'd expected to see anyone, with Sin working them so frantically on the vessels.

Satisfied that she wouldn't be disturbed, she undid her wrap and let it slide to the ground.

Achates stretched out on the bank.

She waded into the surprisingly cool pond and lowered herself to the cushiony bottom. A chorus of whipporwills chirped overhead, and the myriad aromas of flowers drifted on a breeze.

Totally relaxed, she rested her head on the bank and closed her eyes.

Images of Sin danced through her groggy vision.

He stood in his study, his rigid back to her, his anger tangible enough to touch.

She tried talking to him, but he ignored her. She attempted to explain, but he wouldn't turn around, wouldn't listen.

She cried and yelled. Nothing affected him.

Then she touched him.

The room exploded with the violent fury of a hurricane.

Achates growled.

Her eyes shot open, her heart pounding painfully. What a vivid nightmare. Having had enough of what the *healing* pool offered, she climbed out and quickly dressed.

But as she and the panther made their way to the house, she mulled over the dream again and again. Why had everything erupted when she touched him?

Her steps slowed. *Because you make him lose control.* Her heart began to pound heavily. What if she could turn his loss to her advantage? Keep touching him, seducing him, until he was forced to listen . . . or make love to her—*and then listen.*

Her morals demanded she stop this at once, and for just an instant, she did hesitate. But she knew what she was about to do was right. For both of them.

Callie staggered from the bed, her legs barely able to support her. Pain lanced through her stomach, and she stumbled down the outside stairs. The potion was wearing off earlier than it had before. The burning ache in her belly felt like it had grown claws, and the nightly visits to Mudanno were beginning to threaten her sanity. It was as if her brain had shut down. She had no thoughts of her own—no will.

Shakily she gripped the railing. She had to see Mudanno, even if it wasn't dark yet. She had to have something *now* to stop the tearing pain, the emptiness, the uncontrollable shuddering.

With unsteady steps she stumbled across the lawn, making sure she wasn't seen, then staggered into the north woods.

The trip through the trees was torture, the need for Mudanno's potion growing with each step, and by the time she reached the thatch huts, tears streamed down her cheeks and fire burned in the pit of her stomach.

"Please . . ." she managed, grabbing on to one of the men who'd come to the edge of the clearing to meet her.

He leered at her, then cupped her breast and squeezed hard.

"The potion, please," she whimpered.

Mudanno, her naked breast gleaming with sweat, walked up to her. She flicked her long black hair over her shoulder. "You come early. Why? Does the one called Moriah follow?"

"No. It's the potion," Callie repeated through thick lips. "I need . . ."

The priestess laughed huskily. "I see the urge for *tom-coo* grows. Good. Good." She clapped her hands. "Mudanno will give."

Someone hurried to the leader and handed her the bowl Callie knew contained the opiate that would ease her pain. She grabbed for it.

Mudanno held it out of her reach. "Not yet. First you bring the woman."

"I can't." She couldn't take her eyes off the bowl. "Moriah won't come. Sin made her promise. I heard him."

Swirling the dark liquid, the witch stared, smiling evilly, her head moving slowly from side to side to work the medallion. "She will come."

Light from the gold disk moved back and forth across Callie's eyes. She blinked and tried to concentrate on what they were talking about. Moriah's promise. "She won't break her word," she repeated sluggishly, her limbs beginning to quiver, her gaze returning to the bowl.

Mudanno dipped the tip of her finger into the liquid, then ran it around the edge of the bowl. "She won't?" the priestess said softly. "Not even to learn of the one who killed her sister?"

For the barest instant Callie's head cleared and she forgot her pain. "You know who killed Sara?"

The voodoo queen sent her a sly smile. "Tell the white whore Mudanno ended the fair-haired one's life."

No, Callie wanted to scream, but agonizing pain ripped through her, stilling the words. Her desperate need for the opium became unbearable. She licked her lips. "Yes, yes." She would have agreed to anything to stop the burning. "I'll tell her. I'll bring her. But first I've got to have potion. I have to . . ."

"You go."

"Noooo. Oh, please, let me have some now. I can't stand it anymore." Nothing mattered but stopping the hurt.

Shrugging, Mudanno handed the bowl back to the old woman who still stood beside her. "No Moriah—no *tom-coo.*"

The old woman scurried away, taking Callie's only means of relief.

Desperate, she tried to run after her.

A man's hand snagged her waist.

"Go!" Mudanno demanded. "Now."

Sobbing hysterically, Callie ran toward the manor.

CHAPTER
18

Sin still hadn't made an appearance for supper, Moriah noted angrily. Tossing her napkin down on her half-empty plate, and completely ignoring Lucas, she rose. It was time to stop this nonsense. Sin would listen to her. Right now.

Lifting her chin to bolster her courage, she stalked off in the direction of his study. She knew he was in there. She'd seen Beula carry a tray in earlier.

She paused outside his door, suddenly reluctant. The magnitude of what she was about to do staggered her. Was offering herself, *her body,* really the answer?

Her mother's face swam before her, but she quickly shook the image away. No one's opinion, not even *hers,* mattered. Moriah knew she loved Sin. She wasn't sure when she realized it, but the fact was irrefutable. And she would not allow their differences to keep them apart any longer. Determined, she didn't bother to knock as she entered his private world.

Evidently he didn't hear her. He stood with his back to the room, his hands in his pockets, his gaze fixed on the foliage outside the veranda door.

"We need to talk," she declared in an assertive tone.

He stiffened. "Get out of here."

"No."

He whirled around, his eyes fierce. "No one disobeys my orders on this island." His cold gaze raked her. "Especially not some lying little would-be slut."

Moriah felt the sting of his words all the way to her heart. But she felt more, too. His pain. "I'm not leaving, Sin. Not until you've listened to me."

He stormed toward her, gripping her arm. "That's what you think."

Instead of pulling away, as she knew he expected, she turned in to him and wrapped her arms around his waist.

His breath caught. A tremor shook him. "Don't touch me." He jerked away. "Get out of here."

Even knowing he spoke out of hurt and anger, the cruelty of his words nearly cut her in two. Tears sprang to her eyes. Barely able to breathe, she whirled around to run.

The door slammed shut.

Startled, she spun toward him.

He stared in stunned surprise.

Excitement filled her. He'd stopped her from leaving without even realizing he'd done so.

She threw herself into his arms.

He instinctively caught her, then immediately set her from him. "I said, don't touch me."

Knowing his resistance hung by a thread, she ignored his warning and burrowed again into his arms. She brushed her lips over the bare flesh exposed through the gap in the front of his shirt. "I'm going to do a lot more than just touch you."

"You don't know what you're doing," he rasped.

She lightly flicked his nipple with her tongue.

He shuddered. His hands gripped her upper arms, and the fireplace burst into flames.

Undaunted, she pressed more fully against him. "I love you, Sin."

A jolt skipped through him, but his voice remained harsh. "I don't want your love."

"Yes, you do."

The full dinner tray on his desk fell to the carpet.

"Don't," he half groaned, but his arms went around her.

Satisfaction urged her on. She was winning. "I knew after the first time you spoke of my sister that you couldn't have hurt her. The warmth in your voice told me everything I needed to know. You cared deeply about her." She rubbed her cheek on his smooth flesh, enjoying the feel of silky hairs and the intoxicating scent of his earthy maleness. "You couldn't have hurt her any more than you can hurt me. For days I've tortured myself, wanting to tell you the truth."

"Damn you." He gripped her hair and pulled her head back. "Damn you." He crushed her lips with his.

Books toppled from the shelves.

Moriah shivered beneath the force of his sensual attack, her heart racing. Her flesh warmed to the heat of his. She parted her lips, offering him the intimacy that would reveal just how much she was willing to give.

A low moan rumbled from his chest. His tongue pressed between her teeth, taking what she offered, giving even more in return.

The world spun out from beneath her.

A vase crashed to the floor.

"Damn you." He pressed her against the door, his mouth ravaging hers, his hands touching her everywhere at once.

The wrap slid to her feet.

He molded himself to her nakedness, his chest laboring, his lips taking hers again and again. "I can't stop," he breathed raggedly. "I can't."

Heat raced to her core, and she arched her spine, offering everything she possessed. "Then don't."

His fingers dug into her hips.

The door vibrated behind her.

He trailed moist little kisses from her mouth to her ear, then traced the outer edges with his tongue. His hot breath sent shivers through every vein in her body even as his fingers moved to the spot between her legs, sending stabs of excitement to her very center. Dear God. No one had ever made her feel so good.

He lowered his head, nibbling her neck and shoulder with tiny bites. "You taste like honey," he whispered, moving lower. Gently he drew the tip of her breast into his mouth.

Pain-pleasure lanced through her abdomen. Sweet, sweet desire tightened her nipples. Urgently she pressed closer to his hot mouth.

A chair tumbled over.

His hands left their intimate task to slide up and down her sides, then around to cup her bottom. He lowered himself to his knees, his lips and tongue still feasting on her breast. Then slowly he withdrew to trail fiery little kisses over the flesh covering her ribs, down to the tiny indention in her belly.

Her legs nearly folded when his tongue drove into the recess, pressing, then withdrawing, then plunging forward again.

His fingers tightened on her bottom, pulling her closer as his attention moved downward, nibbling her lower stomach, the tops of her thighs.

Her head fell against the door, her strength depleted. His lovemaking took her breath away.

His lips brushed her inner thigh. So hot, so gentle. Oh God. So wonderful. He traced the backs of her legs with his fingers as his mouth moved higher.

She gasped when his tongue slipped into her curls. Her senses spun crazily.

He cupped her rear, pulling her closer.

Nothing had ever felt so good. Nothing could compare to the sweet torture, the taunting little strokes that took her to frightening heights. His breath grew hot, heavy, searing her sensitive flesh.

Reality spun away from her. A tightness banded her stomach, then burst free in an avalanche of quivers that shook her existence. Exquisite shudders pushed her to the edge of a precipice so high, so jagged, she knew she'd die from the fall.

Then she fell. Down. Down. Faster. The incredible speed snatched her breath away. She hit the ground in an explosion of sweet pain and cried out. Her muscles shook with savage spasms.

After an eternity, the turbulence ebbed to modest tremors, and groggily she became aware of him stripping off his clothes, of him lowering her to the floor and covering her with his body. "We're not through yet, princess."

Slowly he ran his leg up and down between hers, then parted them. With a single clean thrust, he drove deeply inside her. A flash of pain made her cry out, but the discomfort quickly faded when another rush of pleasure consumed her.

He thrust again. Again.

Reason spun out of control. She arched wildly, joining his carnal rhythm. He quickened, thrust savagely.

Then, through a haze, she felt him stiffen, heard his hoarse moan, and reveled in the pulsing shudders that drove him deeper into her heat, taking her to a place even higher than before. Gratefully she dove over the ledge, to the ecstacy that she now knew awaited her below.

For several long minutes neither of them spoke, and she became aware of the sound of his ragged breathing, and her own. Of the weight of his damp body pressing down on hers, of the musky scent of their lovemaking, of the heat throbbing through her lower body, of the firm warmth of him still nestled inside her.

Embarrassment tried to rear its head, but she forced it away. She loved him. And she wasn't ashamed or embarrassed about what they'd done. Thoughts of her mother again intruded. But she simply smiled into Sin's shoulder. To hell with Mother.

"If you cry," he said softly, his breath caressing her ear, "I swear, I'll beat you."

Her grin widened. "I won't. I'm too happy."

He rose up and looked down at her. He searched her

face, then his own smile brightened the room. "Well, I'll be damned." He rose, pulling her up with him. "You never cease to amaze me."

She allowed her gaze to wander shamelessly over his perfect form. He was nothing like Clancy O'Toole, not in any way. She shuddered from the mere memory.

"Are you cold?"

"If I am, will you warm me?"

"With pleasure." His straight white teeth flashed against his tanned face. "But I think we should talk first." He moved away, then picked up her wrap. "And I can't do that with you in your present state of undress." Slowly, taking great pleasure in the deed, he drew the garment around her and tucked it between her breasts. His fingers lingered for just a moment, then he withdrew and pulled on his breeches. His shirt, she noticed belatedly, lay on the floor where they'd been entwined minutes ago. Proof of her innocence spotted the garment.

He, too, stared at the shirt.

This time she couldn't stop the rush of heat that stung her cheeks.

Tenderness filled his eyes as he picked up the garment and shoved it into a drawer, then righted the chair behind his desk. "Come over here."

For the first time, she became aware of her surroundings. The room looked as if it hadn't survived the hurricane. Papers, broken glass, books, and splintered wood were scattered everywhere. Embers smoldered in the vacant fireplace. She cleared her throat. "Did we do this?"

"No, *we* didn't." His mouth drew into a thin line. "I did it." She could feel him slipping away from her.

Not about to let him retreat behind that wall again, she quickly moved to his side and placed her palm on his shoulder. "I understand. Honest, I do."

"You only *think* you do, princess." He shoved his hands into his pockets. "What you just witnessed is mild compared to what I'm capable of. Believe me."

She squeezed his shoulder. "Tell me."

"I can't." He moved away. "Maybe later, but right now, I can't." He met her gaze. "Talking isn't such a good idea at the moment, after all. Go, Moriah. I'll see you later."

"Please don't shut me out again," she pleaded, her fear of losing him growing by bounds.

"I'm trying, princess," he said softly. "But I have to think. I need to come to terms with what's happening between us. What can happen in the future." His eyes begged her for understanding. "I want to be alone. Just for a little while."

He both frightened and encouraged her. What if he still wanted her to leave? She softened. But what if he didn't? Knowing only he could make that decision, she fought a surge of nervousness as she walked to the door. Without turning, she spoke to him. "The power you have is much more than just the ability to make things happen with your mind. You also have the ability to destroy with just a word. Think on that very carefully before you make a decision."

She closed the door and walked numbly down the hall, praying he loved her as much as she did him. Their entire future depended on it. Sick with fear, she entered her bedchamber and curled up on the bed. There was nothing to do but wait.

Achates lumbered into the room and climbed up beside her.

Absently she scratched behind the panther's ear. "What if he tells me to leave?"

The leopard made a noise that sounded suspiciously like a disgusted snort.

"Oh, Achates, I love him so much. And this power he has, it doesn't frighten me anymore. If he'll only give me a chance, I know I can convince him that he possesses a gift rather than a curse. That he could do so much good if he only allowed himself the freedom."

The panther nuzzled her hand, then licked gently.

She smiled and glanced at the clock on the mantel. Eight o'clock. Releasing a sigh, she wondered how long it would take him to decide the balance of her life.

Suddenly Achates bristled, then leapt off the bed and raced out the door.

Surprised, she stared after him.

A shadow moved across the veranda.

Oh, no. Not again. Apprehensive, she rose and walked to the doors.

Callie stood just outside, her hair matted and streaked with dirt, her wrap stained and torn. She must have been running wildly through the underbrush.

"What happened? Are you all right?" She reached for her friend's arm.

"Don't," she slurred, jerking away. "I'm not hurt. I came to get you." Her glazed eyes avoided Moriah's. "Mudanno wants you."

Stunned by the revelation, but frightened, she gaped at her friend. Callie's entire manner was scaring her. "What's wrong with you?" She tried to touch her shoulder.

Immediately the girl slapped her hand away. "No. Please, just come."

"For the love of God, Callie. Where are you going? Come in here. Let me wash you." She was becoming genuinely alarmed.

Her friend took several steps back, shaking her head. "No. Mudanno said bring you. I have to. It's the only way."

Feeling as if she'd walked into some kind of nightmare, she stared at the mulatto. "Why would she want to see me? She doesn't even know me. Besides, I can't go there. You know I promised Sin."

The girl rubbed her stomach, trying to concentrate. Suddenly her head came up. "Mudanno murdered Sara. You have to come. Now."

"What?" Moriah couldn't grasp the enormity of the remark. "How do you know? Did someone tell you? Did you overhear? Callie, what's going on?"

Her hands shook as she clutched Moriah's arm. "It's

true. Please, you have to come. Mudanno told me she killed her."

"How? Tell me that. *How* could she have done it?"

"I don't know. Maybe she used the canoes. Maybe she snuck aboard the sloop. All I know is she said bring you. Please, Moriah. Please go now."

A hundred thoughts whirled through her mind, but only one rooted. *Mudanno admitted to murdering Sara.* The sultry, man-hungry bitch had mutilated her sister.

Fury nearly blinded her. Every former thought disappeared from her mind; Sin's lovemaking, the vital decision he was making this moment, even the promise she made, disintegrated beneath an avalanche of hatred. For the first time in her life, she wanted to hurt someone.

Clenching her teeth, her blood running hot with fury, she nudged her friend out the door. "Let's go."

Not bothering with her shoes, she quickly followed Callie into the woods, praying the girl knew the way. A branch snagged her wrap, and she slapped it out of the way. But the more she walked, the more she calmed, giving her a chance to think.

She had to make plans. She and Callie couldn't just go barging into the village. She'd seen how many men protected the voodoo priestess.

No. They had to approach secretly, take Mudanno captive, then hold her until Sin's sloop was ready to sail, which shouldn't be more than a day or so. Then it would be up to the magistrate in Nassau to see the witch punished. *Hopefully hanged.*

She stopped. "Callie, wait."

The mulatto plodded forward, not even slowing her hasty stride.

Moriah raced ahead and grabbed her wrist, spinning her around. "We can't go in there like this. We've got to lure Mudanno away from her men. Capture her."

Desperation was tightly etched around her friend's eyes. "I *must* take you to her. She demands it." Callie rubbed her stomach. "It's the only way."

The glassy look in her friend's eyes scared her more

than confronting Mudanno in the village. Something was drastically wrong. What had that witch done to her?

Self-loathing claimed Moriah. She'd gotten her into this, and she'd let her down. Well, no more. "Callie, go back to the house. I'll find my way to Mudanno's."

She shook her head frantically. "No."

"Don't argue. Just go."

Horrified, the girl swung her gaze wildly for support. Then, in a frenzied burst, she bolted into the trees, straight for the north woods.

"Callie! Callie, come back here!" The low squawk of a parrot was her only response. She battled for control, trying to think of a way to stop this madness.

Capturing Mudanno was the only answer.

For the barest instant she considered following her friend, but decided against it. Mudanno wanted her there for some reason, and when Callie returned alone, Mudanno or her men would come looking for Moriah. And she would be prepared. Determined, she headed for the stream.

Moonlight glinted off the trickling water as she approached. Figuring she had only a short time, she searched for something to use as a weapon.

A rock, a branch, and some sturdy vines were promising. If she could make a club . . . or a spear . . .

Finding a fairly straight, stiff branch, she sat down on the bank and began rubbing one end against a large stone. When she'd flattened one side of the wood to her satisfaction, she turned it over and worked on the other, then the edges.

She surveyed her handiwork. The makeshift spear was crude, but serviceable. Now for the club.

After tying a stone securely to the end of a stout branch with vines, she swung it a few times for practice, then hid it in a thicket of underbrush nearby. As prepared as she would ever get, she sat down to wait for Mudanno.

All too soon the rustle of ground ivy announced the witch's approach several moments before Moriah actually saw her. Deftly she stood and shielded her spear behind her right hip; it wouldn't do her any good until the woman was within reach.

But it was Callie who stumbled into view.

Moriah gasped. The girl was naked. Brutal, bleeding scratches marked her breast and abdomen. Smeared, dried blood darkened her inner thighs. "Oh, my God! Callie, what's happened?" Dropping the spear, she ran toward her.

"Moriah . . ." The girl crumpled in a dead faint.

Horrified, she reached for her.

A man's bare foot stepped into view—an instant before the point of a lance pressed against her throat.

CHAPTER

19

Sin rested his head on the back of his chair and relived the last hour. Damn, how quickly his anger had dissolved at Moriah's touch. The little minx, she would stand up to him when no one else dared. Her courage and intelligence astounded him. She knew of his power; still she didn't fear him.

He stared at the ceiling. But she should. God, if she only knew how dangerous he was. A killing ache pressed in on his heart, reminding him of the beast's viciousness.

Rubbing his throbbing temples, he turned his thoughts to his feelings for her. She had been right when she said he loved her. He'd been fighting that growing realization for quite some time. But he couldn't afford to love her—or *anyone*. Love meant commitment, a life together, and he knew that wasn't possible. He couldn't share his life with her. He couldn't trust himself.

He slammed his fist down on his knee and closed his eyes. Damn it. Why him? What had he done to deserve this curse? What had he done that was so bad that he was forced to live a life of loneliness, a life without a wife and children? A life in constant fear of destroying another human being?

The memory tried to surface. He could hear the angry

shouts, feel the fury building inside him. Dear God, he could even hear those last gasping breaths. Pain and self-damnation ripped through him.

He jerked upright in the chair, his eyes open, blessedly open, dispelling the horrible image he'd seen in his mind. He rose to pace the room. If he'd had any doubts about sharing a life with Moriah, he didn't now. He couldn't chance hurting her. Not like he had—

"Sin?" Lucas said from the veranda. "We just found another crack in the sloop's hull. It doesn't look as bad, but it'll take at least another week to fix this one."

Staring at his friend, he shoved his fingers through his hair. "Damn it. What else can go wrong?" But inwardly he knew, and he groaned. Another week near Moriah. Another week to pray that he didn't lose control, didn't hurt her. Not that God listened to his prayers anymore. *He* hadn't since that day so long ago.

Jamming his hand into his pocket, he closed his fist around the crystal, knowing he had to find the strength to stay away from her.

"Sin?" another voice interrupted.

He swung around, as did Lucas.

Dorothy stood in the main door. "Have you seen Moriah? I went to her room to see if she was ready for her bath, but she wasn't there. No one knows where she went."

A tiny jolt of concern skittered through him. "When was the last time anyone saw her?"

Dorothy shrugged. "Not since supper."

"The last time I saw her," Lucas supplied, "she was heading for your study."

A remembered warmth seeped into his lower stomach. "She was here. But she left over an hour ago. Perhaps she went down to the beach, or possibly even Woosak's village. She and the old woman formed quite a friend-ship."

"What about Mudanno's?" Lucas asked with unease.

He shook his head. "She gave me her word she wouldn't go there. I believe her."

"Then I'll check the beach," the overseer announced, striding out.

"I'll talk to the help again," Dorothy mumbled in a hasty retreat.

Bringing a hand to the nape of his neck, he rubbed at the sudden tenseness. Something didn't feel right. Ah, hell. He'd go to Woosak's village. But somehow he knew he wouldn't find her there.

And he didn't.

Slapping through the underbrush on his way to the manor house, he swore angrily. Didn't he have enough problems without searching for a damned woman who was probably out somewhere having a fine time gossiping or *whatever* women did when they were together?

Entering the house, and seeing that the others hadn't returned, he made his way to her chamber, hoping she'd slipped in unnoticed. A quick survey of the room revealed its emptiness.

He walked out the veranda doors, hoping to find her, or at least some indication of which way she'd gone.

The panther was sitting beside the chair Moriah favored, his head resting on the seat.

A ball of panic bounced through Sin's gut. Achates had acted the same way, done the same thing, after Sara left.

Clamping down on his rising concern, he returned indoors. He was being ridiculous. Nothing was wrong with her. Damn it, she was just out walking somewhere.

Without Achates.

The door opened, and Lucas strolled in. "She wasn't at the beach, and none of the men have seen her."

Sin nodded, praying his growing unrest didn't show. "Maybe Dorothy's learned something."

Fifteen minutes later, the housekeeper came into the study, where he and Lucas waited.

He came to his feet instantly. "Did you find her?"

Dorothy shook her head. "Donnelly's been searching, too. No one's seen her."

"What about Callie?" Lucas asked. "Has anyone talked to her? Maybe Moriah's with her—or she knows where Moriah went."

All three of them rushed toward Callie's chamber.

Sin reached the door first and threw it open.

The room was messy, the bed tumbled, soiled clothes were strewn everywhere, a full dinner tray sat on the table untouched, but neither Callie nor Moriah was there.

His nerves had reached the breaking point. He began to shake.

The dishes on the tray rattled.

Dorothy retreated a step.

"Take it easy, Sin." Lucas spoke softly, but his tone was edged with concern. "She's somewhere on this island, and we'll find her."

"I sent her away because I wanted to be alone. Wanted to think. She didn't want to go, but I made her. What if she was so upset, she went into the woods? What if she's hurt? Maybe lying somewhere bleeding." The vision nearly folded his knees.

A lantern on the bedside table quivered.

Lucas didn't move, nor did his tone change in timbre. "I'm sure she'll explain that when she returns . . . or when we find her." His voice lowered meaningfully. "But we can't do that until you calm down."

Grasping for control, he dragged in a deep, cleansing breath. The trembling eased. He sucked in again, desperately willing the beast into its hiding place. When he was certain he'd succeeded, he faced his friend. "Sorry."

"Don't be. Now, come on. Let's start looking. I've already sent the men who'd been repairing the sloop to the east side of the island. Why don't we take the west? Other than the north woods, that's about all that's left."

"*You* take the west," Sin countered. "I'm going to search her room one more time for anything that might lead me to her. If that fails, I'm going to Mudanno's."

Lucas hesitated. "I thought you said she'd given her word."

"So she did," he agreed, yet with growing uncertainty. "But she's lied before."

One of Lucas's dark brows rose, but he didn't comment. Instead, he nodded and left the room.

Sin's gut twisted into knots as he hurried to Moriah's chamber.

When he still found it unoccupied, he swallowed his disappointment and strode into the connecting one, finding that room, too, deserted.

A slow drumming began in his temples. Images of Moriah came rushing in. He could again see her the way she was that first night, down at the cove, her hair all tangled and matted, refusing to slip from that tight knot she kept it in. He could almost hear her proper little voice the next morning. *Please, sir, clothe yourself. I abhor lewd displays.*

He smiled, recalling their poker game, and her multitude of losses. But even that hadn't set her back. She'd taken his declaration of payment with astounding grace. And most of all, he remembered the abandoned warmth of her passion, just hours ago. She had been an innocent. Still, she'd given generously—and feared nothing. She trusted him.

It was becoming hard for him to breathe. How could anyone put that much faith in another? Lay her life in the hands of one who, with just a look, could destroy her? Love, that's how. *She loves you, idiot.*

"Oh, princess," he breathed softly. "I don't deserve you, but I damn sure love you." And he would tell her so, *after* he found her, and *after* he strangled her for driving him nearly out of his mind with worry.

He started out the connecting door, but something on the bed caught his eye. Slowly, uneasily, he approached the massive piece of furniture.

The voodoo doll that resembled Moriah was tied to the headboard.

He began to shake. "No. Oh, God, please, *no.*"

The doll hung from a rope around its neck.

* * *

Moriah's gaze shot upward to see one of Mudanno's men holding the lance at her throat. Fear trapped her breath. Slowly, afraid to make any sudden movements, she eased to her feet.

Three more men encircled her.

Every nerve in her body tightened. She couldn't reach her weapons, and by the look in their eyes, they were going to kill her. She would die by the same hands Sara had.

"You are right to be afraid, whore," Mudanno said triumphantly as she stepped from the concealing trees. "My men will end your life with a single word from me." She said something in a strange language, and the men instantly grabbed on to Moriah's arms, holding her captive.

"Why?" Moriah cried. "Why are you doing this to me? Why did you kill my sister? What do you want from us?"

The priestess laughed. "The other one was of no consequence. But you, whore, are valuable. The powerful one will come now."

"Don't you have any pride? He doesn't want you."

She smiled satanically. "But I want him. I have watched him for many years, waiting to reach womanhood. Dreaming of the day we would mate. Now the time has come. The Creator has spoken to me this season. My soul and body are ready." Her gaze raked Moriah. "He will not resist. Not if he wishes his woman to live."

Moriah never knew such overwhelming hatred as she did in that moment. To use people in such a despicable way for her own gain. Was this, too, the reason Sara was killed? Mudanno did say this season. Meaning this summer? And what about Sin? She couldn't bear to watch him succumb to this witch's demands. Fury took her reason. "I'll kill you for this."

Mudanno laughed, and clapped her hands twice.

The men holding Moriah started dragging her toward the village. One of them spit on Callie's still form as they passed.

"You *vermin*." She kicked out in rage, only to have her arm twisted viciously behind her back. Hurting and momentarily defeated, she stumbled between the men.

A fire burned hotly in the center of Mudanno's hamlet. The native women danced in pagan joy around the flames.

One of the men shoved her to a pole near a hut and tied her securely with her spine to the beam. A rope, fashioned like a hangman's noose, was lowered over her head and the pole, then tightened around her throat. Another man stood close, holding the long end of the hemp.

She knew if she so much as moved, a swift jerk on the rope would crush her windpipe. Worn-out from her struggles, she rested her head against the beam and watched the proceedings going on in front of her. Even from this distance, heat from the flames warmed her skin where it was exposed by the flowered wrap.

Burning pine mingled with the damp air. Mosquitoes buzzed, joining in the chorus with chattering monkeys, while lazy drums thumped in rhythm to the dancers' steps.

The fire blazed higher, fueled by layer after layer of dried branches. The men had entered the women's dance, unconcerned that their every movement revealed their nudity beneath the open sides of the skirts they wore.

Mudanno stood in the center of her worshipers, her arms raised to the heavens as if in prayer, her spine arched, her head thrown back, her naked breasts jutting toward the fire.

Embarrassed, Moriah shifted. The rope tightened immediately, tearing into her tender skin. Gasping, she glared her hatred at the man who held the other end.

She heard a soft chanting sound and saw several dark, bare-breasted women, each carrying a wooden bowl, walk into the center sphere. In turn, they each placed the bowl they held at their priestess's feet.

The pagan witch didn't move, didn't change her position. Not even when one of the men removed her skirt and spread it out on the ground near Moriah's feet, or when the women dipped their hands into the bowls and began rubbing thick oil all over her naked body.

Still singing as they worked, they massaged the greasy substance into their queen's long hair until the strands gleamed like polished onyx. When finished, they rose and tossed the remaining contents of their bowls into the fire.

Flames hissed and flared, burned brighter, hotter.

Mudanno rolled her head, arching closer to the blistering heat as if to absorb the inferno inside her body.

Suddenly an unnatural hush fell over the crowd. The very air grew still.

Slowly, oh, so slowly, the priestess turned to face the trees. A seductive smile graced her mouth as she fixed on something in the shadows.

Moriah shifted so she could see.

Sin stood just beyond the ring of firelight. He still wore no shirt, a fierce reminder of their recent lovemaking, but his flowing white breeches stood out like a beacon in the moonlight.

Relief flooded her. She opened her mouth to cry out, but he silenced her with a hard look. His eyes flicked to the man beside her holding the rope. Realizing what she'd almost done—*what the man would have done*—she clamped her lips together.

Giving her a tiny, nearly imperceptible nod, he moved forward until he stood fully in the light. His gaze made a rapid survey of the village, then settled on Mudanno.

"You have come, my powerful one," she cooed in a throaty welcome as she moved, shamelessly naked, to stand in front of him. She trailed her fingers lazily down his chest. "Mudanno is pleased."

"You knew I'd come. That's why you left the doll," he said coldly. "What do you want?"

Her hand slid lower, cupping the generous bulge between his thighs.

He didn't flinch. Didn't move.

Moriah nearly exploded with fury.

Smiling wickedly, the priestess caressed him. "Tonight you give Mudanno your child."

Straining against the bindings encircling her wrists, Moriah tried to free her hands.

Sin didn't take his eyes off the priestess. "What makes you think tonight's any different from the other times you tried this?"

A malevolent smile widened the witch's full lips, and her gaze drifted to the man beside Moriah. She nodded slightly.

He gripped the rope and pulled.

Pain stabbed into Moriah's windpipe. She gagged and gasped for air. A hoarse cry wheezed from her throat. She couldn't breathe! She slammed her head against the pole, struggling wildly. Darkness swirled before her eyes.

"Enough!" Sin roared.

Suddenly the rope loosened, and she sucked in great gulps of oxygen, burning her raw throat. Her chest labored heavily. Slowly, groggily, as if coming out of a long, drugged sleep, her senses righted, and her hazy vision cleared.

Sin had grown pale, his jaw clenched tight.

Mudanno's wicked laugh echoed around the village, and her hold on Sin tightened. "You will mate with me—" her black eyes slid to Moriah "—or she dies."

He didn't move, didn't allow his expression to reveal even a hint of his thoughts.

"I'd rather die!" Moriah croaked out. The rope tightened, and she nearly strangled on the words. Defeated, she lowered her head. Dear God in heaven, Sin wouldn't . . . right here in front of her? He *couldn't*. Tears blurred her vision. She moved her head loosely from side to side. She'd rather die than watch him make love to another woman.

Numbly she met his gaze for the last time, knowing she couldn't watch the horror that was about to take place.

Warmth and reassurance filled his eyes.

It didn't help. She could feel the nausea threaten. She lowered her lashes.

The rope cut into her windpipe.

She strangled, and her eyes shot open.

Instantly the cord went slack.

Mudanno laughed with satisfaction, then reached for the ties at Sin's waist.

He didn't lift a hand to protest, not even when she slid the breeches down his naked length, and lifted his feet, one at a time, freeing him of the restriction.

Firelight danced over the sleek planes and angles of his magnificent body.

The witch stared greedily, her features revealing awe. Her breath left her on a sigh. "Such power." She lifted her head and nodded with supreme gratification, then raised her arms to him. "Come."

Through a wall of tears, Moriah watched him move into the woman's arms and willingly press his body to hers. She tightened her bound hands into fists, knowing that if he made love to that woman at her feet, he'd kill any love she felt for him—could ever feel. *Oh, please, Sin,* she begged silently. *Don't do this to us.*

She bit her lip to keep from crying out to him. Vaguely felt the man beside her loosen his hold on the rope.

Suddenly he screamed in hysterical terror. His hand, the one that had been holding the cord, waved frantically in the air. Blue flames licked his skin, searing it to the bones.

A woman cried out, and Moriah swung her gaze.

Fire leapt up the length of Mudanno's long hair. Wildly, screeching hysterically, she charged toward the stream beside the village, slapping the flames, clawing at her head.

Spears flew toward Sin.

Moriah screamed.

The weapons shattered in midair.

His eyes, now bright gold, moved over the village, setting fire to everything within range. Destroying at will.

In a chaotic panic, the villagers ran for their lives.

As quickly as it started, the rampage ended. His eyes darkened, then focused on her. "Are you all right?" he asked in a hoarse voice, his arms shaking.

Unable to speak, she nodded, tears streaming down her cheeks. He'd used the powers he so detested to save her. *For* her. For them. Her body shook with sobs.

"Don't," he whispered raggedly, pressing his length to hers as he untied the ropes. "I had to do it or lose you."

He thought her tears were because of the destruction he'd wreaked. She sniffed. "I'm not crying because you used your powers. I'm crying because you did it for us."

He lifted the rope from her neck and tossed it aside, then untied her and pulled her into his arms. "You still don't fear me or my curse?" He gestured at the smoldering village. "Even after this?"

She gave him a watery smile. "I love you, Sin. Nothing will ever change that. I know that now." She nuzzled his bare chest. "But I wasn't so sure a few minutes ago when you were about to make love to that woman the way you did me."

He brushed the hair from her wet cheeks. "If I had taken Mudanno, it wouldn't have been *making love*. But I never would have let it go that far. I couldn't have done that to you. The pain in your eyes nearly destroyed me." He kissed her gently, then drew her to his side. "It's been a long day, princess. Let's go home."

Home. What a wonderful word. "Yes," she whispered, enjoying his warmth. "After you put on your clothes."

"If I must." He chuckled, then quickly complied.

As they turned to leave, Moriah saw Mudanno sitting in the creek, naked and trembling, her hands clutching the few frizzled strands of wet hair she had left. Smoke still rose from her head in little puffs. Pitiful wails shook her.

Even after what the woman had done to Sara, what she'd nearly done to Moriah, she still couldn't stop a wave of sympathy. Her gaze went to Sin.

An iced-over lake couldn't have looked colder. He

glared at the priestess with undisguised hatred. "I will return in the morning, Mudanno. You and your people had better be off my island."

She didn't even acknowledge the threat. She just continued to cry.

Ignoring her as he would an insect, he swept Moriah closer and moved into the woods.

She had never felt more contented in her life. Suddenly she froze. "Oh, God, Sin. *Callie.*"

CHAPTER

20

"What about Callie?" Sin asked urgently, trying to dispel a jolt of fear.

"She's hurt," Moriah answered, gripping his arm. "Mudanno—"

"Goddamn it!" he bellowed.

A branch exploded from a pine and plummeted to earth.

He took a stabling breath, and guided her into the trees. "Take me to her." They hadn't taken more than a few steps when Lucas nearly ran into them.

He glared at Moriah. "Where the hell have you been, woman? We've been turning this place upside down."

"Stop it," Sin ordered.

Lucas clamped his mouth shut, then gaped in surprise at their battered condition. "What happened?"

"Not now. We've got to find Callie."

Lucas tensed. "She's lost?"

"She's hurt," Moriah corrected, her voice unsteady.

Lucas paled.

Wanting to reassure him, but unable to, Sin turned to continue on. "Get Donnelly to round up the men to help find her."

"Who saw her last?" The overseer demanded, ignoring his order. "Where was she?"

Moriah pointed downstream. "She's by the river, that way."

Lucas broke into a full run.

Sin grabbed Moriah's hand and raced after him.

When they reached the spot she'd last seen the girl, Callie was gone.

"Are you sure this is the right place?" Lucas snapped.

Sin watched her glance around, then stare at a pointed stick lying on the ground. "I'm very sure."

"Well, where in the hell did she go from here?"

He had to clench his teeth to keep from lashing out at his overseer, knowing the man's harsh attitude stemmed from concern. But it was hard to keep silent when Lucas demanded answers from Moriah like that. "Perhaps we should search instead of talk."

They made a wide sweep of the area, then probed farther downstream.

Still nothing.

"Maybe she went to the manor," Moriah said, brushing her hair out of her eyes. Her hand trembled, and he knew exhaustion was taking its toll. She'd been through a lot tonight.

"We're only a few yards from the healing pool, princess. If we don't find her there, we'll check the house."

Lucas became apprehensive. "Sin, you don't think . . . " He glanced fearfully in the direction of the pool, then broke into a run.

Knowing Lucas feared Callie had met the same fate as Davie Waller, he held on to Moriah and hurried after him.

"What is it?" she asked on a winded breath.

"Let's pray it's nothing." Circling a thick-based pine, they emerged from the trees.

"No!" Lucas bellowed.

Frantically Sin searched the pond.

Then he saw her—floating facedown in the pool.

"Oh, God!" Moriah cried.

His limbs were in motion before his brain. He dove into the water, swimming fiercely. Both he and Lucas reached the girl at the same time.

Urgently Lucas yanked her face up out of the water.

She looked dead.

"No!" He shook her. "Damn you, no!" Encircling her neck with his arm, he swam wildly for shore.

Feeling sick, Sin followed.

Moriah raced around the bank to meet them on the other side.

Lucas dragged Callie up onshore, then rolled her onto her stomach and pressed down hard on her back.

Water trickled out of her mouth.

Again. Again. He shoved his full weight against her. "Spit it out, honey. Come back to me." The urgent plea in his friend's voice shocked him until he realized how much the girl must mean to Lucas.

More water gushed out.

He pushed harder, quicker.

Nothing.

As he remembered when Moriah had nearly drowned in the cove, Sin's nerves began to tingle. "Breathe," he whispered. His heart labored with heavy beats. His eyes grew hot. "Come on, Callie. *Breathe.*"

Her body jerked. She gagged and vomited, then convulsed into a fit of strangled coughs.

His own chest tightened in empathy, but his bearing relaxed.

Moriah crumpled to the ground. "Oh, thank God."

Suddenly Callie cried out and curled into a ball. "Nooo," she groaned. "Why didn't you let me die? I can't stand the pain. I want to be dead. Dead doesn't hurt."

Lucas shook her soundly. "What the hell's the matter with you? Snap out of it!"

She curled over, pressing her wet head into his stomach. "Let me die," she begged. "I can't take any more."

The genuine defeat in her voice scared the hell out of Sin.

Fear claimed Lucas's expression. "What are you talking about?"

"The pain. The men."

Sin reacted first. "What pain? *What men?*"

"Mudanno won't give me potion, won't make the pain stop."

"Oh, Jesus," Lucas groaned. He lifted her face, searching her eyes. It was there for all of them to see. The dazed, glassy look, the torture.

"Oh, Christ, honey," his friend moaned. "What has she done to you?"

Callie let her head drop onto his chest, her body shaking.

Sin didn't want to put her through any more, but he had to ask. "What about the men, Callie? What did they do?"

She jumped in terror and clutched Lucas's waist. "No, don't let them."

"Let them what?" he asked in a gentle voice that belied his anger.

"Don't let them hold me down anymore. Don't let them hurt me. I can't take it. So many of them. Over and over again. They're tearing me apart." She grabbed her head and shook it violently. "Oh, God. Mudanno, stop laughing!"

Shock held Sin immobile for a split second, then turned to blinding rage. "Those *bastards!*" He'd never experienced such fury. Such an overwhelming need to destroy another human being.

A cluster of bananas exploded from a nearby tree.

He dragged in a breath, trying to gain control.

Lucas looked like a man who'd been on the rack. Then he began to shake with fury. "I'll kill them."

Knowing exactly how he felt, Sin touched his shoulder. "You can't leave her, Lucas. She needs help. Mudanno and her men can wait."

Swearing harshly over what had been done, Lucas nodded and picked up his precious cargo. "I'll take her to Woosak."

"I'm coming, too," Moriah insisted.

By the stubborn set of her jaw, Sin knew Moriah would put up a helluva fight if he tried to argue, so he handled it the only way he knew how. He scooped her up in his arms and strolled off toward the manor.

"Sin! Put me down."

He hoisted her higher. "No. Lucas will take care of Callie . . . and I'm going to take care of you."

Her voice softened. "I've got to know she's all right. Don't you see, this is all my fault. I was so frightened of coming to your island alone, I brought her with me. If anything happens to her, I'm to blame." She leaned her head on his shoulder, and he felt her tears. "I'm responsible for what she's suffered already." She buried her face in his neck and cried until he thought his heart would break.

"Shh." He brushed his lips over her damp cheek. "You didn't cause this, Mudanno did. And I'll see to it the bitch gets her due." Holding his anger in check, he rubbed his jaw along hers. "Right now what you need is a hot bath and a warm bed. Then, after your friend's had a chance to heal some, you can see her." He didn't want her suffering along with Callie.

She sniffed. "Promise?"

"Yes. And, unlike you, I don't break my word."

A wince crinkled her adorable features. "When Callie told me Mudanno killed Sara, I went crazy. Otherwise I'd have never broken a promise."

His control slipped a notch. "Mudanno did *what?*"

"She admitted to Callie that she was the one who murdered my sister."

"I don't believe it. That bitch might be evil as Satan, but I can't imagine her committing such a brutal crime."

"Then why would she admit to it?"

"I don't know. But I'm damned sure going to find out." *As soon as you're asleep.*

Concerned over Lucas and what he'd do once Callie was settled, Sin quickly took Moriah into his room, then ordered his harried housekeeper to help her bathe, forgoing the pleasure, just this once. He knew if he saw her without her clothes, his visit to Mudanno would be drastically delayed.

When she was at last bundled beneath the quilts, he tested his restraint by lying beside her.

"Mmm, this is nice." With a contented sigh, she snuggled deeper into his hold.

Nice wasn't the word he would have used. *Torture* was more like it. Still, he continued to embrace her and trail his fingers lazily up and down her spine.

"As soon as I rest a little, I'm going to see Callie," she announced on a yawn. "You promised . . ."

Hearing the sound of her deep, even breathing, he pulled her closer, enjoying the feel of her warmth next to him, the sweet lilac scent of her flesh. But over her slender shoulder he saw the first rays of dawn lighten the tops of the trees and knew it was time to go.

He nuzzled Moriah's silky black hair, gave her a light kiss, then eased from the bed.

As he made his way to the witch's village, he tried to control the hatred he felt. Until now, Mudanno had been a nuisance, but restrainable. The episode with Davie Waller had been a volatile one when he learned of her part in the man's death, and he'd nearly tossed her off Arcane then. Only the fact that she didn't *force* him to take the drug prevented her exile.

Still, he wished he had. Too, he was trying to deal with his guilt over his own actions last night. How easily he could have killed all those people when he saw what they'd done to Moriah. And nearly did. He'd known he was capable of violence, but never to such an extent. Never like what he'd displayed at the village. And it was damned hard to deal with.

And the worst part was, he knew he'd do it all over again if he had to. When he'd seen Moriah tied to that pole, and that bastard holding on to the rope around her neck, he had nearly gone insane with fury.

An unusual stillness caught his attention. His steps slowed as he veered into the shadows of several magnolia trees.

Uneasiness tingled through him.

Up ahead, he saw something lying on the ground. Something that looked human. Edging cautiously toward the form, he brushed aside a branch for a closer peek. Numbness held him immobile.

One of Mudanno's men lay in a crumpled heap, his head twisted nearly around to his back, his neck obviously broken.

Oh, God. What had Lucas done? He swallowed a rush of nausea and straightened.

Moving deeper into the woods, he came upon another of the men. This one had a rope around his neck and was hanging from a tree.

His guts in knots, Sin slipped farther into the forest.

The next man he found had been castrated and stabbed through the heart.

Another had been staked out on the ground, a sharp branch rammed through his groin.

Sickened by the grotesque sights, he pushed on, knowing he had to find his friend. He passed several more bodies, all men, before he finally came to the edge of the village.

Then he saw Mudanno.

She had been speared through the chest with a lance and pinned to a tree. Her lifeless body hung in a slump, her charred, nearly bald head drooped to one side, her mouth slack.

"Jesus Christ." Bile rose in his throat, and he lifted his chin to drag air into his lungs. But out of the corner of his eye he saw another form and quickly whirled toward it.

Lucas sat against a tree, his head back, his eyes closed. Blood coated his bare chest, arms, and legs.

"Lucas!"

The overseer's eyes snapped open.

Sin nearly buckled over with relief. His hands shook as he dropped down beside his friend and touched his arm, reassuring himself that he was really alive. "What happened?"

Lucas stared blankly, his expression drawn. "I killed them, Sin. All of them." He shook his head. "No. Not all. The women and children left in the canoes. I had no fight with them. But I killed the men. And Mudanno."

Though he'd known Lucas had done this, hearing the words staggered him. He jerked his hand away. "Why, Lucas? Damn you, why couldn't you let me handle it?"

"If it had been Moriah instead of Callie, what would you have done? Let *me* handle it?"

The image of Moriah fighting wildly as one man after another brutally raped her cracked his control.

A branch crashed into the stream.

"No. Not you—*or anyone else.*" And he knew exactly how Lucas felt. Filled with loathing, he glared at Mudanno's corpse.

The tree that pinned her uprooted, then slammed to the ground.

Lucas touched his shoulder. "She's been dead for hours, Sin. You can't hurt her anymore. Neither can I." He swiped at the dampness on his cheeks. "I just wish I'd done this sooner . . . before Callie . . ." He swallowed. "Before that evil slut killed Sara."

Regaining his senses, Sin shook his head. "Moriah told me, but I just don't see how Mudanno could have. You've known her for as long as I have. Did she strike you as the type that would *dissect* someone? Play with their minds, yes. But mutilation? And *how* did she do it?"

"The canoes. They could have followed the sloop to Nassau. And if she did kill Sara, she killed Beth, too."

That thought had already occurred to Sin. "But why carve up the bodies?"

Lucas raked his fingers through his hair. "Maybe it was some kind of tribal ritual."

Shock waves rippled through him. He'd never thought of that. And if that was the case, this was all his fault. He'd brought those women to the island, and by doing so, had caused their deaths. Goddamn his lust. Goddamn his *stupidity*. He should have known. Should have realized. Mudanno had given him all the signs.

After several minutes, when he'd finally regained his composure, he rose, offering his friend his hand. "Come on. Let's get the hell out of here. I'll send the men back to dispose of the bodies." He glared at the fallen tree lying on Mudanno. "In the ocean. I don't want that vermin contaminating my soil."

"I've got to go to Callie," Lucas said, taking the outstretched palm and coming to his feet. "She's suffering the hell of withdrawals. I need to be with her."

He watched his friend for a long moment. "You love her, don't you?"

A small shrug lifted the man's shoulder. "I don't know what love is. But if it's the need to protect, to absorb another into your soul, to comfort, to share, to laugh . . . and cry with her, then yes, I guess I do." He gave a sheepish smile. "And as soon as she can understand me, I'm going to tell her so." Tiredly he strode off toward Woosak's village.

Glancing once again at Mudanno's body, Sin checked the urge to swear, then headed for home. His need to see Moriah, to hold her, was as crucial as his need to breathe.

CHAPTER

21

Moriah yawned and rubbed the sleep from her eyes, then glanced at a beam of morning light casting its glow through the trees at the edge of the east veranda, wondering where Sin had gone so early. She'd felt him leave the bed a while ago, but she hadn't realized the hour.

She bolted straight up in the bed. *Mudanno.* He'd gone to make sure she'd left the island. Scrambling out from under the covers, she shoved them aside and sprang to her feet. Naked, she hurried across the room to fetch her clothes. Sin couldn't let Mudanno leave. She wanted the vicious monster behind bars—*or at the end of a rope.*

The door swung open.

She whirled around.

Sin stood in the opening, his features haggard and worn, but his eyes were alive with appreciation as they roamed over her bare figure. "Oh, princess," he said in a rough voice. "You're magnificent."

Heat rushed to her face, but she couldn't suppress the urgency she felt. "You've got to stop Mudanno from leaving. Tie her up, or lock her in a room, whatever it takes to hold her until we can get her to the sheriff."

"I can't." He moved toward her, his features tight with something she couldn't define. "She's dead."

Moriah backed up a step, suddenly frightened. Something was dreadfully wrong. "How did she die?"

"From a spear through the heart."

"Who—"

"We'll talk about it later." His voice rasped like rough velvet.

Horrified, she stared at him. *Not you, Sin. Oh, please, not you.* He'd never be able to live with Mudanno's death on his conscience. Trying desperately to think, she turned around.

His fingers closed over her shoulders. "Right now," he continued, "I need you like I've never needed anyone in my life." His grip tightened. "Let me love you, princess."

She tried to cover her nakedness. They needed to talk. She had to reassure him that . . . what? It was all right to take another's life?

"No, don't cover yourself." He grasped her arms from behind. "I need to look at you." His breath feathered over her shoulder, his hands trembling. "I need to touch you. To lose myself in your sweetness and forget . . ."

She heard the despair in his voice, felt it in his shaky hold, and knew, right now, he needed *her* more than words. Talk would come later. She pushed thoughts of Mudanno from her mind and closed her eyes, relaxing against him.

Slowly he slid his palms along the length of her arms, lowering them to her sides. "Your skin is like satin," he whispered thickly, nibbling her ear and neck, sliding his fingers up and down. "I could drown in your softness." His hands eased upward until they cupped her breasts. Erotically he brushed his thumbs back and forth over her tingling peaks, while his mouth nuzzled her hair. "So damned soft."

She swallowed, trying to think of something to say. No words came.

He pressed into her back, while his hands lightly massaged a path down her stomach, leaving behind a trail of fire. Her breath quickened. Flames of need spread through her.

Then his fingers touched the juncture of her thighs, their warmth sending flutters through her belly. Gently, oh so gently, he eased into the curls that shielded her most intimate part.

It was more than she could stand. A small moan escaped her throat, and her head fell onto his shoulder.

Hot little kisses rained over her neck and cheek, then his mouth came around to capture hers. He stroked between her thighs with slow, tormenting caresses while his tongue penetrated the recess of her mouth, taunting her with the same sensual rhythm. A cool breeze from the open veranda doors played over her flesh, and she shivered at this second erotic assault.

His thumbs drew little circles on her belly. "I need to be inside you, princess."

Through the haze of arousal, she caught a hint of urgency in his voice. She turned in to him, wrapping her arms around his waist, offering her lips more fully.

He gripped her bottom, pulling her against his hard, hot need while his fingers continued their provocative invasion from behind, his mouth open on hers, hungry, ravaging.

Desire licked through her, and suddenly the barrier of his clothes between them became an obstacle she couldn't tolerate. She tore at the confining garments, desperately needing to feel his bare skin next to hers.

The ties at his waist broke beneath her impatient hands.

"Sweet Christ," he groaned. He gripped her hair, holding her head while he savagely plundered her mouth again and again. He arched into her, his hardness pulsing against her belly.

On fire for him, she clumsily shoved his breeches down over his hips.

His stomach jumped, and he impatiently pressed his firm, smooth flesh between her legs, over her damp center. She tightened with anticipation.

"Oh, princess," he whispered thickly, clutching her, lifting her to receive him.

"Love me, Sin. Love me," she moaned into his throat. She wrapped her legs around his waist, giving him access to what they both sought.

He drove up into her, crying out her name.

A whirlwind of sensations claimed her. Joy, heat, pleasure, and scalding need. She constricted around him, drawing him fully inside her.

The veranda doors slammed shut.

Grabbing her waist, he pressed her farther down over him, then rotated her hips, pushing deeper and deeper into the center of her fire.

She clung to his neck, their mouths wildly mating, imitating the rhythm of their bodies. Their chests slid erotically against one another as perspiration formed a thin sheen between them.

Then she felt it, the frenzied pulsing between her legs, the explosion that had her arching convulsively, crying out her fulfillment.

"Oh, Jesus. Yes." He thrust violently. Deeper. Faster. He tensed. Shudders racked his body, and he buried his face in her chest, his guttural groan rumbling against her hot flesh.

For several minutes neither of them moved. Only the sound of harsh breathing, and the occasional twitter of a bird, echoed in the silent room. Then, slowly, reluctantly, he withdrew from her and lowered her feet to the floor, but he still held her close, his lips brushing her temple. "It can't get much better than this, princess, or I won't survive."

Too weak to move, she could only nod in agreement.

He smiled, then swooped her up into his arms and carried her to the bed. "But I'm willing to chance it."

Several hours later, they emerged from the room and attacked the noon meal as voraciously as they had each other only minutes before.

Exhausted, yet full of euphoric energy, and knowing their conversation about Mudanno and visit to Callie could wait until later, Moriah laughingly stole bits of food from his plate and ate them greedily.

He retaliated by swiping her muffin.

She filched a grape and popped it into her mouth.

With a devilish gleam in his eyes, he went after it.

Their play turned into another rush of desire, and she nearly wilted, hardly able to believe that after so much lovemaking, she still wanted more. She would never tire of him, she realized. Everything about him set her blood on fire, from the way he spoke in that low, seductive voice, to the deep rumble of laughter that shook his broad chest. The way the light danced through the silky strands of his ebony hair, or the way his lean cheeks creased when he smiled, how his muscles rippled and bunched when he moved.

But she wasn't fooled into believing everything between them was perfect. It wasn't. What happened with Mudanno might very well destroy Sin in the end.

"What's wrong, princess?" he asked suddenly, easing back from her.

"Nothing."

"When my woman goes stiff in the middle of a kiss, *something* has got to be wrong."

She avoided his gaze. "I was just thinking about us. About our future together." She sensed the sudden coolness in his manner.

"There won't be one, Moriah. You've got to understand that. What we share will have to be enjoyed one day at a time. And at the end of each day, we'll pray for one more."

The pain behind those words tore at her heart. It must be because of that witch. "You killed Mudanno, didn't you?"

He shoved a hand into his pocket. "No. But I think I would have."

Relief surged over her, and with it came understanding. "Lucas?"

Sorrow etched his handsome features. "Yes. He killed Mudanno . . . and her men."

"Oh, God." She clamped a hand over her mouth. The poor man. Tears stung her eyes, and she blinked rapidly. "Is he all right?" What a stupid question. Of course he wasn't.

"He's as well as can be expected. And he's with Callie. She's suffering from withdrawals, but she'll survive. He'll see to it."

"I'm going to her."

Sin touched her arm. "No, princess. Right now she needs Lucas more than anything else. Give her a little time."

"Are you sure?"

"Positive. Now, please, sit down and finish your meal."

Knowing she wouldn't be able to force another bite down her throat, she moved away from the table. "Do you think he's in love with her?"

"It seems so." His mouth curved into a wry smile. "I guess we've both been stung by the same bug."

Her heart kicked, but quickly righted. "Then why is our future so uncertain?"

His eyes lost some of their sparkle. "Until I'm free of this curse, it can't be any other way."

"It's not a curse," she insisted determinedly.

He watched her for a long moment. "Would you care to elaborate?"

She smiled, loving him more than her own life. "Yes. But I'd rather go for a walk. Find a quiet, secluded place where we can discuss your problem . . . without being disturbed."

He sent her a rakish grin. "We could return to the bedchamber."

"I want to *talk,* and it's extremely difficult to do something that mundane while lying in bed next to you."

His gaze smoldered with sensual messages. "A bed isn't a requirement."

Her cheeks grew warm. "Well, that may be true, but out in the open, like in the woods, we could always keep a tree between us while we talk."

He laughed. "Oh, princess. How naive you are."

Not sure whether to be offended or pleased, she merely watched him.

He cleared his throat in an obvious effort to control his mirth. "Okay, we'll walk." His expression turned serious. "But don't expect too much from me, sweetheart. Talking about my . . . problem won't come easy."

"Yes it will."

"Are you willing to make another wager?" He glanced down at her as they walked toward the veranda. "Say double or nothing on those sixteen favors you owe me?"

"Fifteen."

He grinned. "Fifteen." Then he suddenly changed his mind. "No. Fourteen."

"Why?"

He brushed a wayward strand of hair off her cheek. "Like you, I want to save one."

"All right. Under one condition."

"And that is?"

"That you allow me to help you."

"How?"

She touched his cheek. "Any way I can."

Cupping her hand with his, he turned his mouth in to her palm. "If only you could, princess. If only you could."

She stared at his bent head, tingling from the heat of his breath on her skin. "Do we have a deal?"

"Sure. Believe me, sweetheart, I've got nothing to lose."

They found a spot in the woods, near the stream, and she perched herself on a fallen log, then motioned for him to sit on a stump some distance from her. It was the only way she could keep her mind on the topic at hand. "When did you first notice your problem?"

"Which one? I have several at the moment."

Knowing that the time had come for them to stop playing games, she straightened her shoulders and faced him squarely. "The one where you make things happen with your mind."

Those velvet brown eyes darkened with bitterness. "I

don't *make* things happen. They just do." He rose and paced. "Damn it, Moriah. I have no control over this thing."

"Then you need to learn how to use your gift," she said softly.

"Gift? If *that's* what this is, I'd rather have a curse."

"Spitefulness doesn't suit you."

"Neither does this conversation."

She ignored the remark. "How old were you when you first discovered you were different?"

"Three or four."

That young? She smoothed down the hem of her skirt. "How many times have you deliberately used your powers?"

"Deliberately?" He considered it, then shoved a hand in his pocket and turned away. "Several times when I was younger. Tripping an adversary, causing a wind to lift a lady's skirt so I could glimpse an ankle, hiding lessons from my tutor, things like that."

"What about after you were grown?"

Pain flashed across his features. "I haven't intentionally used them at all since my mid-twenties, except on a few rare occasions." He swung around to face her. "I don't want to discuss this anymore. It's going nowhere."

"Yes it is," she countered, wondering what happened that caused him to fear his gift so much.

"I don't see how."

She needed something he would understand and be able to use as a comparison. "Think of your powers as a—" she thought for a moment "—a saw."

"What?" His features revealed a mixture of surprise and humor.

Not wanting him to make light of the situation, she glowered. "When someone picks up a saw for the first time, with no knowledge of how to use it, he could do a lot of damage. Destroy the wood he's trying to cut, injure himself, or someone close by, and so forth. But once he's practiced, learned skillful techniques, that same person can accomplish a great many things. He could build homes, fences, barns, even bridges and ships."

The amusement faded from his eyes. "Are you saying I should practice using this thing?"

"Yes."

"No."

Moriah wanted to gnash her teeth. "What are you afraid of? That I'm right and you'll lose the wager?"

"Of course not." He stared at the afternoon sky. "But you don't know what I'm capable of, princess. You don't know how evil this thing is."

"I have a pretty good idea," she said quietly. "I saw an example last night."

He swung a hostile gaze on her. "And you *saw* how I destroyed everything in sight."

"You could have done a lot more, but you didn't. You didn't even hurt anyone."

"What about the man holding the rope? And Mudanno?"

"At the time, your actions were necessary. Besides, neither was severely injured." She crossed to him and placed a hand on his strong cheek. "You could have killed them."

The muscle beneath her palm tightened. "I wanted to."

"But you didn't." She drew her fingertips over the firm outline of his mouth. "Please, Sin. Let me help you."

The warmth of his breath rushed past her fingers, and he kissed them tenderly. "I know you mean well, princess. But I'm just not sure I'm up to it."

Filled with love for this vibrant, troubled man, she smiled and lowered her hand. "Will you at least make a small effort?"

He didn't answer.

Not put off by his silence, she glanced around and spotted a white orchid several feet away. "Would you pick that for me?"

His gaze roamed her face, then reluctantly slid to the orchid. He stared at the blossom for several seconds.

Then, in awe, she watched the flower bend to the side, its stem snap, then slowly glide through the air toward her. She caught it and smiled at him.

But he didn't look pleased. His hands were clenched into fists, his arms trembling.

She became instantly concerned. "Does it hurt when you do this?"

"Not physically."

But inside it must hurt a lot. Knowing she had to get him out of his reluctant frame of mind, she turned the tables on him. "Have you ever tried to use your gift to do something good?"

"Like what?"

Pretending a nonchalance she didn't feel, she shrugged and walked over to the log she'd been sitting on earlier. "Like chopping firewood from a fallen tree, or rescuing an injured animal from an impossible place to reach."

"I used it when I rescued you from the sloop," he admitted softly.

She smiled to herself and brushed the petals of the orchid back and forth over her chin. "Yes, you did. And I certainly thank you for that." She met his hard features squarely. "You also saved me from that tiger . . . and Mudanno. But I still don't think it's ever occurred to you that *if* you hadn't possessed your gift, I might not be here now."

The shocked expression on his face gave her the answer.

"Your powers are a much greater gift than you know, Sin. So much more. Think of the things you could do. Why, you could close a man's wound without the use of a needle. You could stop a raging fire with nothing more than a glance. Or prevent an accident before anyone was injured. The possibilities are endless."

"So are the repercussions."

"Not once you master the power." She arched an ironic brow. "And you can't do that unless you learn to use it."

With a look of resignation, and just a hint of anticipation, he hesitated, then slowly nodded. "Okay, princess. I'll give it a try."

Their eyes locked. "Thank you." She rubbed her cheek with the orchid, not taking her gaze from his. "What do you want to try first?"

A lazy smile curved his lips. "How about making love?"

She narrowed her eyes. "You don't need practice at that."

Amusement deepened the lines bracketing his mouth. "Oh, I don't know. I've never undressed a woman . . . without using my hands." Huskiness rippled through his words. "Or brought her pleasure."

Fiery tingles shot to her belly at the mere thought. Her heart picked up speed, and when she spoke, her voice sounded like a breathless rasp. "You haven't?"

He lowered his gaze to the front of her wrap. "No. But I'm willing to make an attempt." The pupils behind his dark lashes grew bright and fixed on her chest.

She felt a slight tug between her breasts, then watched, hypnotized, as the end of the silky wrap pulled free. Slowly the garment unwound itself, then slid to the ground at her feet. Shivering with excitement, she peeked up.

His eyes flamed into hers, and she couldn't look away. It was as if something hot and tangible held their gazes locked.

Suddenly it felt as if a hand cupped her breast, yet he hadn't moved. Arousing tingles stiffened her crest, and she drew in a shaky breath, her eyes still held by his. Maybe this wasn't such a good idea, after all. She tried to tear her gaze away, but couldn't.

An unseen entity feathered up and down her spine, her sides, then fluttered across her lower belly. She swallowed, nearly overwhelmed by a rush of desire. "Sin, I . . . Oh!"

Something warm brushed over her secret part, stroking so gently, so slowly, so tauntingly, she thought she'd die from sheer pleasure. Shudders ruffled through her, and her eyes drifted closed. Her head fell back, and she let the sweet sensations consume her.

Suddenly a hot mouth captured hers, a hair-roughened chest pressed against her aching nipples. Her eyes sprang open to see him staring down at her. And he was naked.

"I like the old-fashioned way better," he murmured, teasing her lips.

She wrapped her arms around his neck, and sighed beneath his very passionate, old-fashioned kiss. Yes, she thought, caressing the thick muscles along his shoulders, feeling the heat of his lower body nudging hers. She liked the old way better, too.

CHAPTER

22

James Cunningham surveyed his hotel with pride. Everything from the black and white tiled floor to the glistening oak banisters bordering the stairs gleamed from his recent polishing. The entire place was in readiness for the aristocratic guests docking in less than an hour, except the refuse littering the rear alley, and his son, Jamie, was seeing to that now.

The lobby door opened, and a gust of hot wind ruffled papers on the counter. He looked up to see Walter Crow amble into the common room. "Good evening, Father. What brings you out on such a sultry afternoon?"

"The same query, I'm afraid."

James shook his head. The man was tenacious, he'd give him that. "Miss Morgan still hasn't returned. If she had, I'd have sent round a note, like you asked."

The priest's head bobbed up and down. "I'm sure you would have. But I was just returning from mass, and I thought I'd check while I was so near."

"Well, like I said—"

"Pa!" Jamie screamed. His footsteps thundered down the hall. "Pa, come quick!"

The terror in his son's voice jolted him into action. He raced around the counter and toward the hall.

Jamie ran into him, nearly knocking him off his feet. "Oh, Pa. She's dead. The lady's dead!"

James grabbed his son's thin shoulders. "What lady? What are you talking about?"

"In the alley. Her throat—"

Shoving his son aside, James rushed to the rear door and out into the narrow dirt lane behind his hotel. Beside a stack of firewood lay a woman's lifeless form.

"Is that her?" Father Crow huffed as he ran up next to him.

"Yes. Yes," Jamie squealed from the doorway.

James inched closer. Though her head was turned toward the building, he could see the line of crimson darkening her neck. "Jesus."

"Amen," Father Crow whispered.

"Get the sheriff, Jamie. Quick!"

A burst of pounding footsteps told him the boy had obeyed. Feeling frightened and queasy at the same time, he approached the body.

"Do you know her?" the priest asked, sidling up beside him.

"I can't tell." He knelt and rolled her over.

A hole at the base of her throat gaped in the dimming sun, reminding him sickeningly of the wound on the woman they found last year. Beth Kirkland.

The Priest dropped to his knees. "Oh, Blessed Virgin." He crossed himself. "It's Blanche, my sister."

Sin watched Moriah toss the banana high in the air, wishing to hell she'd stop this nonsense. For almost a week now, she'd coerced him into *performing* for her, and he didn't like it. This "gift" scared the hell out of him. And with good reason, he painfully recalled.

Not wanting to think about *that,* he concentrated on the banana, stopping its descent just inches above the ground, then raising the fruit to her hand. "That's enough for today."

She swung those incredible violet eyes on him. "But we've barely started."

He slipped his hands around her waist, loving the way her flesh warmed beneath his touch. "I'm not in the mood." His gaze roamed her curves, and he remembered all the passion they'd shared last night—and this morning—and the shambles he'd made of the bedchamber. He grinned rakishly. "I want to do something else."

"What?" she asked breathlessly, not unaffected by his meandering hands, which were now just below her breasts, his thumbs brushing the soft under-swells.

"Show you the island."

"I've seen it," she returned, then sighed when his thumbs stroked higher.

"Not all of it." He nibbled the flesh exposed above her wrap. His loins responded instantly. Blood pulsed heatedly. They'd just left the bed only a few hours ago, and already he wanted her again. No matter how many times they loved, he just couldn't get enough of her. "Come on." He forcibly extracted himself from her sweet temptation. "I want to show you something."

"I think I've already seen it."

He laughed. "Not *that*. Something else."

Her cheeks flushed. "Oh." She ducked her head, causing her thick hair to waver in the sunlight and catch golden beams among the blue-black strands.

Taking her hand, the only part of her he felt safe enough to touch, he pulled her along behind him and headed for the east side of the island.

When they emerged from the last of the woods, into the clearing he sought, he stopped and turned to face her. "When I was growing up, my father would sometimes come to Arcane, probably to get away from social pressures, and he always brought me and Lucas. This was our special place. We built it ourselves." He gestured toward a massive structure sitting high in a Catalpa tree.

She stared curiously. "How extraordinary. I've never seen anything quite like it; the tree, I mean."

"It's called a Catalpa or sausage tree." He pointed to the nearly two-foot-long, sausage-shaped fruit hanging from sturdy branches by what looked like thin strings.

"Those things weigh about ten to twelve pounds each, but they're not edible. Lucas and I used to pretend they were missiles. We scared the daylights out of more than one unsuspecting animal . . . and servant."

"How long has it been since you were up there?"

"Quite a few years," he said, strolling toward the long, branchless trunk. "But if I recall correctly, there's a pair of chairs, some old chintz curtains we sneaked from a box in the attic, and a chest containing our secret treasures."

Moving to stand beside him, her eyes bright with anticipation, she glanced up. "How do you get up there?"

Sin ran a hand down the length of her silky hair, loving the feel of its softness. "I'm not sure I should tell you. Lucas and I took a blood oath not to reveal our special secret."

Mock seriousness darkened her mischievous eyes, and she leaned close, her tone conspiratorial. "I promise not to tell."

"Your promises aren't worth a fig."

She punched him. "Stop that. Now, tell me."

Enjoying the game, he rubbed his chin thoughtfully. "Well . . . I don't know."

She laced her fingers through the hairs on his chest and nuzzled his skin. "You can trust me."

"All sorts of horrors are sure to befall one who breaks a blood oath. It's too risky."

She chuckled, and her small pink tongue darted out to flick over his bare nipple. His sex sprang to life.

"But for you," he said huskily, "I'll chance the dire consequences." Anxious to get her alone in the tree house, he scanned the area for the row of gardenia bushes where they had hidden the ladder. Spying the cluster of white blossoms closer than he recalled, he clawed through them until he found the aging wood.

The ladder wasn't as sturdy as he remembered. Two long, narrow pine trunks were held together by smaller cross branches that had been tied and nailed rather haphazardly. "I'm not sure about this, princess."

She came up behind him and touched his back. "It'll be fine. In fact, I'll go first. That way, if the ladder breaks, you can . . . catch me."

He wasn't fooled for a minute. What she really meant was he could use his powers to save her neck. Not sure he wanted to do this, but mesmerized by her sweet woman's scent, her throaty voice and smoky violet eyes, he found himself nodding in agreement.

A moment later, it was damned hard to concentrate as he watched the sensual movement of her small derriere when she climbed. The short wrap rode up with each step she took, revealing an intriguing amount of enticing white thighs and the smoothly rounded curve of her rear. He could well remember how that soft flesh felt in his palms. Sweet desire ran rampant through every organ in his body.

"Come on," she called down to him.

Dragging his thoughts from the pleasureable meanderings, he eyed a rickety rung and grabbed hold. Moments later, he joined her, surprised by the sturdiness of the ancient ladder and the smallness of the room he and Lucas had built so many years ago. Thank God they'd both been tall, even as boys. The generous height of the structure was the only thing that kept him from feeling claustrophobic.

"This is magnificent," she breathed out on a sigh. "Just look at that view." She pointed to a part in the branches where the tree house towered over an inlet, almost completely encircled by moss-draped cypress. There was just a small, possibly thirty-foot, opening where waves cascaded through the trees onto a silvery white beach.

"Lucas and I used to call that Treasure Cove. We once found a gold coin there and were both convinced it belonged to pirates. We just knew their treasure was buried beneath the sand." He chuckled. "I can't even begin to guess at how many holes we dug looking for a chest."

A tender warmth filled her beautiful eyes before they

drifted again to the cove. "It must have been so exciting for you."

He slid his arms around her waist from behind and propped his chin on top of her head. "At the time, I'm sure it was. But since then, I've discovered much more *exciting* things to do." He worked his hands up her curves until they met the softness of her breasts. He lazily explored their beautiful shape.

She cleared her throat and eased away to inspect the ancient room. "Is that the trunk where you hid your treasures?" she asked a little unsteadily, nodding to a scarred, crudely built box.

"Yes." Hell, even his own voice wavered.

Kneeling, she carefully raised the warped, ill-fitting lid. Almost reverently she brushed aside a mat of cobwebs and reached inside to pick up a small canoe with two tiny oars. "Yours?"

"I carved them from a piece of driftwood when I was ten. Lucas made the anchor." He watched her lift the miniature anchor with small, delicate hands, her fingers tracing the tiny nicks and gouges in the roughly whittled piece.

"They're quite good. Do you still carve?"

A little embarrassed, he shrugged and jammed his hand into his pocket. He closed his fingers around the crystal. "I do, once in a while. Mostly just designs on tables, doors, furniture, or what have you. I'm not sure about Lucas. If he still does, he never says anything."

"With this knife?" She gestured to one of two small pocket knives in the chest. His and Lucas's.

"No. I have a better one in my study."

A spark of satisfaction that he couldn't define lit her eyes, then she lowered them to the hand in his pocket. "What *are* you fidgeting with?"

Suddenly becoming aware of his unconscious habit, he withdrew the crystal. "My worry-stone, or so my mother called it. I guess I have a habit of fondling the thing when I'm uncomfortable about something. She gave it to me when I was six to replace an ordinary stone I'd used previously and lost. I guess I've never outgrown the need to hold it." He stared down at the blue teardrop-shaped rock. "Too, I think it's my way of keeping her close."

Shoving the crystal in his pocket, and wanting to change the subject, he dropped down beside her, curious about what else was in the chest.

Seashells of every shape, size, and color littered the bottom.

"What's this?" she asked, picking up an old cherry-wood pipe.

"I stole that from my father's study. Lucas and I used to smoke when we came here. I guess it made us feel more adult, somehow. I still do occasionally—but not for the same reasons."

"Didn't your father ever miss it?"

"I'm sure he did. But he never said anything. We were pampered by him. Father was a hard taskmaster to his workers, but he adored the two of us."

"Didn't you think it strange how he took to Lucas so well? I mean, you were his son, I could understand that. But Lucas was a slave, wasn't he?"

"Yes. He came from Hank Fowler's plantation in Virginia. His mother had been a slave there for years, and my father had been a frequent visitor." Sin stared down at her. "It was rumored that Lucas was sired by my father."

Her eyes widened. "You mean you're . . ."

"Brothers?" he supplied. "Maybe." He waited for her reaction to him possibly having a brother of color.

Her expression grew soft, concerned, and she touched his arm. "Does Lucas know?"

"I'm not sure. We've never discussed the subject."

"Why not? Are you ashamed of him?" Her tone sounded brittle.

Love for Moriah filled him, and he stood, pulling her into his arms. "No, princess. I'd never be ashamed of Lucas. I just don't want to press him. If he wants to talk about it, I'll be more than happy to oblige." He rubbed his nose over her tiny button one. "And I'd be honored to call him brother in front of anyone."

Tears sparkled in her eyes, and she threw her arms around his neck. "Oh, Sin. No wonder I love you so much."

"Not nearly as much as I do you, princess." Hungrily he claimed her mouth, anxious to explore the sweet recess, and fill himself with her goodness and love.

She moaned and pressed her small body into his, moving sensually against his hot shaft.

Fiery explosions erupted, and he pressed her to the wall of the tree house, desperate to make her a part of him. Their mouths ground together, as if each would devour the other.

The chest lid slammed shut.

He eased away, breathing heavily. He needed to see her naked. Let his eyes make love to her satiny flesh. With trembling fingers he undid the wrap and slid it from her luscious curves. Perfection. That was the only word he could think of that described her incredible beauty. Her dark hair tumbled over her shoulders, surrounding her small ivory face. Her eyes were dark with passion, her cheeks a creamy pink flush, her lips full, still moist from their kiss, and slightly parted.

He tightened unbearably. His gaze roamed her exquisite figure, from the full upthrust of her coral-tipped breasts to slender ribs, an unbelievably tiny waist, and firm, flat stomach.

The curtains billowed.

Moisture beaded on his brow, and he moved his attention lower, to a nest of soft black curls at the apex of her thighs that shielded from him the place he'd loved so thoroughly only hours ago. The place he desperately wanted to be again.

The musky, sweet scent of her body rose up to taunt him, and he reached for her, touching the soft skin of her breasts with reverence, watching eagerly as the peaks pebbled into hard little nubs. Unable to resist the urge, he bent his head to taste her, to tease the tip with his tongue, then nurse gently.

Her head fell back, causing her hair to brush the roundness of her rear where he'd slipped his hands to massage greedily, to slide his fingers between the sweet flesh. Needing more, so much more, he lowered himself to his knees, drawing her nipple deeper into his mouth, nuzzling, suckling, savoring the delicate treasure.

The floor quivered.

His fingers worked to pleasure her while his mouth nibbled a moist path down her stomach. Heat from her woman's mound beckoned him, and he slid his hands down the backs of her legs to part them, to give him access to her fire. The scent of her pulsed through every inch of his body, and he covered her with his mouth, pressed his tongue between the sweet pink folds.

She cried out, and her hands went to his hair. Her whole body shook with need, and he knew just how to satisfy it. Gripping her small rear, he pulled her more fully to his mouth, moved lower, and thrust his tongue inside her.

The ladder fell.

She arched, pressing into him. He drove deeper. Again. Faster and faster. Eagerly he moved upward to explore the tiny nub pulsing for attention. He deliberately slowed the pace, and tauntingly brushed loving strokes over the delicate bud, then flicked gently.

He pressed his fingers into her tight, hot passage from behind, and she constricted around him. Lightly, yet hurriedly, he pleasured her with urgent caresses while his mouth took her to the height of ultimate sensations.

His own body was near bursting, and he knew he couldn't hold out much longer. He darted his tongue rapidly, increased the rhythm of his fingers.

She gasped, then moaned hoarsely, her body shaking wildly, her hands gripping his hair as she cried out, convulsing with tremors that grew stronger and stronger.

Without stopping the motion of his hand, he lowered his breeches and rose, then replaced his hand with his pulsing need. She was so hot, so damned tight, she took his breath away. He drew her legs up around his waist and drove up into her, pressing her into the tree house wall with each hard thrust. Her fingers clawed the muscles on his shoulders, sending fiery shock waves through his shaft.

The tree shook. Heavy thuds struck the ground.

"Oh, Christ," he groaned, driving deeper. Harder. Pleasure burst over him with the force of a volcanic eruption. Every muscle in his body responded, shook, tightened, and snapped. His seed spewed forth, the pain-pleasure so intense, he arched his spine and groaned deeply.

Slowly, lazily, the quaking subsided, and he became aware of their hearts pounding in unison, of the dampness clinging to their bodies, of the scent of gardenias and sex, of the slow pulsing in his member, of her lips buried in his neck.

He eased back, giving her room to breathe, but he couldn't bring himself to withdraw from her. Not just yet. "Are you all right?" he asked a little shakily.

"I'm more than all right. I'm in heaven."

He smiled. "You were incredible. I've never experienced anything like that." He moved inside her, already feeling himself grow hard again. "Never that wild, or that savagely sweet." He thrust upward.

She inhaled sharply, then tightened her legs around his waist. Her hands dug into his shoulders. "Oh, Sin. Anything that feels this wonderful must be illegal."

Chuckling, he captured her lips and eased them both to the floor. He kissed her thoroughly, hungrily, then whispered against her moist mouth, "Some laws were meant to be broken, princess."

Much, much later, they emerged from their haven and headed home, but not before they'd swum at Treasure Cove and made love on the silvery sand, then again on the shaded grass. The sky had darkened to a dusky amber, and he held her close to his side as they negotiated the shadowy path.

When they reached the yard, they saw Lucas walking across the lawn.

"I've been searching for you," he announced happily. "Jonas couldn't find you, so he came by Woosak's. The freighter's finally finished—and ready to load."

"It's about time," Sin returned sternly, but he couldn't keep the delight from his tone. "I was becoming concerned about the cane." He nodded to his overseer. "Tell the men to start loading and be ready to sail at dawn, then join us for supper." He stopped suddenly. "How's Callie?"

"Tired. But much, much better. She should be up and around soon."

"That's even better news. Get to work, man. Time's a-wastin'."

Lucas gave a comical salute, then sprinted toward the village.

"Are you going with them to deliver the goods?" Moriah asked challengingly.

"No. Lucas will."

"Why not you, Sin? Surely you aren't still afraid of being around people."

Though her words were said gently, it didn't stop the flood of anger that gushed through him. "Yes, Moriah," he said coldly, stepping away from her. "I *am.*"

Her mouth drew into a thin line, and she crossed her arms over her chest. "And you'll continue to be frightened as long as you stay hidden out on this island. Damn it, why can't you see there's no evil in you? That you wouldn't hurt anyone?"

"You don't know that. And neither do I."

She stomped her foot. "You infuriate me with your stubbornness. You won't even give yourself a chance. You're so mulish, so pigheaded, you make me want to shout!"

More than anything, he wanted to pull her into his arms and kiss her senseless, stop the words that were churning his blood to a boil. Damn her, why couldn't she just leave the issue alone? "Let's go inside," he said tiredly, urging her beneath the arch of the veranda.

She dug in her heels. "No. I want to discuss this here and now. Sin, you've got to come to terms with your gift. You can't spend your entire life hiding on Arcane."

Her words stung. Anger hit him swift and hard. He whirled on her furiously. "I *have* tried living around people," he shouted, the blood pumping through his veins, his muscles shaking with helpless rage. "And because of it, a man is d—"

Something cracked overhead. His glance flew upward. A portion of the balcony rail toppled toward Moriah. "No!" he bellowed, diving for her.

He hit her hard, knocking them both to the ground, then rolled away from the porch.

The heavy rail crashed to earth, splintering under the force of the impact.

He began to tremble. If she'd still been under it, she'd be dead. Then an even more horrifying thought hit him. *He* had done this. The one thing he feared above all else had happened. He'd nearly killed her with his anger. Pain nearly tore him in two. No matter how much she talked, no matter how much she coerced him to use his gift, he knew he'd never be able to control the beast.

Thick air forced its way into his lungs as the awful realization struck him. He had to send her away. Now. He couldn't risk another confrontation.

Hurting as if he'd been stabbed, he rose to his feet and pulled her up with him. "Are you okay?"

She nodded, at a loss for words. Perhaps at last she understood.

He pulled her back into his arms, and for one long, last moment, he held her close, dying inside. Then, drawing on every speck of reserve strength he possessed, he set her away from him. "Go pack, Moriah. You're leaving at dawn."

"Leaving for where?"

"You're going home."

She clutched his arm. "What are you saying?"

He withdrew and turned away from her, knowing he couldn't look into her beautiful face and maintain control. Then he sounded the death knell that would surely end his own life. "I want you off my island."

Unable to look at her, he started walking. His feet felt leaden, like the weight that pressed in on his heart. Vaguely he heard her anguished cry, then her footsteps racing into the house. His own misery nearly strangled him, but he kept walking.

He stopped at one of the bordering trees and leaned against the trunk, pressing his forehead to the rough bark. Tears stung his eyes. "I love you, princess," he whispered raggedly. "More than my life. But I have to let you go."

Tears ran down Moriah's cheeks as she tossed her few toiletries into the trunk. *How dare he order her off his island.* Just because of a piece of broken baluster. The damned thing was probably old and could have fallen at any time. It had to have been there for a good twenty years or more if Sin had been coming here since he was a child. And what about the hurricane? The force of the wind could have loosened the rail.

She slammed the lid on the chest. Perhaps Mama was right after all. Now that he'd gotten what he wanted from her, he'd probably grown tired of the game and would use any feeble excuse to end their relationship. Well, fine. She didn't want to stay, anyway. The ache in her breast expanded, and fresh tears tumbled down her cheeks. Damn him. Damn him to hell. She never wanted to see him again. Never again wanted to feel this intolerable ache in her heart.

She sniffed and rubbed at her damp cheeks, vowing not to let him see how close he'd come to destroying her. No. She would hold her head high, draw on some of that Morgan pride, and appear totally unaffected by his decision throughout supper.

Supper. Their last meal together.

Lifting her chin, she hardened her resolve. She *would not* go mushy inside. And as soon as the wretched meal was over, she'd go see Callie. Her throat tightened. Her friend still wasn't well enough to leave. Oh, how hard it would be to say good-bye to her. Even temporarily.

When Moriah appeared, though reluctantly, at the supper table, all remnants of her distraught state had been washed away, or at least concealed by a layer of rice powder. But the facade was all for nothing. Sin wouldn't be joining them, Lucas advised her.

Though she wasn't much company, he made a valiant effort to keep up the conversation throughout the meal. But she could do no more than occasionally respond with a nod or shake of her head. When the unsavored meal came to an end, she asked him to walk with her to Woosak's village, knowing he was still unaware of her departure.

"Tonight?" He was obviously surprised at the request. "Wouldn't it be better if you went in the morning? Crossing the island at night isn't advisable."

"I won't be here in the morning."

He was stunned, then his glance shot to Sin's empty chair. His eyes narrowed, then returned to her. "He's sending you back, isn't he?"

Unable to speak for the knot in her throat, she nodded and lowered her eyes to her clenched hands.

"Why?" he demanded. "He's in love with you, for Christ's sake. Anyone can see that." He took a breath as if to control his burst of anger, and his voice softened. "And, if I'm not mistaken, you're in love with him, too."

Again she nodded, and tears spilled down her cheeks.

He made a noise that sounded like a snarl, then lunged to his feet and kicked his chair aside. "That jackass doesn't deserve you." He offered his hand. "Come on. I'll take you to the village."

They found Callie seated in the same chair Moriah had occupied the night of Woosak's birthday party. The night

Sin carried her home. Forcing back another wave of heartbreak, she glanced at her friend's lovely face.

Immediately she noticed how much better Callie looked. She'd regained some of the weight she'd lost. There was a healthy sheen to her long hair, and a glow in her emerald eyes.

"How are you feeling?" she asked, taking the girl's hand as she dropped down beside her.

The mulatto's sparkling eyes moved over Lucas, then returned. "I've never been better."

The flush of love was written all over her face, and Lucas was the recipient. Happiness for Callie and the overseer engulfed her, and for a moment, her troubles with Sin were insignificant. Then the reason for her late visit intruded. She squeezed her friend's hand. "I'm glad you're doing so well. And I wish you all the happiness in the world." She shot a sly glance at Lucas. "You deserve it."

She met Callie's gaze and found her expression puzzled.

"That sounds like a farewell, Moriah."

"I'm afraid it is. The cargo ship's sailing at dawn, and I'll be on it."

"Why?" Callie demanded, much as Lucas had.

Not wanting to upset the girl, she concocted a tale she hoped sounded believable. "I've enjoyed my stay here on Arcane, I really have. But now that Sara's murder is solved, I find myself restless. This solitary life isn't for me. I miss the theaters and parties and operas and balls offered by civilization. I'd never be happy in a place like this for long. Surely you know that?" The lie tasted bitter on her tongue. Social gatherings had never been of monumental importance. They were enjoyable, but the serene beauty of Arcane offered so much more. "Besides, we'll see each other soon. As soon as you're able to travel, that is."

Callie glanced at Lucas.

He cleared his throat. "She won't be returning, Moriah. I'm going to marry her." He hesitated and avoided Callie's surprised face. "If she'll have me."

Moisture glimmered in the girl's eyes, but she quickly blinked it away. "We'll see."

Knowing her friend was only speaking out of embarrassment of the moment, and certain she'd eventually take Lucas up on his offer, she pushed her own despair aside and hugged Callie fiercely. "I wish you all the best." She tried desperately to hold on to a sob. This really was good-bye.

Rising quickly, afraid she would start crying at any moment, she spoke to the overseer. "Would you take me back now, please?"

He nodded, then bent and gave Callie a quick kiss. "I won't be long."

Once again installed in her room and left to herself, Moriah paced the chamber, kicked a chair on the veranda, cried, swore to the best of her ability, then finally fell exhausted into bed. She detested that sniveling coward, Valsin Masters, with all her heart.

The next morning she awoke with a pounding headache and to a bustle of activity as Dorothy entered the room, ordering the servants to prepare a bath, setting out that damned orchid gown for her to travel in, and commanding Donnelly to take her trunk to the freighter.

With the break of dawn, she was hugged fiercely by the staff, then dispatched to the vessel by two very efficient seamen and ensconced in a cabin. But all she could think of was the fact that she was sailing out of Sin's life forever. And he hadn't even come to see her off. She hadn't seen him once since he told her to leave.

Numb with pain, she stumbled up to the deck and clung to the rail for one last look at her island paradise. She never knew, never even dreamed, that loving someone could hurt so much. Through a blur of tears, she focused on something white near the edge of the trees, then clamped a hand over her mouth to stop a cry.

Sin stood among the foliage, his gaze locked on her face. Oh, God. She could see his pain. Feel it. Hot tears coursed down her cheeks. How could he do this to them?

The ship lurched, then moved slowly toward the

mouth of the cove, but she didn't take her eyes off him, not until he became nothing more than a tiny white speck in a forest of emerald green. Not until her heart had lumped into a ball of cold, hard clay.

Arnold, their new captain, had his first mate show her below, and like a machine, she followed, uncaring whether she was locked in as on her previous journey. But they didn't—and she was encouraged by the fact. At least Sin trusted her enough not to reveal the location of his island. Of course, he didn't know she'd already seen his map and had pretty much figured Arcane's position, anyway.

After she'd settled, she strolled to the deck and met Donnelly standing by the rail amid stacks of crated sugarcane.

"Good morning, miss," he greeted kindly.

She forced a weak smile. "I'm pleased to see you aboard."

The graying man shrugged his thin shoulders. "I hadn't planned to be. But Lucas didn't want to leave his lady at the moment, so Sin asked me to come. Lucas will come for me when the sloop's repaired. Shouldn't be more than a few days."

"I'm sorry to put you to such an imposition. But it wasn't necessary. I'm certain that Captain Arnold could have handled my departure without incident."

"The boy knew that, missy. But he didn't want you to make the long trip with a boatload of strangers. He figured you'd appreciate a friendly face."

The lump of clay in her chest softened just a little. "I appreciate his concern. And I'm glad of your comforting presence."

Donnelly smiled. "Thank you, Miss Morgan. I'm glad to be here."

The trip passed slowly, and though Sin's manservant did his best to keep her entertained, she was certain she was poor company in return. Then, all too soon, the huge cargo freighter anchored in Nassau Bay.

From there, crewmen loaded her trunk into a longboat and took her ashore. Donnelly came with her and hired a carriage to take her to her hotel, then pressed a purse, heavy with coin, into her hand. "This is not for services rendered," he quickly explained. "Sin just wanted to make sure you were taken care of."

She pushed the purse away. "I don't want his money. What I *do* want, he obviously can't give." Through a haze of tears, she vaguely heard Donnelly's feeble apology and heartfelt good-bye as he closed the door to the carriage—and shut away all of her hopes and dreams.

Wondering if death was as painful as love, she made her way to the desk and procured the same room as before from Mr. Cunningham, then ordered a bath, and her clothing to be brought down from the attic. After sending a quick note to Carver, making certain he understood their engagement was over, she headed upstairs.

An hour later, in the warmth of the tub, Sin's image rose again and again to haunt her. She could still see the way his eyes crinkled at the corners when he smiled, and how they narrowed in anger. The way lights danced in their velvet brown depths when he teased her, or how they darkened to nearly black when they made love.

She could hear the gentle timbre of his voice when he talked about his animals, or chuckled in that husky way of his, or whispered all the delicious things he wanted to do to her.

Sniffing, she rose from the now cold water. After toweling off, she retrieved one of her dressing robes from the clothes closet, wondering why she didn't feel as pleased about wearing her own clothes again as she should. Too, she never thought she'd truly miss the island wear. But she did.

Overlapping and tying the front of her pristine blue and white striped wrapper with its lacy, high-necked collar, she moved to the second trunk, the one she'd brought from Arcane, and lifted the lid to get out her hairbrush.

A gold chain lay on top of the garments.

She picked up the necklace to examine it more closely. From the bottom of the loop hung a beautiful blue crystal. Her breath shuddered in her throat. Sin had been in her room last night while she slept . . . and he'd given her the gift he cherished. Tears sprang to her eyes. "Damn you, Valsin Masters. You're tearing me apart."

With trembling fingers, she clutched the chain to her breast.

Someone knocked on the door.

Assuming it was the proprietor, she crossed the room in swift strides.

A thin, neatly dressed man in a black suit stood on the other side. "Miss Morgan?"

"Yes?"

"I'm Father Walter Crow."

Blinking, she noticed the stiff white collar beneath the neck of his black tunic shirt. A priest. She opened the door wider. "How can I help you, Father?"

"I've been sent to see to your welfare."

"By whom?" There was only one person it could have been. "My mother?"

"Yes, child." He stepped inside, then closed the door behind him. "It's her wish that I see you safely ensconced in one of my parishioners' homes."

"Why?"

"I'm afraid, with that murderer on the loose, she fears for your life."

Since when has Mother become so concerned? "Well, thank you very much, Father Crow. But that won't be necessary. The killer's been caught . . . and punished."

Pencil-thin brows shot up in surprise. "What? When?"

"Nearly a week ago."

"Oh, dear." He looked upset.

"What's wrong?"

"Whoever captured that poor soul got the wrong person. The killer struck again just days ago. Right here, behind the hotel." He shook his head. "I'm sorry, my dear. But I think it's best I do as your mother asks. Now, please, gather your things."

She was too shocked to move. Mudanno wasn't Sara's murderer? That maniacal bastard was right here on

Nassau? She began to tremble with anger. "Thank you again, Father. But I prefer to stay here." She'd find that vermin if it was the last thing she ever did.

He gripped her arm, startling her. "You're coming with me now, miss."

"How dare you!" She tried to wrench out of his hold.

His fingers tightened. "It won't do you any good to fight me."

The frigid tone of his voice scared the hell out of her. *Something wasn't right.* "My mother didn't send you."

His thin lips curled into a smile. "No. She didn't."

Pain throbbed beneath his gouging fingernails. "Then why are you really here?" Her heart bumped crazily; she feared she already knew the answer.

"I've come to rid your soul of Satan."

"I wasn't aware he'd entered my soul."

The priest smiled. "I know." He pulled her toward the door. "That's why you're coming with me."

When the clouds turn green, she thought wildly, looking around for some means of escape.

"Come now. Don't try to resist. It won't do any good. I must lead you to salvation. Only through prayer and repentance can I rid you of this demon." His bright gaze lowered to her stomach. "Rid you of his evil."

Though fear was choking her, she kept her voice steady. "I'm not going anywhere with you." She tried again to draw away. The chain she held caught on the button of his coat, snapping the gold in two. The chain and crystal dropped to the floor.

His eyes narrowed on the object, and his viselike grasp became brutal. "I *will* save your soul, whore. Whether you want it or not."

The man was insane! Frantically she lashed out with her free hand and raked long furrows down his cheek.

A vicious oath burst from his lips, and he drew back his fist.

Pain exploded in her jaw. Blood spurted from a cut on her lip. Then slowly, hazily, everything slipped away into swirling black. . . .

CHAPTER

24

Sin paced the confines of his study, trying to ease the pain eating away at his heart. It didn't help. His gaze drifted over the destruction he'd wreaked, the upended furniture, broken window glass, torn curtains, and scattered books. That hadn't helped, either. But at the time the pain had been unbearable. Now he felt shame on top of everything else.

Automatically he shoved his hand into his pocket and reached for the crystal. It wasn't there. Just as Moriah wasn't there anymore. But he was glad he'd given it to her. It was a part of him, and he'd wanted her to have it. Maybe when she looked at the necklace she'd know how much he loved her, how much he hated this thing that kept them apart.

He'd mounted the stone on the chain that held his Saint Christopher medallion, then made his cowardly jaunt into her room to put the gift in her trunk. He'd wanted to give the crystal to her personally, place it around her neck, but he knew if he touched her, kissed her, he wouldn't have been able to let her go. He just wasn't that strong.

How achingly beautiful she'd looked lying there amid the satin covers, her billowing hair forming a thick, black cloud around her sweet face, her long lashes making tiny crescents on her smooth pink cheeks, her luscious mouth slightly parted. He'd watched her for hours, dying inside with each little breath she took, with each despairing moan she'd made in her troubled sleep.

"Sin?" Lucas called softly as he knocked.

Startled, he swung toward the door. "Yes?"

His friend peeked inside. His eyes widened as they traveled over the destruction in the room, then he cleared his throat. "May I come in?"

Waving a hand, he kicked aside a pile of books and strode to his chair behind the desk. After righting it, he sat down and faced the overseer. "Well?"

Shifting uncomfortably, Lucas made an obvious effort not to glance at the carnage all about him. "I've been warring with myself all day. Telling myself to stay out of your affairs. But goddamn it! I want to know why you sent her away."

He leaned back in his chair. "I'd grown tired of her."

Lucas's hands drew into massive fists. "Don't lie to me. We've known each other too long for that. I know you love her, and she loves you. Any fool could see that." His voice trembled with emotion. "Damn it, why are you doing this to her? To yourself?"

Sin's insides crumbled. "Because of this curse!" he bellowed in frustration. "Damn it, Lucas. I can't chance hurting her."

"You wouldn't have. You couldn't hurt someone you love. Hell, you couldn't hurt anyone, period."

"I not only could, I did," he spat viciously, his insides twisting with guilt. "I killed my own father."

For a stunned moment, silence filled the room. Lucas stared in disbelief, then slowly, cautiously, eased forward. "What makes you think that?" he asked so softly, Sin barely heard him.

"You were there. You saw his body crushed beneath that chandelier." He braced his elbows on the desk and stabbed his fingers into his hair. "But what no one knew was how the accident happened. No one knew how

Father and I had argued over something so senseless, I can't even remember. Or how, in a surge of anger, I caused the damned thing to fall on him."

Lucas remained so quiet, Sin could almost hear the man's heartbeat. When he at last spoke, his voice shook with pain. "You did not kill *our* father."

Sin's head jerked up. For the first time, Lucas had admitted their blood ties. *And he had denied Sin's part in their father's death.* "You weren't in the room when it happened, Lucas. You don't know—"

"Yes, I do," he ground out. "The accident was my fault. Do you hear me, Sin? *My* fault. I was the one who should have replaced the bolts holding the chandelier the day before . . . after I finally got the nerve to speak to him about my mother . . . about me. He became so distraught, he nearly shook it down with that bellowing voice. But I just didn't realize how loose the thing was." He rubbed the back of his neck and paced. "When the sheriff called Father's death an unfortunate accident, I saw no reason to announce my part in it. My overwhelming guilt was punishment enough for me to bear alone. But if I'd thought for one minute that you blamed yourself . . ." He shook his head, his eyes bright with unshed tears. "Ah, God, Sin. What have I done to you?"

The enormous burden he'd carried for the last five years slowly slid from his shoulders. He hadn't killed his father. He *hadn't*. That damned chandelier was loose and it just fell. *Oh, God. Thank you.* His watery eyes met Lucas's. "You can't blame yourself, either. It was an accident. That's all. No more, no less."

"Didn't you hear what I said? I should have checked the bolts."

He rose and moved to stand beside his brother. *Brother.* How good that sounded. A warm feeling encompassed him, and he touched Lucas's shoulder. "It was Father's time to go, or it wouldn't have happened, and I think we've both suffered enough over it. Put it aside, and let's get on with the rest of our lives."

"You didn't when you thought yourself responsible."

"I know." He squeezed his shoulder. "But I thought I killed him deliberately . . . in my anger. That I'd unconsciously used this curse of mine to destroy him."

"That doesn't excuse what I did, setting him off that way when I knew deep down he'd done everything he could for Mama. Then forgetting the bolts . . ."

"No, it doesn't excuse you," Sin agreed. "But ask yourself this: Did you want Father dead?"

He made a gruff sound in his throat. "Of course not. I loved him."

"So did I. And I could have lived with what happened if I'd believed it wasn't intentional."

Lucas's throat worked. "I never thought of it that way."

"Maybe it's time you did."

A half smile pulled at his lips. "Maybe I should at that." He lifted his chin, staring squarely at Sin. "Are you going after Moriah?"

Swift, sharp pain cut into his chest, and he turned away. "No."

"Why the hell not?" he demanded. "Why are you still torturing yourself? You didn't kill Father with your curse, and you wouldn't hurt her, either."

Sin had taken all he could. He swung on Lucas like a viper. "I damn near killed her last night! We were arguing near the front door. In my anger, I caused the rail above her head to fall. It nearly hit her. If I hadn't knocked her out of the way, she would have been crushed beneath it!"

Lucas's temper, nearly as volatile as Sin's own, rose to horrific proportions. "The hell you did!" he bellowed. "You goddamn jackass. Delta, the little maid who's been hobbling around here for the last few weeks on a broken ankle, caused that. She came to Woosak this afternoon, frightened to death that you'd punish her when you found out. She'd been up on the balcony, eavesdropping on your conversation, and was bending over the rail when the damned thing broke under the pressure of her weight. The storm had loosened it. Now, stop being such a pigheaded fool and go get my future sister-in-law!"

Relieved, and filled with renewed hope, Sin wasn't about to argue. "Anything you say, little brother."

Together they sprinted toward the cove.

By the end of the day, his confidence was beginning to sag. He jammed his paintbrush into the pail of transparent resin, then slapped it on the hull of the sloop. "Two more days of this. At least. What if she's gone? What if I can't find her?"

Lucas, who knelt beside him, swiped at a seam with the liquid hardener. "She'll be there. But if you don't stop pushing the men, they'll all be dead and you won't have anyone to sail your ship."

Lucas was right, he was being impossible. Knowing that neither he nor the men could keep up such a brutal pace much longer, he tossed the brush into the pail and stood. "Send the crew home. We'll start again in the morning."

Lucas let out a heartfelt sigh.

Feeling the heavy weight of loss, and the growing knot in his gut that hadn't let up since Moriah left, he headed for his room and a hot bath, wondering if they could finish tomorrow—if they worked hard enough.

As he made his way through the undergrowth between the cove and the manor, Moriah's image rose again and again. He could almost hear her sweet voice. *Haven't you ever used your powers on purpose?* He smiled, recalling his answer about tripping adversaries, lifting women's skirts, and hiding papers from his tutor.

Your powers are a greater gift than you know. Think of the things you could do. You could close a man's wound without the use of a needle, stop a raging fire with nothing more than a glance, or prevent an accident before anyone was injured. The possibilities are endless.

His step faltered. His gaze swung back to the cove. *The possibilities are endless.* "Son of a bitch! Why didn't I think of that sooner?" Renewed energy surged through his blood as he raced toward the sloop.

By the time Lucas and the others arrived at dawn, the ship was finished and in the water, waiting for its crew—and his brother was still trying to explain the strange phenomenon to the men when they docked at Nassau late that afternoon.

Leaving the sloop before it had been secured at the moorings, Sin headed for the hilltop town. It took him less than an hour to discover where Moriah had been staying.

But the proprietor was no help at all.

"What do you mean she's gone? Gone where?" Sin demanded.

The thickset man shrugged a beefy shoulder, causing the evening light from the open front door to waver over his green chambray shirt. "Don't know. She came in a couple days ago, then disappeared the same night. She hasn't returned."

"How do you know she left the same night?" he snapped, feeling in his gut that something was very wrong.

"Got a message from Charleston that night. Took it up to her room to deliver it. Her clothes were still there, but she wasn't. The lady is making a habit of disappearing."

"Which room?" he asked urgently.

"Six."

He bounded up the stairs, taking them three at a time. When he reached the room, he burst through the door and shot a frantic glance around. Her trunk lay open on the bed. A used towel sat on the end of a dresser. The disarray had all the appearance of someone who'd bathed and changed, then gone out. *For two days?* his logic demanded. But there was no other explanation.

He turned for the door. Maybe if he rode around town . . . His foot hit something, and he glanced down. The crystal he'd given her lay on the floor, the chain broken. Beside it, a spot of red blotted the carpet.

With shaking fingers, he touched the dried crimson stain. Blood. His insides curled in denial. *It can't be Moriah's blood.* But it was. He knew it.

"No! Damn it. What's happening?" He began to shake.

The tapestry-covered stool in front of the dresser pitched over. A bedside lamp crashed to the floor.

"What's going on here?" the proprietor screeched from the doorway.

Sin snapped to his senses and dragged in a deep breath. He couldn't find her, couldn't help her, unless he regained control. After another cleansing lungful, he faced the confused hotel owner. "Did she have any visitors?"

"No. Least not that I know of," he answered warily, eyeing the broken lamp. "I wasn't here the whole time. Had to run down to the barbershop around five that day, about an hour after Miss Morgan arrived. I haven't seen her since."

"There was no one at the desk, then?"

The man puffed out his barrel chest. "Of course there was. I don't leave my customers unattended. My son, Jamie, was here."

"Where is he?"

"In the basement, bringing up some linens."

Without waiting for the proprietor, Sin charged down the stairs. Just as he rounded the bottom railing, he ran into a scrawny adolescent carrying a load of towels in his arms.

He steadied the boy. "Jamie?"

The kid was startled. "Yeah?"

"Did anyone come to see Miss Morgan in room six, the day she disappeared?"

Thin, scraggly brows crumpled into a vee, then rose high. "I ain't sure, but when I was haulin' the trash outta room nine, I thought I saw that priest headin' upstairs."

Sin's fingers dug into the kid's shoulders. "What priest?"

"Walter Crow, most likely," the huffing proprietor said, hobbling up next to them. "He's been coming round

264

here for the past few weeks asking about her. Real nice man. Said her folks wanted him to see after her."

Some of the panic left him, and he eased his fingers out of the kid's shoulders. "She must be with him. Or he knows where she is."

"I hope so—with that murderer still on the loose. The scum killed a woman behind my place, just a few days ago. And of all things, she was Crow's sister. Imagine that."

He stared at the man in shock. The killer hadn't been Mudanno! The bastard was right here. His hands trembled. He had to find Moriah. "Where's Father Crow's church?"

"Couple blocks down. Saint Anne's."

He nodded. "If she returns before I do, keep her here. I've got to talk to her."

It only took him a couple of minutes to sprint the distance to Saint Anne's. After belonging to the Catholic church for so many years, he instinctively bent one knee and crossed himself before entering the ethereal high-domed room.

Statues of the Savior and his Mother were inset at intervals along both sides of the main cathedral, just beyond the rows of hardwood seats. Multicolored lights filtered in through a stained-glass arch cut into a brick wall behind a pulpit at the end of the room. He remembered the place well. He'd come here for confession two years ago.

A door opened, and a robed clergyman came into the room carrying a candelabrum. He spotted Sin and set the holder on the back of an organ, then walked toward him, a smile of welcome on his kindly face. "How may I be of service, my son?"

"I'm looking for Father Crow."

The priest's smile faltered. "I'm afraid he's no longer with us."

"What do you mean?" He battled a surge of alarm. "He was at the Nassau Hotel two days ago."

"I mean," the robed man said gently, "that he's no longer a member of this parish."

"He moved to a new one?"

"I'm afraid not. The church was forced to . . ."

"Excommunicate him?" Sin supplied incredulously.

A nod was his only answer.

Feeling the same urgency he'd experienced in the hotel room, he stepped closer. "Why?"

"I'm sorry, I'm not at liberty to discuss—"

He touched his arm. "Please, Father. It's very important. A woman's life may be at stake."

Kind blue eyes searched his. Apparently finding what he sought, the clergyman nodded. "Two years ago, after Father Walter talked with a man in the confessional, he became convinced the man had unnatural powers and therefore was Satan in the flesh."

The floor wavered beneath Sin's feet.

"Father Walter followed the man to the docks and learned his name." The priest arched a brow. "Which I will not divulge, so please don't ask. Anyway, Father Walter became crazed with finding the 'devil's lair,' as he called it, and destroying Satan. Fortunately, no one knew where the troubled man lived. But Father Walter wouldn't accept that. He began haunting the docks, ignoring his duties, the boys in his charge, everything. When he did deign to join us, he rambled on about nothing else. He became irrational, started frightening his students with maniacal preachings. In the end, the bishop had no choice."

It was becoming hard to breathe. "Where does he live?"

"Why, my son?"

There was no way he'd lie to a priest. "I'm the man he thinks is Satan. It took me three years to get up the nerve to come to confession after an accident killed my father. An accident I thought I caused. But I never dreamed . . . Oh, God. He's got the woman I love. May try to kill her." His gut twisted at the realization that Crow may have already—*No! Damn it, no.*

The priest crossed himself, his eyes filled with compassion and concern. "He lives on Thompson Lane. Last house. I'll go with you."

Sin barely heard the last of the man's words as he bolted from the church, his heart nearly bursting with fear for Moriah. He had to find her. This was all his fault. If he hadn't gone to confession that day, none of this would have happened. None of it. Not to Sara. Not to Beth. Tears blurred his vision. Not to his beautiful Moriah. *Oh, Jesus. What have I done?*

CHAPTER
25

Moriah came awake to a stinging ache in her lip, a pain in her wrists, and the rancid odor of bird droppings. She wrinkled her nose at the offensive smell and tried to move. She couldn't. Blinking wildly to clear the haze from her vision, she glanced at first one of her arms, then the other. Her hands were pulled wide apart, each tied to steel pegs imbedded in the wall behind her, holding her in an upright position. She straightened, easing the pressure on her wrists.

Still dazed, she gazed around the small, empty, dark room. White and gray fowl droppings coated the dirt floor. Through the dim light, she could see a closed door on either side and a tiny window in front of her that emitted the last rays of evening.

She didn't remember how she'd gotten here, but she certainly hadn't forgotten Walter Crow's maniacal rantings, or the beatings he'd inflicted. *And would again.* She twisted frantically, trying to free the bindings. Her feet went out from under her, and she sagged, plunging all her weight onto her bound hands. Oh, God. The pain.

Scrambling quickly, she planted her feet under her. Her heart slammed into her ribs. Why was she here?

Where was the priest? What did he want with her? Why was he doing this?

Suddenly Carver's words came back to haunt her. *The women had rope burns on their wrists.* Fear curled up her spine. No!

A door opened on her left, and she jerked her frightened gaze toward it.

The clergyman, still dressed in black, walked in carrying a lighted candle and a bowl filled with yellow kernels. He set both on a crate by the door that she hadn't noticed in the shadowy dimness.

His calm, satanic eyes turned on her. Eerie shadows flickered over the scratch marks on his cheek. The ones she'd put there. "Well, my dear. I see you've finally awakened."

"Please, please let me go. I haven't done anything to you. I don't even know why you've taken me."

He smiled, not a nice smile. "I told you why. I'm going to rid you of the devil. And in turn, you're going to do something for me."

"What, for heaven's sake?"

"Tell me the location of his lair."

"I don't know what you're talking about."

"Oh, yes. But you do. Satan's a smart one, I'll give him that. But he didn't fool me. Not two years ago when he tried to trick me by coming to confession, claiming he was cursed with the ability to make things happen with his mind, and he won't now. You know, all right, and very soon, *I* will know."

Panic seized her. Sin. He was talking about Sin! "Please listen to me. Sin—" She gasped, not daring to use *that* name. *"Val*sin isn't what you think. He's not a devil. He's troubled, that's all. He does have this 'curse,' as you call it, but he's a good man. He would never use it to hurt anyone. Please, you've got to believe me."

"Well said, my dear. But I would have expected nothing less of the evil one's followers. Such a devoted lot. And I now realize the mistake I made with the other two. I ended their lives much too quickly."

Shock and fury stole her breath. "You admit it!"

"Of course. Unfortunately, I should have put more effort into attaining information from them first." He shook his head in self-recrimination. "But I was so anxious to redeem their souls and rid the world of their filth, of the seed they possibly carried, that I became impatient." He smiled mockingly. "I won't this time, though. Before I'm through, you'll gladly shout the location of hell's own hideaway to the heavens."

Realizing the man's severely unbalanced state, she struggled to push aside her hatred. She had to reason logically with him. Stop this madness, somehow. "How do you know Sin—Valsin *is* Satan?"

"I told you, he came to confession. He admitted to killing his own father."

She stared at the man in shock, knowing Sin couldn't possibly have committed such an atrocity. But if he did say the words—*believe them*—no wonder he feared his gift so much. She glared at the priest. "Why would the devil admit something like that to you—or anyone?"

The priest leaned on the door and crossed his arms. "He knew how powerful I was, and he wanted to destroy me. And it nearly worked. After he left the cubicle, I broke the first law of the church. I followed him, learned his identity from a dockworker when I saw him board a vessel. I was terrified and elated. I'd actually spoken to Satan. It wasn't until later, when I told the bishop, that I realized the demon's evil plan. By me following him, learning who he was—and reporting it—the bishop thought I was crazed. I should have known *he* would twist the clergyman's mind. Make them think *I* was the one deranged. I'm sure the evil bastard thought he'd won when I was excommunicated from the church. But he didn't know how deep my faith went, or how I would make it my life's work to obliterate him."

He's truly insane, Moriah thought through a veil of horror. *The man's mind is completely twisted with madness. And he killed Sara and Beth.* There was no doubt now. Tears welled in her eyes, and she tried not to visualize what sheer terror her sister must have known. What horror she herself would undoubtedly endure.

For the second time in her life, she knew what it felt like to truly hate another human being. "I hope you rot in the fires of hell."

His eyes flared wildly, and he lunged at her. His hand gripped her throat. Squeezed. "Shut up, whore! Don't try your curses with me."

She sucked wildly for breath. No air reached her lungs. She kicked out, her chest burning, blood pounding viciously through her head. She needed air!

Suddenly he snatched his hands away, his face twisted into a grotesque smirk. "Almost," he rasped. "You almost won, didn't you? You wanted me to kill you, wanted me to end your life before you weakened and betrayed that heinous vermin. But it didn't work." He leaned back, smiling, the tips of his muck-covered shoes touching her bare toes.

She gasped heavily, taking great gulps of air to feed her starved lungs. But in her heart she knew it was only the beginning of the end. She wouldn't survive this.

His hands lashed out, striking her hard across the face. "Tell me where he lives!"

"Get away from me!" She kicked and twisted like a madwoman. Tried to ram her knee into any part of him she could reach.

Again he viciously struck her.

Numbed from so many blows over the last days, she didn't even cry out. "Go to hell."

"Demon's whore!" the priest screeched. "We'll see which of us is stronger."

With jerky movements, he tromped through the muck to the door and lifted the bowl of kernels, then returned and dumped them at her feet.

Frightened, but not sure why, she tried to kick out again, but the pressure on her wrists was becoming unbearable. "W-What is that?"

He lifted the candle. Then turning, he smiled evilly. "Corn."

Moriah stared at him in surprise. Did he think that would hurt her? Well, she certainly wasn't going to tell him any different.

Then she heard it, the sound of geese squawking on the other side of the opposite door. The smell of corn had stirred them, would send them into a feeding frenzy—*at her feet.* "Please, Mr. Crow, don't do this, I beg you. I've never done anything to you."

Ignoring her, he shifted the empty bowl under his arm, then picked up a towel and wiped his shoes. Not looking at her again, he left the room.

The squawks were growing more frantic, more savage, as the scent of the corn obviously taunted the birds. Wings flapped. Low, hissing sounds echoed on the other side of the closed door.

Do something, her mind screamed. *Before he lets them in.* In quick, panicked motions, she tried shoving the kernels away from her feet. Switching from one foot to the other, she dug her toes in the dirt and muck, then kicked until the flying dust and droppings nearly gagged her.

The door on her right flew open.

She caught just a glimpse of Walter Crow's hated face as flapping, wildly squawking geese surged into the room in a tidal wave of dirty white feathers and open orange beaks.

She screamed hysterically and kicked out as one beak after another stabbed into her feet and she was clawed with webbed feet and tiny, sharp nails.

Nearly insane with terror, she lifted her legs, trying to avoid the snapping animals. Her bound wrists bore the weight. Burning pain sliced into her skin, forcing her to stand. "Oh, God. Help me!" she cried out hoarsely. Her senses spun. Swirled. Pain . . . wings . . . feathers everywhere . . . the sounds. The horrible sounds . . .

Pull into yourself and draw on the powers of good. Her old priest's words vaulted through her mind. Squeezing her eyes tightly shut, she forced back the horrendous waves of pain. She shut out the sounds and focused her mind on Sin. He was good. No matter what he thought. No matter what Walter Crow thought. And if she was going to die, she wanted her last thoughts to be of Sin. Forever him.

She wasn't aware of when the geese retreated, but she couldn't hold her head up any longer. It took too much effort. She was too weak. A dullness had finally claimed her body and her mind, relieving her of the gnawing ache . . . the thirst. No. She wouldn't think about that. During the last days and nights without food or water, she thought she'd go insane. Now she realized the madman had only begun.

Wearily she laid her cheek against her shoulder, wondering how much longer she could survive. Her strength was nearly gone. Soon her will to live would follow. She was so tired . . . .What she'd give to sleep in a bed one more time . . . next to Sin. Unshed tears burned her eyes; it could never be. He wouldn't even know what happened to her until he read it in the newspaper.

She was vaguely aware of Walter wrapping his arm around her waist and cutting her down. Of him dragging her to the door and cleaning her feet, then jostling her inside the house. He probably didn't want her tracking blood on his floors, she thought giddily.

His huffing and puffing as he struggled to pull her into what appeared to be a tiny church made her nauseous. His breath was as foul as the geese droppings.

When he reached a makeshift altar, he shoved her to the floor, then picked up a bowl of water. In low, murmured words, he blessed the liquid.

She licked her dry lips, praying he would give her a drink.

Instead, he gripped her by the hair and jerked her head back. Smiling, he trickled the holy water over her brow. When she didn't move, he drizzled it over her nose and mouth. She gulped wildly.

Laughing, he dumped the contents full in her face.

She coughed and sputtered, then blinked rapidly. "You bastard," she croaked.

The humor left his face. Still gripping her hair, he pulled her up to her knees. "Pray for your eternal soul, whore. Ask the Savior to forgive your sins—your blasphemous fornicating with Satan."

She shook her head numbly.

Angrily he shoved her face against the wood of the altar. "Pray, harlot!"

She whimpered, then moved her lips to form the words she'd spoken so often over the years. "Forgive me, Father, for I have sinned. . . ." She closed her eyes, her lips still moving in silent prayer.

Evidently satisfied, he released her hair and stood, then waited for her to finish.

"Now, Satan's own, where is your master's island?"

She didn't move. Didn't speak.

"Tell me now, little whore, or return to the geese," he threatened softly.

Her eyes widened in horror, and shudders ran through her body.

"Where is the island?" he demanded again.

With a strength she didn't know she possessed, she pushed away from the pulpit and sat on her heels. She held her head high and met his gaze squarely. "Out of your reach, *vermin.*"

Rage bulged the veins in his temples. "You demonic bitch!" He grabbed a dagger that had been lying on the altar.

Hysteria bounced through her stomach.

Viciously he grabbed her by the hair and yanked her head back. With a maniacal wail, he arched the blade and thrust it toward her throat.

"No!" Sin's voice roared.

The man's arm slammed to a stop in midair, the point of the blade just inches from her windpipe. He shot wild eyes toward Sin and released her, pointing the knife in his direction. "So, Master of Darkness, we meet again."

Through a haze of fear and relief, she watched the robed man rise to his feet, his eyes bright with a feral gleam. "I've waited a very long time." He edged forward.

"When I rid your whores of your demon's seed and buried their wombs, I knew you'd come to me. See that my faith was stronger than yours and accept defeat. But I didn't expect it to take so long. I should have known you'd have a loyal lot. Not one of them would tell me the location of your heinous lair."

Sin paled, but his eyes remained wary, watchful. "Why did you kill your own sister? She wasn't one of my . . . women."

"You know why," he snarled. "She was going to the church, just like you planned. She would have found out about my dismissal. It wouldn't have taken her long to figure out that I was the one who killed those women. She would have turned me over to the authorities to save her filthy business. You *knew* that." He laughed insanely. "But your scheme didn't work. I killed her, just as I would any other harlot." He took another step. "Just as I'm going to kill you."

She watched Sin lift his arms, holding them open in invitation. "Come get me, Crow. I'm all yours."

"In due time." The man's glazed eyes narrowed, and he stared down at her still huddled into a ball at the foot of the pulpit. Without warning, he lunged.

She threw up her arm to ward off the attack.

Suddenly Crow flew sideways, slamming into a wall of statues. A magnificent avalanche of pottery crashed to the floor. Candles bounced and rolled like spilled marbles.

The maniac screeched insanely and lurched to his feet.

"What's the matter, *priest?* Don't you want me?" With a burning glare, Sin pitched him into the rear wall. Ceramic statues burst all around him. The shelf next to him crumbled.

He scrambled to his feet, clutching a finely carved replica of the Virgin Mary. He held it out in front of him as if for protection from Sin's evil. His eyes moved rapidly, searching for some means of escape. But there was only one way out—through Sin.

"Afraid of me, Crow?" he taunted softly. "You should

be, you know. I want to kill you more than anything I've ever wanted. Come on. Make it easy for me."

Terrified for Sin, she gained her voice. "He's not worth it."

"I'll fight my own battles, bitch!" Crow roared, then raising the dagger, he charged.

Fear for Sin exploded. She reacted instantly. Her leg shot out in front of Crow's.

He tripped and fell forward. A sickening thud pierced the stillness, then a strangled, gurgling sound. His thin body jerked spasmodically. A second later, he slumped . . . lifeless.

Slowly, warily, Sin approached the inert man. When he saw no movement, he placed a booted foot against Crow's shoulder and rolled him over onto his back.

The man's eyes stared unseeingly, his mouth slack. His own dagger protruded from the center of his chest where he'd fallen on the point of the blade.

She clamped a hand over her mouth.

Instantly Sin was beside her, pulling her to her feet, holding her close, as if to absorb her pain and horror into his own body. She was safe, her mind repeated over and over, but still she shook with emotion, allowing all her earlier terror to rise to the surface.

"Oh, princess. I thought I'd lost you." He hugged her fiercely, his cheeks damp against her own. Then he raised his gaze heavenward. "Thank you, Father."

At that moment, another priest stumbled through the door, his chest heaving. He froze, surveyed the carnage, then dropped to his knees. "Lord have mercy."

Sin buried his face in her hair, and held her tight. "He has, Father. Believe me, He has."

CHAPTER

26

Moriah rested her head on Sin's strong shoulder and toyed with the crystal at her throat. Her bandaged feet still ached a little, and all the bruises hadn't faded, but nothing could stop the burst of love she felt for the man beside her. "I adore you," she whispered, rubbing her cheek over the soft texture of his white shirt.

Lucas, sitting across the parlor from them, cleared his throat and rose from the sofa. "You can discuss that later. Right now the whole island is waiting for an explanation." He made a sweeping gesture with his hand toward Dorothy, Beula, Donnelly, Callie, and Captain Jonas, who had just walked in and now stood immobile under the arched entry, their gazes expectant.

Sin sighed and withdrew his arm from around her, then moved to stand beside his brother—a fact he'd confirmed on the return trip to Arcane when he told her about their father's death. Quickly, in that low, resonant tone of his, he explained to the others about Walter Crow.

"What did the authorities say?" Donnelly asked.

"They were glad to have the murders solved, and exceedingly pleased that another one had been prevented." He slid her a warm look. "But not nearly as pleased as I am."

Callie frowned. "How did the priest know about your women?"

"Blanche Rossi. When he heard his sister mention my name, he questioned her frequently about her business, learning the identity of the women who visited my island." He met Callie's eyes. "If you had gone with Moriah, I imagine Crow would have taken you, too."

Callie shuddered, and edged closer to Lucas. He slipped a protective arm around her.

"What about Mudanno?" Dorothy asked, her lined features revealing confusion. "Why would she say she killed those women?"

"She knew it was the only way Moriah would break her word to Sin and come to the village," Callie supplied with a slight shiver. "Moriah was Mudanno's ticket to Sin's bed. The only way she figured she'd ever conceive the child she so badly wanted." Her troubled gaze slid to her friend. "I'm sorry for my part in it. If I'd been in control of my senses, I'd have never betrayed you like that."

Moriah smiled. "I know that, and I never once blamed you. In fact, I blamed myself for getting you into this mess." Anger at what the girl had suffered ignited. "After what that heathen did to you, I hope she spends eternity burning in hell."

Lucas tightened his arms around the beautiful mulatto. "Not nearly as much as I do."

"I still don't see why you sent the lass to Nassau," Donnelly spoke up. "You loved each other. Why would you do that, boy?"

Sin winced at the servant's pet name, the same one Lucas detested so. "I was afraid of harming her." He offered her his hand, then pulled her to her feet and into his arms. "I thought I was to blame for that chandelier that fell on Father. I thought, in my anger, I had caused the accident, and if I could do something like that to the man who sired me, I was capable of any atrocity. I couldn't chance hurting the woman I loved."

He glanced at Lucas. "I no longer blame myself, or

anyone, for what happened. Too, thanks to Moriah, I now know I can harness my . . . gift." He hugged her to him, and she was so content, she thought her heart would burst.

Reluctantly he let her go and took her hand. "Now, if you'll all excuse me, I'd like a private word with my future wife."

A thrill shot through her midsection. *Future wife.*

The others ambled out the door, all with a secret smile curving their lips, then a grinning Lucas closed the panel behind him.

Moriah suddenly felt shy.

"Did you send the message?" Sin asked softly.

Knowing he referred to the letter she had Jamie post in Nassau to her mother, informing her she would not be returning any time soon, she nodded.

"Then there's nothing standing in the way of us marrying, is there?"

"Only your fear of being around people and letting them discover your gift. It'll be extremely difficult to marry without a clergyman and witnesses."

Warmth filled those beautiful brown eyes. "I'm not afraid anymore, princess. Not after what happened with that bastard, Crow."

"I don't understand."

He ran a hand down the length of her hair. "I wanted that maniac dead. More than I've ever wanted anything. But when it came right down to the deed, I couldn't do it. I couldn't force myself to take his miserable life." He cast her a resigned smile. "I wouldn't have let him hurt you. I'd have definitely stopped that. But I know in my heart that I wouldn't have killed him.

"I *can* control it, princess—in a manner of speaking. And I can choose who to tell and who not to. Too, I'm going to reopen the house in Savannah. We'll spend half our time there and half here on Arcane."

"What made you decide that?"

He pulled her head down on his shoulder and nuzzled her hair with his lips. "When you went to say good-bye to

Callie, I followed you. I heard what you told her about civilization."

"But it wasn't the truth. I love it here."

He chuckled softly. "I know that. And I knew it then. But it started me thinking when we were on the way back from Nassau. You will eventually miss those things; even I do sometimes. Besides, it's long past time for me to come out of hibernation. I want to see the world again. I want to show you New York, and Paris, and London, and—"

She placed her fingers over his lips to still the words. "How about showing me your bedroom first?"

Air rushed between her fingers with his quick intake of breath, then he kissed them gently and lowered them to his chest. "I'd rather show you the healing pool." He bent his head and brushed his lips tenderly over hers. "I've often wondered what it would be like to make passionate love to you in those magic waters."

Achates suddenly appeared, nudging his way between their feet.

Sin ruffled the cat's ear. "I think he missed you."

"And I've missed him." She gave a small smile. "You know, I wonder how this would have turned out if I hadn't followed in my sister's footsteps and posed as your mistress."

"Posing was all she did, too," Sin reminded. "I never slept with her. When she thought I might want her in my bed, she broke down and told me the truth."

"What about the two men in Nassau?"

"What two men?"

"The one's named on Carver's list as the men who hired Sara for . . ." She swallowed, "I believe their names were VanDeer and Halpin."

A low rumble shook his chest. "Oh, princess, if you think your sister's virtue was at stake with either of those two, then you're in for a great surprise. It's common knowledge that Halpin and VanDeer are . . . er . . . not exactly attracted to women. In fact, they only hire an occasional lady of the night to put up a front, thinking their secret is safe and that no one knows of their little tête-à-têtes after the women have gone home. I'm sure Sara had a lovely time, though. They're usually very gracious and prone to dine in the best supper houses."

"I see." She cleared her throat, anxious to change the subject. "When are we going to the mainland?"

"Why?"

"There's someone I'd like you to meet."

"Not your former betrothed, I hope."

Having explained to him about wanting to marry Carver just to gain her mother's approval, she shook her head. "Heavens, no. Carver would collapse with heart failure. No, definitely not him. I want you to meet my old priest, Father Albert.

"Is that who you want to marry us?"

"I wouldn't mind. But that's not the reason. I know this is going to sound strange, but in a way, he saved my life—or at least my sanity."

His features turned dark at the painful memory. "How?"

"When I was young, I would go to him with my troubles. God knows my mother wouldn't listen. Anyway, Father Albert always told me to pull into myself and draw on the powers of good when I felt despair. That's exactly what I did with Walter Crow. And *you* were the good I concentrated on."

His eyes softened. "Oh, princess, I love you so much, it scares me."

She gave him an impish grin. "Maybe the healing pool would ease your fears."

"I've learned not to doubt your wisdom, woman. I think it just might be what I—*we*—need."

Breathlessly she encircled his neck, her body alive with anticipation, her heart thudding wildly. "What are we waiting for?"

He brushed his lips across hers. "Settlement of a bet. I want to collect on my remaining favor, since you've won back all the others."

"What do you want me to do?"

His fingers traced the edge of the island wrap covering her breasts. "Promise me you'll give me a daughter with shimmering black hair and violet eyes."

Her skin tingled where he touched her, and her heart expanded with love. "If you'll promise to honor my last favor by giving me a son with raven hair and liquid brown eyes *and a new swing."*

He laughed huskily. "The swing is already in place, and this time I used chains." He touched her cheek. "As for a son . . . well, I'll do my best, princess. So help me, I will." Scooping her up into his arms, he sauntered out of the house, his step light, his arms protective and strong.

The others, who still stood on the veranda, talking and joking, stopped to stare.

He cast them a wink. "The healing pool is off limits for a few hours." Whistling, he continued on.

Fighting a blush, she pinched him soundly.

His laughter rang out, blending with the sound of chattering monkeys and Achates' contented growl.